A Valiant Woman

Tabitha & Wolf Historical Mystery Series

Book Eleven

Sarah F. Noel

ISBN - 979-8-9919192-3-4

Cover design by: HelloBriie Creative
Printed in the United States of America

Also by Sarah F. Noel

Tabitha & Wolf Historical Mystery Series

A Proud Woman

A Singular Woman

An Independent Woman

An Inexplicable Woman

An Audacious Woman

A Discerning Woman

An Indomitable Woman

An Intrepid Woman

A Patient Woman

An Enigmatic Woman

An Anointed Woman

The Continental Capers of Melody Chesterson

A Venetian Escapade

Mischief In Morocco

The Amsterdam Enigma

Acknowledgments

I want to thank my wonderful editor, Kieran Devaney and the eagle-eyed Patricia Goulden for doing a final check of the manuscript.

To the lovely people of Pembroke and Lamphey, who made us so welcome.

Foreword

This book is written using British English spelling. e.g. dishonour instead of dishonor, realise instead of realize.

British spelling aside, while every effort has been made to proofread this thoroughly, typos do creep in. If you find any, I'd greatly appreciate a quick email to report them at sarahfnoelauthor@gmail.com

Chapter 1

"Well?" Tabitha demanded anxiously, before Wolf even had a chance to settle himself into the chair opposite her in the cosy parlour, the family's preferred room for everyday living while they were staying at Glanwyddan Hall.

"Can I pour myself a cup of tea first?" Wolf asked, smiling at his wife's impatience.

"I will pour for you while you talk."

Wolf accepted his fate with good grace. "I spoke with Bear, and he took my words seriously."

Tabitha had to tamp down her frustration. "Well, I never doubted he would take them seriously. But what did he have to say about their relationship?"

Wolf understood her impatience. Wolf had known for some time that he needed to have this conversation with Bear, but he had been so uncomfortable broaching the subject that he delayed it much longer than he should have. Both he and Tabitha had been concerned for some time about the obvious growing closeness between Bear and Mrs Rose O'Leary, Tabitha's private secretary. Wolf agreed that, as Bear's long-time friend, employer, and the head of the household, it was fitting that he was the one to raise the issue. However, that didn't mean it was an easy subject for the two men to discuss.

"As you might imagine, Bear was no more comfortable having such a conversation than I was starting it."

Tabitha could easily imagine this; Bear was a taciturn man at the best of times. That he sat in an unusual grey area between employee and closest friend must have made the conversation even more awkward. Was the matter being raised by Wolf, the man he had lived, worked, and often starved alongside for more than a decade, or the Earl of Pembroke, who paid the wages of both Bear and Mrs O'Leary?

"And yet you did start it?" Tabitha asked nervously, suddenly worried her husband might have found yet another reason merely to hint at the issue rather than facing it straight on.

"I did. You need not worry. For the most part, I covered everything we discussed. There is no understanding between them, at least for now. Mrs O'Leary has not been widowed for even six months, and, despite her lack of grief over her husband's death, Bear understands there are some social conventions that must be observed."

Even as Wolf said this, he felt like arguing, yet again, that what might be expected of a woman of their status and rank was hardly a standard to which anyone was likely to hold the widow of a violent street thug. Nonetheless, he understood Tabitha's point: while Mr O'Leary had been a criminal, Rose O'Leary was brought up in a genteel, middle-class household. The standard was one to which the woman would undoubtedly hold herself, regardless of what the world might demand.

Tabitha considered Wolf's choice of words. "So, he does intend to pursue a courtship once society's demands have been satisfied?"

"You can hardly have expected me to ask him that so directly?" Wolf exclaimed. Even as he said this, he knew that was precisely what his wife had expected him to do. The frustration on her face conveyed that very expectation.

His intuition was confirmed as Tabitha set aside her teacup, leaned forward, and said in a tone she might use with Melody to explain why she was in trouble, "Wolf! What else did you think you were talking with him about, if not just that?" Tabitha shook her head; she knew she should have been the one to speak with Bear. As unconventional as it might have been, at least the conversation would have served its purpose.

As Wolf relived the conversation with Bear, he cringed all over again, but forced himself to answer. "You know Bear. And well, you know me. We were never going to get into those kinds of details. But yes, there is a growing attachment between the two, and yes, when her mourning period is over, he is interested in seeing where that leads, and she has indicated her willingness for him to do so. Are you satisfied now?"

Tabitha leant back, a smile on her face. "Very!"

Wolf sighed again, this time in relief. He celebrated his release by taking two of Mrs Budgers's delicious shortbread biscuits to munch on while he sipped his tea.

Just as Wolf had finished his first biscuit and was starting to relax after the stress of his morning conversation with Bear, the door to the parlour opened. Although it was a warm summer day, he could have sworn an icy chill filled the room. One glance at their visitor made it clear why. Though Wolf didn't know what had triggered this particular cold front, he didn't need to in order to realise that it wouldn't bode well for the rest of his morning.

"Mama!" Tabitha said in a cheery voice that belied an intuition of the challenge ahead that mirrored Wolf's own. "You are up and about early."

"Early? What are you implying, Tabitha? Why, it is past eleven o'clock in the morning. Are you insinuating that I am a regular slugabed?"

Tabitha and Wolf exchanged glances; how should they respond to this? As it happened, the Dowager Countess of Pembroke was a notoriously late riser, often not leaving her bedchamber until nearly noon. However, as with many aspects of her character, the dowager appeared to be in denial of this fact, at least when it suited her to portray herself otherwise. It seemed that now was one of those times.

Over the past year, as her relationship with her former mother-in-law had both deepened and broadened since spending far more time together than they ever had when the dowager's son was alive, Tabitha had learned a thing or two about how to handle the usually difficult woman. One of the primary rules of successfully managing her was to ignore the blatantly contradictory statements she made, whenever possible. Once again, it seemed that now was one of those times.

"Nothing could be further from the truth, Mama," Tabitha said in a sweet, conciliatory tone. "Rather, you mentioned last night that you had some correspondence you wished to catch up on this morning, and I expected you to still be in your room working on it. I am delighted that you finished your task early enough to join us."

The dowager harrumphed. She was far too wily an old woman not to realise when she was being placated. Nevertheless, she had no wish to dilute her carefully built ire. She had chosen to rise from her bed early that morning to cloak herself in righteous indignation, and she refused to be distracted from that mission. Instead of continuing to debate her morning routine, the dowager pivoted her frosty irritation towards what had initially brought her into the room.

Tabitha attempted to communicate to Wolf her uncertainty about what they were about to be harangued for, and he gave a slight shrug of his shoulders in response. There was no doubt they had fallen short in some regards. However, even as they racked their brains, neither could figure out how.

Finally, Tabitha decided to take a tentative step to test the ice, even though she knew she was bound to be rewarded with a plunge into frigid waters. "Is there something you need, Mama?"

The dowager smiled, but it was a smile that did not reach her eyes. In fact, it was more a hunter's satisfaction than a genuine smile, as if she had lured her prey into a trap.

"My needs are insignificant. When have I ever prioritised my needs above the rest of the group's?" There was no doubt that this was not only a rhetorical question, but that the only response was a full acknowledgement of the dowager's storied selflessness. Since neither Tabitha nor Wolf was willing to debase themselves so thoroughly merely to have the chance to resume peacefully drinking their morning tea, they chose to remain silent.

Fortunately, the dowager often required no reply, and this appeared to be one of those instances. Instead, she continued, "This is about the needs of the estate; what is owed the title." Now, Tabitha and Wolf were even more confused.

The dowager noted their bafflement and, after a deep sigh to indicate her profound disappointment in both of them, she condescended to explain herself. "Jeremy, as I have emphasised on multiple occasions, it is vital that you fully immerse yourself in the rich history of the earldom. Therefore, a visit to Pembroke Castle must be a top priority for this trip. I overlooked the matter at Christmas because of the weather, but now there is no excuse for neglecting this obligation."

Oh, so this was what was wrong, Tabitha and Wolf both thought. Now, it was their turn to sigh.

"Lady Pembroke, as I believe I mentioned when you last brought up the subject, I am happy to spend a day visiting Pembroke Castle, but it cannot be my top priority. There are crucial estate matters that must be attended to before I can indulge in leisure activities."

As soon as Wolf spoke these words, he realised his mistake. "Leisure activities! Is that what you call visiting the ancestral castle that has stood in one form or another since 1093? To say nothing of walking in the footsteps of some of the most illustrious holders of the title."

By this time, the dowager had settled herself into an armchair. She seemed to have, at least temporarily, forgotten her high dudgeon and had instead fallen into a contemplative mood.

"Of course, William Marshal was known as the 1st Earl of Pembroke, but in reality, the first earl was Gilbert de Clare. Marshal was thus known only because the first creation of the title had become extinct. Therefore, William Marshal was regarded as the 1st Earl of Pembroke of the second creation. Nonetheless, my point remains. William Marshal and many others are ancestors worth honouring and remembering," she mused.

Before he could think better of it, Wolf asked, "But Marshal isn't an actual forebear of mine, is he? My understanding is that the title lapsed multiple times before being awarded to one of my ancestors."

There had been a slight thaw in the ice while the dowager had been distracted by the history of the title, but now the glare she directed at Wolf made it clear it had been only a temporary reprieve.

"Let me ask you, Jeremy, would you feel comfortable sharing that sentiment with our Queen when discussing her own family tree? After all, when George I ascended the throne through the Act of Settlement, the aim was to ensure a Protestant succession to the English throne and exclude Catholics, no matter how close in blood."

The very last thing Wolf wanted was to get sucked any further into this discussion. Instead, he replied, "Why do we not visit Pembroke Castle tomorrow? We can all go, including Rat and Melody. I can ask Budgie to organise a picnic, and we will make a whole day of it."

"Jeremy, this is not to be trivialised, reducing a place of serious history to a site of frivolity. What will you suggest next? Perhaps we might bring a brass band and treat William Marshal's stronghold as if it were the Crystal Palace. Or set up a Punch and Judy show while we're at it and turn Pembroke Castle into the Margate sands!"

Wolf closed his eyes briefly as if trying to summon strength. "Then what would you suggest, Lady Pembroke?"

"That you contact the current owners of the castle, the Pryse family of Gogerddan, and request both access and someone able to provide an expert commentary on the site's Norman and Plantagenet history. I would imagine Sir Pryse must have a local steward or some such person who can give us a tour of the property."

Given that Pembroke Castle was privately held, the courteous thing to do was to ask for such permission, even if they were just going for a picnic. Wolf agreed to send a note to Picton Castle immediately.

"A note? Gogerddan is almost a day's journey. Why do you not telephone? Sir Pryse is no Luddite; I would be amazed if he does not have one installed."

Wolf had forgotten that the dowager had insisted on installing a telephone at Glanwyddan Hall after their last visit. Now, he rose and prepared to find his butler, Talbot, hoping he could help determine if Sir Pryse owned one of the devices and then assist him in making the call. Although Wolf had become more comfortable using a telephone, he rarely made it his first choice of communication, preferring to leave telephone calls to Talbot.

Ten minutes later, he returned to the parlour. "We are to meet a Mr Jeremiah Goodge at the castle tomorrow at noon."

Chapter 2

Once the dowager had achieved her goal, her mood immediately lifted, and by the following morning, she was nearly giddy with excitement. Over a surprisingly early breakfast, for her, she regaled the group with titbits of information about the history of Pembroke Castle.

"I thought she hated it there," Bear whispered to Wolf as the dowager related enthusiastically how Henry VII was born in the castle.

"So did I," Wolf confided. "Perhaps she merely hates this house and does not extend that loathing to the greater Pembrokeshire area."

"Perhaps. Regardless, she seems quite insistent that this visit be educational, at least for me. If I were you, Bear, I would take Mrs O'Leary and the boys for a nice walk around the grounds as soon as you can; save yourselves."

It had been agreed that all the children, including the O'Leary twins, would join the outing, along with Dodo, the dog. This meant that both nurserymaids would be accompanying them and that they needed to take several footmen to carry the food, chairs, and other picnic paraphernalia. It was fortunate that the Pembroke Estate had multiple carriages and some carts that could be used for the footmen and furniture.

No one imagined the dowager would sit on a blanket on the ground, so at least one chair was needed. Once this became clear, Tabitha admitted she would rather not sit on the ground unless it was unavoidable. Now, from what Wolf could see, they were bringing almost a whole dining room set of furniture with them. As he often did in such moments, he thought nostalgically about the days when he and Bear were free from wealth, status, or expectations. Of course, those were also the days when he didn't know or love Tabitha, so perhaps they weren't truly halcyon after all.

The drive from Glanwyddan Hall to Pembroke Castle would take roughly thirty minutes. Just before half-past eleven, the family and their entourage, including children and a Cavalier King Charles Spaniel, gathered on the steps outside the hall. The footmen had already gone ahead with the furnishings and food.

The O'Leary twins were especially excited and ran about, chasing Dodo or sometimes being chased by her. Their mother, Rose, watched them anxiously. "I am so sorry they are being so wild," she said apologetically to anyone who was listening.

"Do not worry yourself, Mrs O'Leary," Tabitha assured her. "They are small boys, and they should get their energy out now, given that they will be in the carriage for some time."

A loud sniff came from beside her, implying that not everyone in their party was as understanding and forgiving. However, fortunately, for once, the dowager said nothing.

The journey to Pembroke Castle was uneventful. Mrs O'Leary and the two nursemaids had squeezed into one carriage with Melody and the twins, and the dowager, Langley, and Rat rode with Tabitha and Wolf, while Bear sat up top with the driver.

"What do we know of this Mr Goodge?" the dowager asked sceptically. "I hope he is sufficiently knowledgeable to provide insights into the history of the earldom."

"Apparently, he is a local antiquarian. He was tangentially involved with a Mr Cobb, who briefly leased the castle in the 1880s and did some basic renovation. According to Pryse, he is considered the foremost expert on the castle and its history at this point. Or at least he is in Pembrokeshire."

Even as Wolf said this, he realised he had not fully answered the dowager's question. From what little Wolf knew, while the history of the earldom was connected with Pembroke Castle, it was hardly regarded as the most important aspect of the historically significant site; that Henry VII was born there was much more notable. He could only hope that this Jeremiah Goodge could temper his storytelling enough to placate the dowager.

Neither Wolf nor Tabitha knew where the old woman's sudden passionate interest in the earldom's history had come from. The dowager had a complicated relationship with her fellow aristocrats; although she was a snob who believed titles mattered and that rank should be deferred to, in reality, she found most of those in her class tedious and made little effort to hide her contempt.

Beyond her general disdain for most of the aristocracy, the dowager had loathed her husband, the late earl, and had suffered for many years from her father-in-law's obsession with securing an heir for the title. Given this, her interest in the earldom was difficult to understand. Whatever her complicated reasons, there was little doubt she was on a mission to ensure Wolf was appropriately in awe of what he had inherited.

As she watched the Pembrokeshire countryside pass by, Tabitha wondered why this might be. She had failed to produce an heir for the dowager's son, Jonathan, or indeed any surviving child. This inability to have offspring was part of her initial hesitation to marry Wolf. However, he had made it clear that he cared little whether he passed on the title to a child of his own. In fact, Wolf had pointed out, he was evidence that there was usually a male relative somewhere who could inherit.

Surprisingly, the dowager had never commented on Tabitha's likely inability to produce an heir for Wolf. However, she had frequently made such remarks when Jonathan was alive and shortly after his death. Was this sudden interest in the title's history her subtle way of renewing her criticism of Tabitha? If so, it was too little, too late; she and Wolf were now married. What was the dowager hoping to achieve? Did she believe that the ability to procreate successfully was within their control, and that they had simply chosen not to, needing persuasion? Surely, the infuriating woman couldn't really think that, could she?

Tabitha glanced over at Wolf, who was describing some of his recent improvements to the estate to Lord Langley. Did her husband care more than he claimed? Even if he didn't at that moment, would he come to resent her inability to bear him a son at some point? Tabitha sighed; if that was the case, there was little she could do about it now. Every month when her courses came, she sighed and accepted the inevitability of her barrenness.

Perhaps 'barren' wasn't the right word; she had fallen pregnant twice, but in both cases, she had lost the baby before showing any signs of it. Of course, Jonathan's tendency to use her as his personal punching bag probably contributed to at least one, if not both, of those miscarriages. This was the only glimmer of hope Tabitha clung to: she had conceived twice. Surely, she could do so again.

Sighing, Tabitha realised there was no point in dwelling further on this subject. Wolf had assured her he didn't care, and now they were married. Moreover, they had Melody, whom both she and Wolf had come to love like a daughter. While the little girl couldn't fulfil the role of heir, she more than fulfilled that of adored child.

Turning away from such thoughts, Tabitha instead took in the view as they entered Pembroke. As she looked out of the carriage window, she drew a sharp breath. There it stood: Pembroke Castle, vast and brooding, its weathered, silvery limestone walls rising above the river, almost as if it had been carved from stone and had stood there since the dawn of time. The midday sunlight caught the top of the cylindrically shaped bulk of the great keep, but the shadows of the walls remained dark. Despite having visited the Pembroke Estate multiple times, both during her marriage to Jonathan and then at Christmas with Wolf, Tabitha had never visited its namesake town before and so had never seen the castle.

As the carriage descended towards the Mill Bridge, the full scale of the castle was revealed: a fortress carved from time and war, standing guard over the intersection of the Pembroke River and Mill Pond. The vast outer gatehouse loomed ahead, still scarred from centuries of neglect, despite some recent repairs.

Their coach stopped before the barbican. Through it, they could see the main gate, which was shut. The gate bore heavy iron fittings, rusted in places, but it remained formidable, as it had through sieges and revolts for nearly a thousand years.

A small, wiry man of about sixty emerged from a nearby stone cottage. He approached the carriage to greet them. Wolf descended first and was immediately hailed by the man. "Lord Pembroke, I assume." The man's accent was local but also suggested he was educated and middle-class.

"Are you Mr Jeremiah Goodge?"

"At your service, milord. And may I say how delighted I am to have the opportunity to share the history of the castle and the earldom with you." Then, in a voice that hinted at years of disappointment and neglect, he added, "Unfortunately, your predecessors were not as interested in learning about their forebears as one might have hoped. Did you know that the creation of the earldom you now hold only dates back to Tudor times?"

Wolf hadn't known the specific time period and nodded along as he helped Tabitha and the dowager out of the carriage.

The dowager looked Jeremiah Goodge up and down, as if sizing up his suitability for the task at hand. "So, you are the so-called antiquarian?" she demanded.

"Indeed, indeed. Jeremiah Goodge at your service. I assume you are the Dowager Countess of Pembroke. Allow me to say what an honour it is to meet you at last, milady."

This was spoken in such a guileless tone that even the dowager couldn't find anything to be displeased with. Instead, she replied, "Yes, I suppose it must be an honour. I only hope you will live up to my expectations."

"Certainly, certainly. I doubt you will find anyone in all of Great Britain who knows more about the castle, and particularly about William Marshal." Jeremiah Goodge's voice took on an almost reverential tone. "The man is a personal hero of mine, and quite underappreciated, one might even say overlooked, by many historians, if you want my opinion."

The dowager shot him a look that she meant to show she did not want his opinion, but the man failed to read her expression. Or maybe he was just so caught up in enthusiasm for his subject that he couldn't hold back the tide of words.

"Of course, I am not claiming that William Marshal receives no recognition in the history books; after all, he was the regent for a time. Even so, I believe he is one of the greatest men in this country's history. Did you know he served five different English kings?"

The dowager was unaware of this, nor did she care. "Well, you are clearly a fountain of information. Only time will tell how useful it is. I assume you can let us into the castle?"

"I can. I can." With that, Mr Goodge produced a large, rusty key from his pocket and waved it at the dowager. "I already opened it for your servants who have been setting up your picnic."

Chapter 3

As they walked through the castle gates, Jeremiah Goodge began his commentary. "For many centuries, the headland on which this iteration of the castle is built was seen as the ideal spot from which to defend not only Wales but all of Britain from marauders. However, the earliest version of this castle was constructed in 1093 by Roger de Montgomery, the Earl of Shrewsbury, to defend Norman-invaded lands against the Welsh."

"Yes, yes, that is all very well," the dowager said irritably as Mr Goodge stopped just inside the castle walls to begin his lecture. "Can we skip ahead to the Pembroke earldom? I realise that Shrewsbury is considered quite the man about town these days, but personally, I find him a crashing bore."

Jeremiah Goodge looked bemused by her words. "Roger de Montgomery, a crashing bore? I believe the man was quite the opposite. In fact..."

"No, Charles Chetwynd-Talbot, the Earl of Shrewsbury," the dowager said incredulously, as if Mr Goodge was a complete fool for failing to keep up with her train of thought.

Wolf could see this conversation spiralling out of control quickly if he didn't step in. "Mr Goodge, perhaps we might jump forward a few years to the establishment of the Pembroke earldom." Wolf paused as he looked at the picnic setting his servants had gone to such trouble to transport and arrange. "In fact, why do we not settle ourselves and have some luncheon first? Mr Goodge, I hope you will join us for a repast."

The dowager's face revealed her feelings on a lowly antiquarian breaking bread with a dowager countess. Luckily, Jeremiah Goodge had his back to her as he replied he would be delighted to join them.

From what Wolf could see, the footmen had moved an entire dining set to the grounds of Pembroke Castle. As it happened, it was a lighter, more portable set kept in storage for such occasions. Nonetheless, with the table covered in a crisp white tablecloth and china and cutlery neatly arranged, it was hard to tell that this was meant to be a picnic.

Wolf looked at the table in bemusement. As far as he was concerned, the pleasure in a picnic was lounging on the grass, eating cold chicken with his hands, and basking in the informality of it all. Transposing the formality of an aristocratic meal from a dining room to an outdoor setting seemed to miss the point. Wisely, he kept these thoughts to himself.

The adults seated themselves around the absurdly grand table, while Mrs O'Leary and the nursemaids settled themselves and the children nearby. Wolf enviously watched Melody, Rat, and the twins sprawled on a large, plaid blanket, letting the grass run through their fingers as they lay on their backs, soaking up the sun. Well, the twins sprawled out for a minute or two, then Liam stood up and began running around the blanket, quickly followed by Willy, who started chasing him.

"Oh my," Jeremiah Goodge said anxiously. "Do ensure that the children stay well clear of the ruins. While Mr Cobb made many improvements to the castle over a decade ago, most of it remains quite unstable and certainly not safe enough for inquisitive little bodies."

"Thank you, Mr Goodge, for the warning," Tabitha said sincerely. "We will ensure the children stay on the grass and well away from any of the structures."

Their picnic was laid out on the wide stretch of grass inside the castle walls. To their left were the ruins of the keep and what Tabitha assumed were the main castle living quarters from hundreds of years ago. While some towers and walls appeared to be in reasonable condition, she noticed many pieces of fallen masonry and appreciated the words of caution.

As the group enjoyed many of the usual staples of a summer picnic, such as cold chicken salad, game pie, and finger sandwiches, all served with sterling silver cutlery and on fine bone china plates, Mr Goodge continued his history lesson. However, in deference to the dowager's wishes, he moved his narration forward to the creation of the earldom.

"Well, as I am sure you all know, the first Earl of Pembroke was Gilbert de Clare, who was rewarded with the title for his support of King Stephen. It then passed to his son, Richard, known as Strongbow, in 1148. However, Richard Strongbow was predeceased by his son, at which point the title reverted to the crown."

Tabitha noted that Jeremiah Goodge had quickly adapted to his audience of one and sped the story along, being careful to keep the account tightly focused on facts relating to the earldom. Well, at least that was her assumption. However, as cheese and water biscuits were added to the already groaning table of food, Mr Goodge's face lit up and his voice became animated.

The antiquarian placed his knife and fork on his plate and rubbed his hands together. "Now, we come to the most important, and in my view, the most storied holder of the Pembroke title." Tabitha could see the dowager's eyebrows shoot up at what was almost certainly perceived as a slight against her nearest relative.

Oblivious to the danger sitting to his right, Mr Goodge continued, "William Marshal, soldier, knight, statesman, regent of England. To my mind, one of the most underrated heroes in British history."

Tabitha had never enjoyed her history lessons and was unaware of who William Marshal was. She couldn't tell if her lack of knowledge confirmed Jeremiah Goodge's claim or simply highlighted her shortcomings as a student.

Jeremiah Goodge's voice adopted a solemn tone as he delved into his favourite part of Pembroke Castle's history. "As a young man, William Marshal supported himself as a tournament knight, where he became skilled in combat and the laws of chivalry. He also gained wealth and fame across the realm. After proving his honour and, more importantly, his loyalty to the crown, Richard the Lionheart gave Richard Strongbow's daughter and heiress, Isabel de Clare, to William Marshal in marriage."

While this might have been Mr Goodge's favourite part of the castle's history, the dowager's yawn, which she did not attempt to hide, should have been a cue to move the story along.

Indeed, it did seem that, if nothing else, Mr Goodge had quickened his pace as he continued, "Although Pembroke did not immediately come into his possession, in 1199 William Marshal was confirmed as the first in the line of the second incarnation of the Earl of Pembroke by Richard's brother, the new King John."

Tabitha wondered if this was where the story would end. However, it seemed Jeremiah Goodge was only getting started praising William Marshal's many virtues and achievements.

"Certainly, England's greatest knight, William Marshal, served five kings of Britain." Jeremiah Goodge paused, then said almost reverentially, "I believe it not to be an overstatement to say Britain would not be the land of laws it is renowned for without the influence of William Marshal."

The dowager had been sipping her glass of cool barley water. Now, she set the glass down, cast Jeremiah Goodge what was meant to be a withering stare, and said, "That is quite the statement to make, Mr Goodge. Perhaps you are slightly biased towards this William Marshal?" As she said this, the dowager offered him a condescending smile one might bestow on a six-year-old telling tall tales.

The dowager's condescension was known to reduce prime ministers, senior clergy members, and, rumour had it, even the Prince of Wales to quivering piles of jelly. Given this, it was surprising to see Jeremiah Goodge so completely unaffected by her words or glare.

Instead, his eyes gleaming with the fervour of a true believer, he declared, "I do not believe it can be disputed that William Marshal played a quiet but vital role in the story of the Magna Carta. Though not the loudest voice among the barons at Runnymede, he was respected by both sides for his loyalty, good judgement, and long service to the Crown. His influence helped bring about a more balanced agreement, one that aimed to restore peace rather than stir rebellion. But it was afterwards that Marshal's real genius and value became apparent. Indeed, when King John died the following year, Britain teetered on the brink of collapse, torn by civil war and weakened by distrust. Marshal's steady hand and moderate approach helped to restore order."

Tabitha wasn't certain, but she could have sworn the dowager rolled her eyes at this remark. She could only hope Jeremiah Goodge hadn't noticed. The poor man. Tabitha was convinced this wasn't what he'd expected when he was asked to give a tour to the current Earl of Pembroke and his family.

Just when they thought he was finished, Jeremiah Goodge took a deep breath. Then, he continued his proclamation: "As Regent of England during the minority of Henry III, it was Marshal who reissued the Charter twice, ensuring its survival. Without Marshal's care, the Magna Carta might have faded into obscurity eventually. Instead, it endured and became a symbol of law and liberty, and the foundation of government in this country to this day."

There was no doubt the man had an incredible grasp of British history and seemed quite besotted with William Marshal. Were they destined for a day with little other than lauding the man? Even as Tabitha wondered this, she realised the dowager would put paid to that swiftly if it was the direction Mr Goodge intended to take their tour.

Luckily, by the time their plates had been cleared and fruit tartlets and sponge cake laid out, Bear had asked Mr Goodge a question about something unrelated to William Marshal and even Pembroke Castle, and everyone else moved to small talk amongst themselves.

By the time tea and sweetmeats were served, the dowager seemed to have laid down her arms, at least for the moment. She had even thawed sufficiently to address their guide. "Mr Goodge, is that charming little tea shop still in Pembroke? I came once or twice many years ago."

"Indeed, it is milady. Miss Marigold's. Though it is now run by the granddaughter of the original Miss Marigold. Nevertheless, their cream tea remains as delicious as ever."

"Excellent. Should we stop in there before we return to Glanwyddan Hall?" While the dowager had phrased this as a question, neither Tabitha nor Wolf had any illusions that this was more a statement of intent.

Chapter 4

"Let us begin with the keep," Jeremiah Goodge suggested once their meal was over. He pointed to a round tower. "As is the case with so much of what you see left of the castle, this was built by William Marshal. The walls are nineteen feet thick at the base."

Tabitha tilted her head back to take it all in. Even in its somewhat ruined state, the keep was impressive, and its narrow slits seemed quite foreboding.

"We cannot go up," Mr Goodge added, noting her gaze. "Some of the inner stairs have fallen, though the lower chamber is quite safe."

He then led them through a worn arch and into the tower's cool, dark interior. The air was damp but not unpleasant. Shafts of light filtered through the slits, the dust motes in them.

"This would have functioned both as a refuge and as a last stronghold during a siege. You'll notice the spiral staircase and the way it curves to the right. That is a defensive feature." From there, they crossed the bailey, Mr Goodge gesturing towards the crumbling remains of the Great Hall and kitchens, narrating their former splendour with the enthusiasm of a true believer.

Tabitha noticed Rat hovering on the edge of their group. While she had reiterated to the nursemaids and Mrs O'Leary that the children should remain on the grass, Rat was older and an inquisitive child. She was pleased he was interested in the castle's history and saw no need to send him away.

They wandered through the ruins of various rooms. Their guide had captivating stories to share about every aspect of each room, or so it appeared. He brought the castle ruins to life for the group, though it seemed as if he never missed a chance to slip in more anecdotes about his hero, William Marshal. Every time he did so, Tabitha couldn't help but glance at the dowager to see if the woman was about to make another caustic comment. Fortunately, she kept her thoughts to herself, for a change.

At last, Mr Goodge led them to the entrance of a stone staircase that descended into the rock itself. "Wogan's Cavern," he said, voice lowered reverentially. "In place since ancient times. William Marshal used it as a store. Some say it hides treasure, though none has ever been found." Jeremiah Goodge was a natural storyteller, and his tone was so dramatic that Tabitha shivered despite the heat of the afternoon sun.

Mr Goodge paused. "I will not be taking you down there today. The stairs are far too dangerous for females to undertake, and the cavern itself, while fascinating to an old historian like me, is damp, cold, and will be charmless to your group." Tabitha was rather disappointed; the cavern sounded interesting. However, she didn't relish the idea of guiding the elderly dowager down ancient, slippery steps, and she doubted the woman would agree to being left out of an adventure.

Without waiting for any challenge to his statement, Mr Goodge turned and led them back out to near the grassy area. Mrs O'Leary and the children were still on the blanket, but the group kept walking away from the picnic area and towards the high, foreboding castle walls. Just before reaching the walls, their guide stopped and pointed towards a door in one of the towers around the wall. "What do you think happened there?" he asked, clearly warming to his performance. No one answered, and so he continued, "In that room is where Henry VII was born!" He said this with such a theatrical flourish that Tabitha had to stifle a smile. Still, it was clear he expected this news to be a moment of high drama.

Given the reaction the antiquarian appeared to expect, he was probably very disappointed when the dowager sniffed and said dismissively,

"One hardly needs to have gone to Oxford or Cambridge to know such a thing. Indeed, I mentioned it yesterday."

Jeremiah Goodge's face fell at this news. However, he was not a man to be kept down easily. Instead, he forced a brave smile and said, "I always appreciate an educated audience. So much more rewarding to stir the interests of people already familiar with some of the history." Then, he held his hand out towards the door and said, "After you, Lady Pembroke."

Whatever the dowager's view on the antiquarian and his potted history of the Pembroke earldom, the woman could never resist the opportunity to sweep in and out of rooms with almost regal pomp. Given that they were about to enter the birthplace of one of England's most celebrated kings, she felt it entirely appropriate that she be the first in the group to grace the space. She acknowledged Mr Goodge's deference and entered first.

Once they were all in the small round room, the dowager looked all about it, disappointment writ large on her face. "Is this it?"

Jeremiah Goodge was quick to try to explain. "Well, of course, this is merely the ground floor of the tower. Unfortunately, the staircase is not in a condition to allow touring of the other floors. Nevertheless, this is close enough to the actual spot of the birth of the man who united the warring houses of York and Lancaster, ended the War of the Roses, and founded the illustrious House of Tudor."

There was another sniff, usually a sign that a contrarian view was about to be expressed. "The House of Tudor, indeed. A usurper, if one is being strictly accurate. Certainly, history has been kinder to him than he deserved. Let us be truthful: the man was no warrior-king in the grand tradition. He fought only one battle and founded a dynasty from it. However, I will acknowledge that he understood the importance of sound governance, a well-managed purse and, perhaps most importantly, a carefully chosen marriage; the match with Elizabeth of York was a masterstroke. It quite erased the stain of his upstart origins in the eyes of the masses."

Jeremiah Goodge seemed unsure how to respond. He was accustomed to being regarded as the ultimate authority locally on historical matters, especially those involving Pembroke Castle.

After momentarily appearing stunned into silence, Mr Goodge

regained his composure and delivered a proud and spirited defence, as if his own family lineage was under attack. "With all due respect, milady, you do the man a disservice. It is easy, from the comfort of the drawing rooms of modern times, to scoff at a Welshman who rose by merit and strategy. But to those of us here in Pembroke, Henry Tudor is not a usurper; he is a native son and a hero."

From her vantage point, Tabitha had a clear view of the dowager's face and wondered if the mild-mannered Jeremiah Goodge had any idea of the lion's den he was walking into.

It seemed he did not, as he continued, "Born within these very walls, almost on this very spot, in a tower that has withstood centuries, Henry came into the world in uncertain times, an heir to a lost cause, scarcely expected to survive, let alone reign. And yet, he reigned wisely and with restraint. He restored order after decades of bloody division that tore the country apart. King Henry restored peace and order in Britain, not through the sword but through good governance."

The man's words were spoken in a tone that brooked no dissent. However, the dowager was unaccustomed to being on the receiving end of such a diatribe and was determined to have the last word.

With one more signature sniff, she proclaimed, "In the end, Henry left the realm better governed than he found it, I will give you that much. Though I've always thought the glory of the Tudors began with his son and ended with his granddaughter."

It seemed as if Jeremiah Goodge didn't know when to bow out graciously and gratefully accept that wounds that might have been fatal were instead merely superficial. Instead, he looked ready to continue the debate. Tabitha was about to signal silently to Wolf that he should step in, when they heard shouting from outside. Tabitha immediately recognised the voice as Rat's and the tone as one of emergency.

In a panic, Tabitha ran out of the tower to find Rat on the grass, looking around him. "Milady Tabby Cat," Rat said between deep breaths. "There's a body."

Tabitha approached the clearly shaken boy, put her hand on his shoulder, and said, "Rat, start at the beginning."

"I know that man said not to, but I crept down to the caves. I just wanted to see if I could find the treasure. I'm sorry I didn't listen."

"We can discuss that later, Rat. For now, what do you mean there's a body?"

"The cavern has windows and a doorway that lead outside, though, so it's not completely dark, and I could see quite a bit. Though it was a little scary down there," the boy admitted.

"Well, that is one reason Mr Goodge suggested we not go down," Tabitha couldn't help but say. "However, carry on with your story."

"I found a stick and dug around for a bit, looking for the treasure, but I couldn't find anything. Then, I wandered into one of the darker corners, and suddenly I realised there was a body there. I think he's dead. I felt him, and he's very cold."

By this time, the rest of the group had emerged from the tower, and Wolf had come over and heard the end of Rat's story. "Bear, Langley, we'll take two of the footmen and go down to the cavern," Wolf directed.

Chapter 5

Tabitha protested Wolf's plan to take Rat back into the cavern. "If he describes where he found the body, I am sure that will suffice. It is bad enough that he saw the corpse once; I do not believe we should make him relive it."

Finally, they reached an agreement; Rat could stay above ground for now, but Wolf would bring the boy down if it became necessary. In the end, it was easy to follow Rat's description of where he had found the body. As the boy had said, some openings allowed enough natural light for Wolf, Bear, Langley, and the footmen to navigate the space.

The openings offered a clear view of the Pembroke River and the steep, wooded banks opposite. While the cavern itself was damp and musty, when Wolf stood near the openings for a few moments, looking out onto the water, he could feel a welcome cool and fresh breeze. Then, he heard one of the footmen, Charlie, shouting, and he moved further into the body of the cavern.

While the openings to the cavern offered some minimal light, it was still quite dark, and Wolf's eyes had to adjust to the gloom. When they did, he discerned the shape of a body on the ground. He stooped beside it. From what he could see, it was a young man. Wolf felt for a pulse. Rat was correct; the body was icy cold and stiff. It was clear the man had been dead for some time.

"I don't think we should try to move him yet," Wolf said. "There must be a local police constabulary in Pembroke. Let us send word." The last time they were in the area, Wolf had dealt with the police in nearby Pembroke Dock. He assumed that the town of Pembroke had at least one of its own police officers. Jeremiah Goodge hadn't descended into the cavern with them, and now, Wolf instructed the footmen to stay with the body while he returned up the stairs with Bear and Langley.

As Wolf emerged from the stairs to the cavern, he saw Tabitha trying to soothe a panicked Jeremiah Goodge. The dowager was nowhere in sight.

As soon as Wolf came into view, Mr Goodge rushed over. "Your Lordship, is it true? Is there a dead body down there?" Then, without waiting for confirmation, he cried, "Oh my, however did this happen on my watch?"

"Why would you say on your watch, Mr Goodge?" Lord Langley asked.

"Well, I have been entrusted with the key and allowed access to the site for my research. So, if some ruffians have used the site for their nefarious purposes and have now come to blows here, it will reflect poorly on my stewardship."

There was something so pointed about the immediate assumption Mr Goodge jumped to that Tabitha felt compelled to ask, "Do you believe you know who our corpse might be, Mr Goodge? Have there been problems previously at the castle?"

Now, Jeremiah Goodge's tone shifted slightly from outright panic to shifty agitation. "No, no. Well, perhaps. I really couldn't speak to the motives of local criminal types. But you know how these things go: boys sneaking into the cavern at night on dares, or poachers who lurk along the riverbanks, even vagrants and drunks taking shelter."

Tabitha hadn't been down to the cavern, so she didn't realise it could be accessed from the river. Given this, she didn't understand Mr Goodge's explanation, but she chose not to press him further and instead waited to speak with the others later.

"Mr Goodge, we need to inform the local police. Can you help us with that?" Wolf asked.

"Yes, yes, the police. We must inform the authorities." Then, the man paused. "Though I cannot imagine what help Constable Tucker will be. The last serious crime the man had to investigate was when someone let Mrs Howell's pigs out to cause mischief."

Wolf had met members of the Pembrokeshire Constabulary during a previous visit to the region. While the various police officers he had encountered had been helpful and accommodating to some extent, he had to agree that none of them were likely capable of conducting a thorough investigation into a death. Let alone a murder, if that was what this turned out to be. Of course, even as Wolf thought this, he realised there was no reason to believe it was murder; it was far more probable that the body belonged to a drunk who had staggered into the cavern.

Even so, Mr Goodge's words of caution gave Wolf pause; was this investigation something he and Tabitha were willing to involve themselves in? As reluctant as he'd been to continue any aspects of his prior thief-taker work, Tabitha had finally persuaded him they might take on occasional cases, especially where they felt they could lend their power and influence to try to right a wrong. Under normal circumstances, this self-imposed mandate didn't include investigating the deaths of random people completely unrelated to anyone they knew or a cause they cared about.

Wolf glanced over at Tabitha. He knew their investigations offered his beloved wife both a challenge and a purpose. This had been the main reason he was persuaded to take on the cases that crossed their path so far. Finally, Wolf decided to see how things unfolded and to follow Tabitha's lead. Three footmen had accompanied them to Pembroke Castle, and now the one who had remained above ground was sent to fetch the local policeman.

"I think the children should be sent home," Wolf said in a low voice to Tabitha once the footman had gone. "This might take some time, and we don't want them getting underfoot."

Tabitha agreed and left to ask Mrs O'Leary to gather the children and nursemaids and return to Glanwyddan Hall.

The dowager had been surprisingly quiet and, in fact, had sat back at the picnic table. What did that mean? Tabitha wondered. Usually, they couldn't keep the woman out of investigations, no matter how much they tried.

As Mrs O'Leary packed away the children's belongings, Tabitha sat down at the picnic table. "Will you be returning with the children?" she asked.

The dowager looked at her quizzically. "And make it easy for you to cut me out of a new investigation? How do you not know me better by now, Tabitha?"

"That was not my intention, I assure you. In fact, there is no reason to believe this is an investigation we will take on. We are uncertain if the death was even caused by foul play. I was merely asking because it is so unlike you to take yourself off like this."

"Not to be poking my nose in, you mean?" the dowager asked, but with a surprising twinkle in her eye. Then she sighed. "It is a warm day, and walking around the ruins tired me out. I was taking the opportunity to rest. Nothing more."

Tabitha glanced at the elderly woman. Although she had never been brave enough to ask the dowager's age, if she did the maths based on what she knew, Tabitha would estimate the woman to be around seventy-three. The dowager was such a force of nature, both within their extended family and society at large, that it was easy to forget she was a septuagenarian.

As she placed her hand on top of the dowager's, Tabitha said in a tone of filial concern, "Why do you not go back? I promise we will inform you of any news as soon as we return. We might be here for quite some time. Wolf has called for the local police constable, and then I assume they will bring the body up. This could all take a long time, and, as you said, it is very warm out.

Initially, it seemed as if the dowager was about to refuse, but then she surprised Tabitha by saying, "Thank you, my dear. Perhaps I will do that. I did not sleep well last night, and a nap might be just the thing." Then she narrowed her eyes. "However, do not take advantage of what you might see as a moment of weakness. I expect to be told everything immediately when you return."

"I promise," Tabitha swore.

With the youngest and oldest members of their party sent on their way, they could do nothing more than wait for the police constable.

"What on earth is keeping the police?" Wolf grumbled.

Jeremiah Goodge looked apologetic. "Perhaps I should have gone in the place of your man. I might have had better luck tracking down the constable."

"I presume that if he is not at the police station, he is out in Pembroke keeping the peace," Tabitha suggested.

"You might be excused for such a reasonable thought, Lady Pembroke. However, Constable Tucker is, how can I put it?" Mr Goodge paused, unsure how to continue. "He is... well, he is known to..."

"Mr Goodge, whatever you have to say, you may say in front of my wife. I assure you, she is no shrinking violet," Wolf assured the stammering man.

With a final apologetic glance towards Tabitha, Jeremiah Goodge said, "The man is fond of his ale and can usually be found either in the pub or asleep at his kitchen table. Either way, by this time in the afternoon, it's likely he has one too many, if not more."

This will not make anything easier, Wolf thought. A quick exchange of looks with Tabitha assured him that his wife was equally worried. "If my footman does not return with the constable within the next thirty minutes, we may take you up on your suggestion that you be the one to go and find him."

Chapter 6

Fifteen minutes later, Constable Tucker arrived. Although Wolf could smell beer on his breath, the man seemed sober enough.

"Apologies, m'lord," the man said, doffing his police helmet. "I was attending to some urgent police business."

"At the Old King's Arms, constable?" Jeremiah Goodge sneered.

Constable Tucker's face reddened. "I had stopped in there to question a witness, Goodge, if you must know. I don't like what you're implying."

Wolf stepped in before the argument escalated further. "I am just glad my man was able to find you, constable. Did he tell you what has happened?"

"Said something about finding a body, not more than that."

"Indeed, in the cavern below. We have not moved the body, but once you are ready, my footmen can bring it up."

"The cavern? Must be some drunkard who stumbled in."

Wolf nodded. "Indeed, this was our thought as well. However, why do we not go down so you can review the scene, and we will move forward from there."

A few minutes later, they returned to the cavern. During the process of being summoned, Constable Tucker had the foresight to gather a lantern, which he now lit. They made their way to the corpse. With the dim light from the river's opening, Wolf had not seen much of the body beyond an outline. Now that Constable Tucker held up his lantern, it became clear the corpse was of a young man, perhaps not much more than twenty.

"He does not look like a vagrant," Langley observed. Wolf had been thinking something similar. The other thing that became clear was how the man had died: a dagger was sticking out of his side. Wolf hadn't seen it earlier because of the gloom of the cavern and because the dagger was on the far side of the corpse. Now, there was no question that this was a case of murder.

Wolf took the lantern from the constable and held it over the body. The dead man was dressed simply, but it was clear he wasn't a labourer. Rather, his clothes suggested he was a clerk of some sort. Apart from the dagger thrust into his body, there was nothing about the corpse that stood out. There wasn't any obvious blood on the body or on the ground. Then, Wolf noticed something. By the man's left hand, there seemed to be something scratched in the dirt. Crouching down, Wolf tried to make it out. It looked like letters; had the dying man written a clue to his murder? It was hard to decipher what was written, and even once Wolf had picked out the letters, he didn't know what they meant: DIG. Or at least, that was what he thought was written.

Whatever expectations, however low, Wolf had for Constable Tucker's ability to handle a murder inquiry were quickly dashed. The man looked genuinely shocked to see a dead body and was hesitant to approach it.

"Do you know who this is?" Wolf asked, trying to keep the impatience out of his voice. When the constable didn't answer immediately, Wolf pressed on, "Perhaps it would be better if you came closer and got a proper look at the face." When the other man still made no move, Wolf snapped, "Constable Tucker, please come over here and look at the body."

Finally, the police officer was stirred into action, and cautiously, he crept towards the dead man. When he got close enough to see his face in the lantern's light, Constable Tucker gasped.

"Can I take it you recognise this man?" The constable nodded silently. Wolf could barely hide his irritation. "And if so, who is it?"

"It's... it's... well, I believe, it's Mr James Truegood." Finally, they were making progress.

Wolf decided to focus on practical matters. "What is your usual process in the case of murder, Constable Tucker?" Even as he asked this, Wolf realised it was unlikely that a sleepy town like Pembroke experienced murders very often. Perhaps the constable had never had to deal with such a situation.

Changing tack slightly, Wolf said in as gentle a voice as he could manage, "When there is a death in Pembroke that is in any way suspicious, what do you do with the body? I assume there is no mortuary in town."

This appeared to be a question the constable could answer, and his relief at this was evident as he shook his head vigorously. "You're so right, m'lord. There's no mortuary."

Wolf took a deep breath. "Then where are bodies taken?"

Constable Tucker was perhaps in his mid-forties. Still, Wolf had to assume that there had been barely one or two deaths that were anything more than old men dying in their sleep, no matter how long this man had been in the constabulary. It was too gloomy in the cavern to read whatever expression crossed the constable's face, but he turned his head slightly and gazed off to the side, as if in deep contemplation.

Just as Wolf was about to interrupt the reverie, the man said, "Well now, I remember there was a death when I first took up the uniform. Back then, Constable Jones was looking to retire and brought me on to train me up."

"And? The body?"

"Yes, yes. Well, we put it in the cellar at the King's."

Happy that they were making progress at last, Wolf confirmed, "You mean the public house, the Old King's Arms?" Wolf remembered this as the place Jeremiah Goodge had mentioned when the constable had first arrived. "And would you like my footmen to move the body there now, or do you have another way you would prefer?"

Constable Tucker was more than happy to have all responsibility for the body taken from him. After checking around the body to ensure they had missed nothing else, Wolf instructed Charlie and the other footmen to bring the body up from the cavern.

Wolf, Langley, Bear and the constable preceded the footmen. As they exited the staircase, they were confronted by the sight of Jeremiah Goodge pacing and wringing his hands while Tabitha stood patiently, trying not to let the man's anxiety affect her.

As soon as the men exited the entrance to the cavern, Mr Goodge stopped pacing and hurried to meet them. "Well? Who is it? Was it a vagrant as I thought? Yes, I'm sure it must be. Who else could it be?" Wolf raised his hand to halt the man's continuous prattle. "Constable Tucker has identified the body as James Truegood."

There was no need to ask if Mr Goodge recognised the name; the look of horror on his face was proof enough.

"James? No, it cannot be. He is no vagrant or drunkard."

Between Constable Tucker's ineptitude and Jeremiah Goodge's nervous ramblings, Wolf struggled to contain his annoyance.

"Mr Goodge, there is every reason to believe that Mr Truegood was murdered. It appears that he was stabbed with a dagger."

"Murder! No!"

The use of the deceased's given name indicated that he and Mr Goodge were more than casual acquaintances. "How did you know Mr Truegood?" Tabitha asked.

Before the man could reply, the footmen appeared carrying the corpse between them. At the sight of the dead body, Mr Goodge looked as if he might faint. Wolf instructed the footmen to take the body to the Old King's Arms using one of the carts they had brought the furniture in. There seemed little point in testing Mr Goodge's queasiness by prolonging his view of the dead man.

With the body out of the way, Wolf considered how best to proceed. Two things were beyond doubt: this was a case of murder, and Constable Tucker was wholly ill-equipped to handle such an investigation. He considered a local landowner, Squire Partridge, who was the Pembrokeshire magistrate. When they met the man at Christmas, neither Tabitha nor Wolf was impressed with him. Their overall view of the bon vivant was that of a man who enjoyed the power and prestige of the magistrate title but had no genuine interest in using his position to promote the common good.

Lord Langley had said little during the examination of the body, but he had witnessed enough to perceive Wolf's inner turmoil. The older earl moved slightly closer and said in a low voice, "Wolf, even if you do not actively participate, as the highest-ranking local aristocrat, you have a seat on the county's Commission of the Peace; you are a Justice of the Peace. If you wish to take on this investigation, you have both the social and legal authority to involve yourself in a suspicious death, if you so choose."

Such a possibility had never crossed Wolf's mind. Now, he glanced at Tabitha, who had been standing close enough to hear Langley's words; did she know this? After all, she was much more familiar with such matters than he was. In response, his wife offered him a gentle, encouraging smile along with a slight nod of her head. It appeared she both understood and approved.

With a sigh of resignation, Wolf said, "Mr Goodge, is there somewhere we might go and talk?"

Mr Goodge indicated he had a home near the castle and would be pleased to host such illustrious guests.

It didn't take long for Tabitha and Wolf to give the servants instructions for packing up and returning to the hall. Constable Tucker followed the footmen to the public house.

"I want you to accompany them," Wolf said in a low voice to Bear. "Just to keep an eye on everything." Bear nodded. Wolf didn't need to say more; it was clear that the constable was not a conscientious police officer who would do things by the book and cut no corners.

Once the footmen had left with the body, followed by Bear and Constable Tucker, the rest of the group left the castle. It was only a short walk down the main Pembroke high street before they turned onto a side street and found themselves outside a small but well-kept townhouse.

Chapter 7

After opening the door and showing the group into a front parlour, Jeremiah Goodge disappeared for a few minutes, saying, "Let me just go and arrange some tea."

Tabitha looked around the room. The furnishings were outdated, but clearly well-made. Everything about the room suggested that Jeremiah Goodge lived a comfortably well-off, middle-class life. The appearance of what looked like a housekeeper bearing a tea tray confirmed this belief.

It hadn't been long since they had lunch, and nobody was hungry, though the tea was very welcome.

"Mrs Wallace's fruitcake is famous throughout Pembroke," Mr Goodge remarked as he reappeared in the doorway and noticed no one eating. "She wins first prize at the church fair every year." The antiquarian seemed to have regained his composure during the walk from the castle. Now, he settled into an armchair that looked well-used enough to be his favourite.

"Mr Goodge, how did you know James Truegood?" Wolf began.

The question reminded the man of why they were all gathered in his parlour, and he immediately became agitated again. He started tapping his knees with his fingers and nibbling on his bottom lip.

Just as they were beginning to worry that the man wouldn't answer,

Jeremiah Goodge said, "Mr Truegood was a fellow historian and devotee of all things Pembroke Castle-related. He is, well, was, a schoolteacher by profession, but history, particularly local history, was his true passion."

"So, you worked together?" Tabitha asked.

"In a manner of speaking. As you may know, the castle was leased in the early 1880s by antiquarian J. R. Cobb, who restored part of it. Along with the restoration, he undertook to survey and document the castle. Most of what we know today is due to his efforts. I moved to the area about fifteen years ago and developed an interest in the castle and its history. I am currently writing a book on the history of the castle, focusing particularly on William Marshal."

"And was Mr Truegood helping you with this book?"

"I suppose you could say that. James's fascination with the castle began when he was a child. We shared resources and collaborated on some of our work. And yes, James was helping me to research aspects of my book. However, he also had his own interests."

Lord Langley interjected, "Given where his body was found, can you think of any of those interests that might have led to his death?"

If Tabitha hadn't been looking at Jeremiah Goodge at that moment, she might have missed the fleeting expression that crossed his face. She couldn't immediately identify it, but filed away the thought to discuss later.

"James Truegood was a decent and honourable young man. I can think of no one who might wish him harm nor anything he might do that would precipitate such an outcome."

Tabitha decided this was a thread to pull on, but later. Instead, she asked, "Did Mr Truegood live in Pembroke?" She was answered with a nod of the head. "And can you point us towards his residence?"

"That could not be easier," Mr Goodge said with a rueful smile. "He rented a room from me. James is, was, a single young man. I live alone. About a year and a half ago, when he was looking for lodgings, I suggested he take my back room. He was a quiet and pleasant tenant, and the arrangement worked well for both of us."

Well, that was useful. It also made clear that the two men shared a more personal relationship than a merely professional one.

"I assume you would like to inspect the room," Mr Goodge guessed. "Why don't I take you up there now?"

He led the way up the stairs to a light-filled room at the back of the house. Although it was very tidy, the room was filled with books and papers. Every surface seemed to be covered with neat stacks of reading material.

"James was a prolific reader," Jeremiah Goodge said, gesturing to a tall pile of books beside the bed. "He would often sit with me in the parlour in the evening and always had a book at hand. Of course, he was especially interested in history, but he was quite the polymath. Sometimes he read a historical biography, but he was just as likely to be reading about the latest scientific discoveries. He had subscriptions to *Nature* and *The Fortnightly Review.*"

"It seems he was a true man of parts," Langley observed.

"Indeed, indeed. His death is a loss to the young minds he opened to the rich possibilities of the known world, but also to the intellectual establishment to which he contributed." At this, Jeremiah Goodge took a handkerchief out of his pocket and dabbed at his eyes.

It was clear it would take some time to go through all the papers and books in the room. "We may be here some time, Mr Goodge. Do not feel compelled to stay. You must have many other demands on your time." Wolf's words were courteous and indicated nothing more than a wish not to inconvenience their host, but his tone suggested this might be an order rather than a suggestion. Whether Mr Goodge picked up on the firm nature of the words, he seemed happy enough to leave them to their task.

Once Jeremiah Goodge had left the room, Langley, Tabitha, and Wolf began searching through the books and papers, trying to find any clue as to why anyone would want to murder the young historian. Mr Goodge hadn't exaggerated; James Truegood's books covered every subject from art history to botany. The man had eclectic interests and read widely. He also subscribed to numerous periodicals. Of particular relevance, they found years' worth of back issues of *The Journal of the British Archaeological Association* and *Archaeologia Cambrensis: The Journal of the Cambrian Archaeological Association.*

Tabitha had taken on the task of looking through the periodicals. She quickly realised that there were slips of paper in some of them as bookmarks. She opened the most recent edition, which had a bookmark, and found an article with various passages underlined and circled. She put that edition to the side and made her way through all the rest that were bookmarked. In all the cases, there were underlines and, in some cases, annotations in the margins.

Wolf noticed the pile growing beside her and asked, "What have you found?"

"I am unsure," Tabitha admitted. "Various articles seem to have caught Mr Truegood's attention. I am struggling to see if there is a common thread linking them all."

"Perhaps the thread is just that they all interested him," Langley suggested.

"Perhaps. Though the underlining and exclamation marks seem quite emphatic, almost as if he believed he had found a justification or confirmation of something."

Langley had been looking through a pile of letters on the desk. "Is one of those periodicals, *Archaeologia Cambrensis: The Journal of the Cambrian Archaeological Association?"*

"Yes. In fact, it is the one with the most bookmarks and annotations," Tabitha answered.

Picking up a letter from the pile, Langley said, "It seems that Mr Truegood submitted an article to that journal recently that was rejected."

He then read the letter.

May 5, 1898, London

Dear Mr Truegood,

Thank you for your recent submission titled "The True Treasure of Pembroke Castle," which I have read with interest and some caution.

Your enthusiasm for the life and legacy of William Marshal is evident, and your references to the Annales Viridimontis, though obscure, are intriguing. I must commend your diligence in tracing those marginal allusions. However, I fear the main premise of your paper relies more on conjecture than solid evidence.

While Archaeologia Cambrensis has never aimed to discourage speculative inquiry, we are committed to upholding a standard that values documentation over hypothesis. The lack of corroborating charters, seals, or even references in known inventories of the Marshal estates makes it difficult for us to justify publication at this moment.

If you uncover additional material in the future, especially manuscript evidence or references in estate rolls or ecclesiastical registers, I would be happy to revisit the matter. I will be visiting Pembrokeshire in August and would be happy to discuss in-person any further discoveries you might make.

In the meantime, I wish you continued success in your antiquarian pursuits, and remain,

Yours faithfully,

John Romilly Allen,

Editor, Archaeologia Cambrensis

"I wonder if Mr Goodge knew about this," Tabitha mused. "Certainly, it seems as if he is passionate about William Marshal. One would imagine that if Mr Truegood were writing about a topic so near and dear to Mr Goodge's heart, he would have mentioned something."

They agreed to ask Mr Goodge when they had finished going through the room. There were so many papers and books that the group was worried they had missed something. It might take days to sift through every single item in real detail. The only other things they found that seemed noteworthy were letters that, at least at first glance, seemed to be love letters of a sort.

"They are signed, Clarice," Langley noted. "There are quite a few. Far too many to read now."

"Let us take those, the periodicals Tabitha has set aside, and the letter from the editor. We can study them all in greater detail back at the hall," Wolf suggested.

They gathered all the items they wished to take with them, then, after a final glance at the room, they returned downstairs. Mr Goodge was still in the parlour, drinking a fresh cup of tea and reading a book. Upon seeing the pile in Wolf's arms, he asked, "Did you find something of use?"

"Honestly, we are unsure. We would like to take these and examine them in more detail. Can we ask you to leave Mr Truegood's room untouched for now, in case we wish to return to continue the search?" As Wolf said this, he wondered whether the young man had any local family who might have a claim to his possessions, and directed this question to Mr Goodge.

Mr Goodge indicated no. "James did not speak much of his family. But from what I gathered over the time I knew him, he was the only son of parents who died just before he moved here. His father had been a vicar who ensured his son was educated, but could not provide much of an inheritance beyond that."

"We have one more question before we leave," Tabitha said. "We found a letter in Mr Truegood's belongings. It was a rejection letter from a periodical called *Archaeologia Cambrensis.* Apparently, he had submitted an article titled, *The True Treasure of Pembroke*, which involved William Marshal. Can you tell us anything more?"

Again, a shadow briefly crossed Jeremiah Goodge's face, but it was so fleeting that Tabitha nearly missed it. "I am afraid I am unaware of what you speak. As I said, James was helping me with my research, but he would have told me if he was submitting an article for publication."

Would he? Tabitha wondered. Or perhaps he did, and Mr Goodge was dissembling for some reason?

Just as the group was about to leave, Tabitha remembered something. "Mr Goodge, do you have any idea who a Clarice might be?"

"Yes. That would likely be Clarice Hill. Her father is a prominent local solicitor. Why?"

"Was James Truegood courting Miss Hill?"

Mr Goodge laughed. "Heavens no! I cannot imagine Cyril Hill allowing his darling Clarice to throw herself away on an assistant schoolmaster."

Chapter 8

The group spoke little during the carriage ride back to Glanwyddan Hall. Everyone was lost in thought about the shocking events of their afternoon. Moreover, as Tabitha pointed out, they would need to rehash everything for the dowager as soon as they returned, so it was perhaps easiest to hold off on sharing their thoughts until then.

As they expected, no sooner had they set foot in the hall than Talbot informed them, "Lady Pembroke is waiting for you in the parlour. She has had us set up your corkboard and requested your immediate presence."

Tabitha nearly groaned aloud. Instead, she replied, "Thank you, Talbot. Please inform her ladyship that I have gone to freshen up and change out of these dusty clothes. I will be downstairs shortly."

Even the usually inscrutable butler couldn't fully conceal his facial reaction to the news, and it was quite clear that he didn't relish being the bearer of these particular tidings.

Out of compassion for the man, Wolf said, "Why do you not all go and freshen up? I will explain to Lady Pembroke that you will meet her in the parlour. I can also take the letters and periodicals into the parlour for us to peruse later."

Tabitha flashed him a grateful smile for his willingness to be the sacrificial lamb. There was little doubt this news would not be well-received, but it would probably be better coming from her favourite, Jeremy, than from any of the others in their group. She retired to the bedchamber she shared with Wolf and found Ginny busy arranging freshly laundered clothes. Tabitha washed the grime of the day off herself and was busy changing into a comfortable gown when Wolf entered the room.

"Thank you," she said, not needing to explain what her gratitude was for.

"Indeed," Wolf replied with a rueful smile. "As you can imagine, she was not pleased to be kept waiting, and I quote, 'Even longer than was already necessary, I am sure'."

"Let us not worsen her irritation any further. Ginny, can you help me button up this dress? Wolf, I will go downstairs and buy you a little time to change."

When Tabitha entered the parlour, she saw that Langley and Bear had preceded her. As she had expected, the dowager was in full flow. "I agreed to return with the children because I expected you to be close behind. Instead, you were gone all afternoon!" the woman whined.

"Mama, we were hardly gone all afternoon," Tabitha said gently. "And did you really expect us to be close behind? We had to wait for the police constable to arrive, which in itself took some time. Then, the body had to be inspected and thereafter brought up to the surface. After that, we retired to Mr Goodge's home to speak with him further and to search the victim's room. Once we had finished, we came straight home."

There it was, one of the dowager's sniffs. As was so often the case, the woman employed them when she realised she might be in the wrong, or at least not on the moral high ground, but still wished to indicate her displeasure at a situation.

"Well, you are here at last. So, let us waste no more time. Tell me everything." Under different circumstances, Tabitha would have suggested they wait a few more minutes for Wolf. However, the look on the dowager's face showed it might be the last straw for her. Instead, she approached the corkboard, took the stack of fresh notecards placed there, and grabbed a pen. Then, she settled into an armchair and allowed Langley and Bear to start the story while she wrote on the notecards.

Langley had scarcely finished describing what they had realised about the death when Wolf entered the parlour. He had anticipated that the dowager would be reluctant to wait for his arrival, and simply gave Tabitha a knowing look before settling into a chair.

The group provided the dowager with a full, though not overly florid, explanation of what they had learned. The elderly woman had told them many times that, at her age, an economy of words was a better use of whatever time she had left on earth.

When they finished their story, the dowager gestured towards the pile of papers and journals Wolf had left on the table earlier. "And so, why have you brought all of this back with you?"

"Well, to be honest," Tabitha admitted, "we are not sure. Mr Truegood had bookmarked certain articles, so those seemed to be as good a place to start as any. In addition, I would like to look through his love letters from this young woman, Clarice Hill. There were so many books and papers in the room that it was hard to know what to focus on. It is possible that we may have to return and do a more thorough search later."

"So, a doomed love affair!" the dowager said with a rather inappropriate glee in her voice. "That seems like a good place to begin. All very Romeo and Juliet if you ask me; a forbidden love, a controlling father, and a final honour killing. Why, the story almost writes itself."

The woman's morbid delight aside, it was hard to argue with her overall point. Tabitha realised they needed to speak with Clarice Hill, but how?

Wolf's answer made it clear he didn't see their conundrum. "Is there a reason we cannot visit the Hill residence and make inquiries?"

"Of course, we cannot. Why would we turn up on their doorstep without any previous introduction? If Mr Hill was unlikely to approve of the courtship, then all our visit will do is expose his daughter to parental censure, and for no reason; Mr Truegood is dead."

Tabitha's explanation was reasonable, but Wolf still pressed, "Would it not be possible for you to visit Miss Hill without exposing her secret?"

"Jeremy," the dowager snapped irritably. "Sometimes you can be shockingly dim-witted. There is no good reason the Countess of Pembroke would lower herself to make such a visit, particularly without any previous meeting somewhere. If Tabitha did turn up, any social climber worth his salt would insist on being part of such a visit. I cannot imagine how a private audience would be obtained without an explanation."

"Then what should we do?" Wolf asked.

"Oh, dear. When will you ever realise the power of an earldom?" the dowager asked as if questioning a small boy. "You will throw a dinner party and invite Mr Hill and his daughter. It will be far easier to peel her off in your home, amongst a large group. Unfortunately, it is too late to plan a dinner for tonight, but tomorrow evening should be more than enough notice to give your guests."

"Will it not seem odd if I invite people at such short notice? Especially those with whom I have no acquaintance? How will I even explain to Mr Hill why he is being invited?"

Tabitha was well aware of her husband's natural modesty and disinclination to throw his weight around as an aristocrat. However, she understood the dowager's point perfectly and explained, "Darling, you are an earl. Do you really believe anyone will not put aside any other evening plans for the chance to dine at your table?"

Wolf shrugged. The dowager took up the explanation. "In my experience, most people overestimate their importance and status in society. A small-town solicitor is precisely the kind of man who considers himself king of a very small hill. I can just imagine how a man who mistakes local deference for real consequence will puff up on receiving the invitation and how it will fuel his sense of entitlement and prestige."

While Tabitha might have phrased her answer a little more charitably, she couldn't argue with the dowager's overall point. "We had that dinner for local neighbours at Christmas and invited people from across the social spectrum..."

"Do not remind me," the dowager interjected with snobbish passion. "Promise me that you will not invite the awful local squire and those simpering, nitwit elderly sisters. What were their names? The Miss Edwards?"

"Miss Edgars," Tabitha corrected. Nevertheless, the dowager's words did make Tabitha consider who else to invite. It would be too pointed to only invite Mr and Miss Hill, and also much more difficult to get Miss Hill on her own.

Addressing Wolf, Tabitha asked, "Were you planning to inform Squire Partridge of your involvement in this investigation?"

Wolf considered the question. Before he could answer, Langley suggested, "I believe you should call on the man and give him the courtesy of informing him yourself. Based on our prior dealings with him, I doubt he will bestir himself to interfere if he does not need to." Wolf agreed with this assessment of the local magistrate and said he would call on him the following morning.

"In that case, I believe we cannot avoid inviting him to dinner." Still, they needed more guests. "Let us invite Sir Jerome and his wife. He was the mayor of Pembroke and likely is well-acquainted with Mr Hill. Perhaps this will make it easier to engage him in a conversation distracting enough for me to talk with his daughter privately," Tabitha suggested.

Although this would result in uneven numbers of men and women, everyone agreed the group was large enough for their purposes, and Tabitha went to speak to Mrs Budgers and the housekeeper, Mrs Jenkins, about the menu. At the same time, Wolf immediately sat down to write invitation notes to send as soon as possible.

When Tabitha returned, she took up James Truegood's letters from his supposed paramour and set about combing through them for any clues while Langley and Bear combed through the marked periodicals. They paused for an early dinner and then picked their reading back up after.

Chapter 9

The following morning, the group minus the dowager gathered for breakfast. Tabitha had read and reread the many letters from Clarice Hill, searching for clues.

Now, she admitted her frustration. "While the letters are certainly flirtatious, I would not call them passionate love letters. In fact, mostly, they are full of social gossip and the kind of silliness one might expect from a sheltered, very young woman. She complains about her father, but equally frequently about their cook, who apparently is quite prone to burning the roast. While it is difficult to imagine precisely what Mr Truegood's side of the correspondence was like, his beloved's responses do not speak of any great urgency to resolve their situation. More than anything, they have the trappings of love letters; the paper is scented, and at least one letter had a lock of hair in it."

"What do you mean by that?" Wolf asked as he buttered his toast.

"Well, there is definitely no talk of elopement or any other drastic actions. If I had to guess, I would say that Miss Hill is quite young, perhaps not even eighteen. She writes as someone who is enjoying the drama of their illicit relationship a little too much. I imagine that Mr Hill is a rather strict parent, and that perhaps some rebellion lies behind this romance just as much as anything else."

"I wonder how they first met," Bear mused. Then, answering his own question, he added, "Although Pembroke is not a large town, so perhaps it is not so hard to imagine."

"Indeed," Tabitha agreed.

Then, their conversation shifted to the articles they had read. "From what we could tell, there were about six articles he had both bookmarked and annotated in some way." Wolf then read the list he and Langley had compiled the previous evening. "On the Custody of Royal Charters in the Marches during the Reign of Henry III, Some Notes on a Sealed Vault beneath the Norman Hall at Pembroke, The Lost Charters of the Abbey of Monkton: A Hypothesis, Duplicitous Drafts: The Distribution of the Great Charter beyond Westminster, Observations upon a Wall-Niche at Pembroke Castle: Shrine or Hiding-Place?, and finally, A Charter Chest at Kidwelly and Its Contents."

"That is all quite a mouthful," Tabitha observed. "Did you read the articles?"

"I tried," Wolf admitted, "but they were turgid, to say the least."

Langley had not had an easier time of it. "The person who might shed some light on why Mr Truegood had marked these is Jeremiah Goodge," he suggested.

"However, you are not sure you trust the man," Wolf said, finishing Langley's thought. "Indeed. Do you all share the same feeling?" They all agreed that Mr Goodge's insistence that he knew nothing about the article James Truegood submitted for publication and which had been rejected lacked credibility.

"While his seeming lack of candour does not mean he is guilty of murder, it does suggest we might not get a full and honest answer from him about this," Tabitha said, expressing their collective thoughts. "However, what other choice do we have?"

"Well, something in the latest edition of *Archaeologia Cambrensis* caught my eye. Actually, it was something else that Mr Truegood had bookmarked. It was an announcement that its editor, the man who wrote the rejection letter, a Mr John Romilly Allen, is leading a guided tour of Lamphey Bishop's Summer Palace. In his rejection letter, Mr Allen said he would be in the area in August. And as luck would have it, the tour is this afternoon!"

"That is fortunate. What time?"

"At two o'clock. It seems it is open to the public. I suggest we have an early lunch and then head over to Lamphey." Langley paused. "Have you ever visited the Bishop's Summer Palace, Wolf?"

Wolf had never even heard of it. Lord Langley left the breakfast room and returned a few minutes later with one of the periodicals. He flicked open to an inside page and read, "Join our own Mr John Romilly Allen for a guided tour of the Bishop of St David's ruined summer palace at Lamphey, where cloister and court once met beneath Pembrokeshire's gentle sky. Let your steps trace the stones of centuries past, as we recount tales of bishops, banquets, and the subtle politics of the medieval Welsh Church. All are welcome."

Wolf wiped his mouth, then stood. "Then, I suppose that is how we will spend our afternoon. Before that, I need to speak with Squire Partridge. I sent him a note last night, and he will be arriving sometime after eleven this morning. Would any of you care to join the meeting?" When no one answered, he said, "Langley, I would appreciate your company. You are far more versed in the legalities of the JP system than I am. I doubt the squire will question my involvement over his, but just in case, would you be prepared to join me?"

Langley expressed his willingness to sit in on the meeting. Tabitha was eager to absent herself from the conversation. She found Squire Partridge distasteful. The dowager had once described him as a "lewd, drunken sot," and for once, Tabitha could only agree with her judgement.

Wolf had received grateful thanks and eager RSVPs from all his invited guests for that evening. Tabitha thought she should take some time to ensure that all their last-minute dinner plans were proceeding smoothly, so she set off to find Mrs Jenkins.

There was some time before Squire Partridge's visit, so Wolf and Langley parted ways, Wolf to review some estate papers, and Langley to check on how Rat's studies were progressing. Bear took the opportunity to head to the nursery to see Mrs O'Leary and the children.

Wolf was absorbed in reviewing a report on the recent renovation of the cottages on the estate when Talbot announced Squire Partridge. The large, red-faced man entered the room with a broad smile on his face.

Standing to greet his guest, Wolf said, "Squire Partridge, so good of you to make time for me." He hoped to see Langley in his wake, but the man was nowhere to be seen. "Talbot, please let Lord Langley know that our visitor is here." Wolf could only hope that the ever-efficient Talbot would find the other man quickly.

"Think nothing of it! After all, the Pembroke Estate has always kept one of the finest cellars in the country."

The man said this with a very definite gleam in his eye, and although it was only mid-morning, Wolf took the hint. "Can I offer you something to drink?" Then, if only for propitiatory's sake, he suggested, "Tea or coffee?" When, as expected, neither of those beverages elicited a positive response, he added, "Or perhaps a brandy?"

"Ah, now that would be very civilised. I miss many things about Philip, but his brandy is high on the list." The squire had regarded the dowager's brutish husband as one of his dearest friends. Aside from all the disgust his personal traits evoked in the woman, this was probably his greatest sin.

Wolf stood and poured a generous measure of brandy into a glass.

"Are you not joining me?" the squire asked.

"I have some work to do this morning and want to keep my wits about me."

"In my experience, most things are improved if you're a little merry while doing them."

Wolf wasn't sure if the squire was joking or not, and so ignored the comment. Instead, he launched into the reason he'd requested the meeting. The squire's company was not something he wished to endure any longer than necessary, especially considering the man was returning for dinner that evening.

Because he was unsure exactly how local magistrates operated, Wolf didn't know if Squire Partridge had already been alerted to the death of James Truegood. It seemed he hadn't been. Nor did he seem concerned about that oversight. On their previous visit, Wolf had judged the man to be lazy and self-satisfied, showing little regard for whether justice was truly served. Nothing about this current conversation changed his view.

After describing their visit to Pembroke Castle and how Rat stumbled across the body, Wolf explained, "I know that I have not been an active JP in Pembrokeshire, however..." At that moment, the door opened, and

Lord Langley entered the room. "Good timing, Langley. I was just beginning to explain the situation to the squire."

Now that Langley had arrived, Wolf felt more comfortable jumping to the pertinent part of the story: that he would be acting as the Justice of the Peace in this case.

He had hoped that Squire Partridge's natural sloth and general disregard for true justice would prevail over any possible ruffled feathers at not being consulted earlier. It appeared he was correct in that assumption.

Squire Partridge took another gulp of his brandy and replied, "Capital! Capital. I am sure you will do an excellent job. While, of course, I am available if you should need any advice on local matters, do not hesitate to move forward without me."

Relieved, Wolf answered, "Actually, there is one question I have for you: what do you know of a Pembroke solicitor, Mr Hill?"

The squire rubbed his copious stomach as he considered the question. "Hill, you say? Not sure I know him. I do know that Jeremiah Goodge. Odd little man. We had a bit of a set to a few years ago. He claimed there were ruins on my land and wanted to carry out an archaeological dig. I told him to sling his hook, so to speak." Squire Partridge chuckled at his own use of nautical slang.

Wolf tried to decide if the squire's assessment of Jeremiah Goodge held any real value. With a glance at Langley, he decided that even a lecherous drunk's opinion was at least worth hearing. "When you say, 'odd little man', what do you mean?"

"Well, for starters, the man doesn't drink. I've never trusted a teetotaller, especially a sanctimonious one. Mr Goodge turned up at my house while I was enjoying a fine bottle of claret, then proceeded to lecture me on the evils of the demon drink! Have you ever heard such rot? Anyway, I sent the man packing soon enough. I received some strongly worded letters from him about the importance of some so-called ruins in the area, but I ignored them all after that."

Once the conversation about the investigation concluded, Wolf was eager to be rid of the jocular squire. However, it took another glass of brandy and far too much talk of apple-cheeked dairymaids before they could get the man to leave.

Chapter 10

As planned, the group gathered for an early midday meal. The expedition to Lamphey Bishop's Summer Palace was to include Tabitha, Wolf, Langley, and the dowager. During lunch, there was some effort to persuade the elderly woman that stomping around a ruined building might not be advisable.

Unsurprisingly, she brushed aside their concerns. "I will bring my walking stick and will be perfectly able to navigate the terrain, I am sure." Then, narrowing her eyes suspiciously, she addressed Tabitha. "You were able to persuade me to absent myself from the investigation yesterday. Do not lapse into the false hope that this acquiescence bodes of similar passivity going forward."

As it happened, in this instance, Tabitha's concerns had genuinely been for the dowager's well-being. They didn't know how safe the ruins were to walk among, and even with a walking stick, she worried about the woman's welfare. However, once her intransigence on the matter became clear, not to mention the implication that Tabitha's concerns were insincere, all attempts to dissuade the dowager were abandoned.

The carriage ride to the Lamphey Bishop's Summer Palace was brief, and before they knew it, they were travelling down a country lane before stopping by an ancient-looking stone wall.

It was five minutes before two o'clock, and a small crowd had gathered. Tabitha presumed they were also there for the tour and lecture. The Pembroke carriage seemed to cause quite a stir among the group. As Tabitha stepped down, she could hear murmurs and gasps of surprise.

Perhaps it wasn't surprising, she thought. After all, these sorts of events were probably rarely attended by local aristocrats. Add to that the fact that Wolf was the new earl, and therefore a figure of particular local interest, and she wondered why they hadn't considered that their presence might turn this lecture into a farce.

As the crowd parted to gaze at them in awe, Tabitha saw it had gathered around a man of medium build, perhaps in his fifties. He sported a neatly trimmed grey beard. His thinning hair, which was greyer than that on his face, was slicked back and parted to the side. He was dressed soberly but professionally and wore round, wire-rimmed spectacles.

The man approached them. "I am John Romilly Allen and am about to conduct a guided tour of the ruins. May I ask with whom I have the pleasure of speaking with?"

Since the man was not from the area, it was no surprise he didn't recognise the crest on the carriage. Wolf inclined his head slightly and replied, "I am the Earl of Pembroke, Jeremy Chesterton. My group and I are here for your talk."

While his first instinct had been to offer his hand, he knew, from many years of observing his grandfather in such situations, that an earl would not typically extend such a courtesy to a commoner. Although Wolf despised adopting aristocratic airs, he understood that sometimes it served a purpose, and suspected that now would be one of those times.

Wolf's expectations were fulfilled when Mr Allen's eyes widened with surprise, and his entire demeanour and tone grew more deferential. "Your lordship, I am most honoured. Now that you are here, we shall proceed. If you would be so kind as to follow me."

Tabitha adjusted her hat against the gentle breeze as they followed their guide through the crumbling gatehouse of Lamphey Bishop's Summer Palace. Mr Allen paused for a moment beneath the weathered arch.

"Here," he said, tapping his walking stick against the wall, "you see the remains of the 14th-century gatehouse, with its projecting turrets and the bishop's arms, or what's left of them. The original residence dates from the early 13th century, under Bishop Bek, but it was Bishop Henry Gower, in the 14th century, who transformed the site into what you see today."

He guided them onto the palace grounds. It was a lovely day; the sky was a perfect shade of blue with the occasional cloud drifting by. The vast stretch of grass they had stepped onto seemed ideal for a lazy afternoon outing, and in the distance, they could see at least one group picnicking.

Even in its ruined state, the Bishop's Summer Palace remained impressive. From their vantage point, Tabitha could see a spread of low stone walls and taller ruins. There was a quietness to the place that made her wish she could explore the grounds freely, rather than being confined to Mr Allen's group. Tabitha comforted herself with the thought that she could always return another day. Today, they had a task to complete.

Pointing toward the ruins, the historian continued, "Lamphey was the bishops' summer palace, a place of retreat from ecclesiastical squabbles in St David's. You'll notice it is not a fortress, at least not in the Norman sense. Nevertheless, the place was quite prestigious."

An older woman in rather severe bombazine raised her hand. "Were the bishops often here, Mr Allen?"

"Excellent question! Excellent," the guide replied. "Indeed, they were. The bishops kept a large household here in the summer. Accounts from the 14th century mention clerks, cooks, stewards, and huntsmen. The surrounding land was well-stocked and productive, with fishponds, an orchard, a dovecote, and fertile arable soil."

"Are we to put up with much more of this heckling?" the dowager asked Tabitha in a voice that was not nearly low enough.

Whispering in reply, Tabitha said, "You could stay in the carriage, Mama."

As the dowager contemplated the rather large expanse of land on which the palace stood, she conceded, "Perhaps I will do that, after all." Tabitha sighed with relief as the elderly woman returned to the carriage. The relief was partly due to concern for the woman's stamina and safety while traipsing through the ruins, but mostly from fear of what else she might have said if she'd continued with the tour.

Mr Allen led them across the grass, towards the ruins of what he explained was the Great Hall.

Gesturing toward the long eastern wall where tall lancet windows opened to sky and field, he continued, "Imagine, if you will, the high table beneath that window, the hearths along the centre line, and coloured cloths on the tables. Gower had an eye for comfort; note the traces of domestic refinement. This is not so much a place of authority, but one of elegance and comfort."

Large dark birds seemed to perch in every high nook, occasionally swooping down and circling the ruins. Mr Allen explained they were jackdaws.

The tour proceeded through each room of the palace. They descended a well-worn staircase into the vaulted room. "This is one of the finest surviving features," their guide said almost reverently. "The undercroft beneath the Great Hall was used for storage and perhaps household functions. Some speculate a private chapel may have stood above, though that's still unproven."

There was no doubt that touring the ruins with the highly knowledgeable Mr Allen was more enlightening than wandering aimlessly on their own. However, Tabitha thought that, in different circumstances, she might have preferred a less educational but more leisurely stroll around the site. There was a mysterious romance to the ancient stones that was somewhat diminished by Mr Allen's extremely detailed explanations of every aspect of the place.

The tour lasted longer than Tabitha and Wolf had expected or hoped. Mr Allen was very passionate about his subject and took delight in going off on lengthy and complicated tangents. Whenever a member of the group asked a question, Tabitha's heart sank, knowing this would add at least another ten minutes of rambling to their tour. She was relieved, however, that the dowager was no longer present to make sarcastic asides at each question and response.

Finally, it seemed they had been in every room of the palace and discussed every possible aspect of the ruined palace. Mr Allen made a small bow, and the group clapped enthusiastically.

As the group disbanded, Wolf approached their tour guide. "Mr Allen, that was a very informative and interesting tour."

Mr Allen smiled appreciatively. "This is one of the most interesting ruins in the area, except perhaps for the castle itself," he quickly added.

"Indeed. In fact, the castle is part of why we hoped to speak with you today. Would you be able to join us for tea at Glanwyddan Hall?"

The man hesitated before replying. "I am staying with Mrs Herbert Jones, who brought me here in her carriage..."

Wolf interrupted. "I would be happy to take you in the Pembroke carriage and then return you to the Jones residence."

"In that case, I would be delighted, your lordship. Let me tell Mrs Jones not to wait for me, and then we can be on our way."

Ten minutes later, the Pembroke carriage had returned to Glanwyddan Hall. It was fortunate that the journey was brief, as the carriage was rather cramped with six people inside. Hoping to impress Mr Allen with the full weight of the earldom, Wolf escorted him into the formal drawing room. From his expression, it appeared the tactic had been successful; he was clearly overawed.

"If you do not mind, Mr Allen, we will leave you here briefly while we all refresh ourselves from the heat and dust of the afternoon," Tabitha said.

They left Mr Allen nervously perched on the edge of a primrose silk couch. Everyone quickly prepared themselves and returned to the drawing room within twenty minutes. In the meantime, Talbot had brought a tray to the drawing room, where Mr Allen was now sipping a cup of tea and nibbling on a shortbread biscuit.

The group settled themselves with cups of tea, and then Wolf began, "Mr Allen, I am sure you are wondering why I wish to speak with you."

"Well, I am curious. Though as I pondered that question while I waited, it did occur to me that perhaps you wish to take a more active interest in local archaeology. Naturally, the field has always benefitted from the curiosity and, of course, the largesse of great men such as yourself."

Wolf was sorry to disappoint the man, but it had to be done. "Actually, I wished to speak with you in my official capacity as a local Justice of the Peace. There has been a murder in Pembroke."

"Oh my!"

"Indeed. The victim was a Mr James Truegood."

"Truegood? Why does that name sound so familiar?" Mr Allen wondered.

"He recently submitted an article to the *Archaeologia Cambrensis,*" Tabitha explained. "Your letter of rejection was found among his effects."

"Yes, of course. I do remember now. It was an intriguing proposition. However, as I believe I said in my letter, his hypothesis was entirely speculative. Mr Truegood found a reference in a 13th-century chronicle, *Annales de Viridimontis*, which he believed referenced a hidden, later copy of the Magna Carta. It seems that Mr Truegood was either descended from, or believed himself to be descended from, a steward in William Marshal's household. Some family lore had been passed down through the centuries, leading Mr Truegood to believe that this other Magna Carta was buried somewhere in Pembroke or thereabouts. He believed it was either somewhere in the Castle, or some other neighbouring ruins."

"The Magna Carta?" the dowager exclaimed. "Why on earth would it matter if there were another copy of that, for heaven's sake?"

"Madam," Mr Allen began.

"It is your ladyship," he was advised sternly.

"Your ladyship, it isn't an unbelievable thesis. William Marshal reissued the Magna Carta in 1216 and again in 1217, further refining it. More importantly, he made great efforts to legitimise it after King John's death. The document, even as we have it today, is one of the most important and radical in British history. It laid the groundwork for the legal system we have today and served as a blueprint for many other countries. A new version, perhaps granting greater liberty or inheritance rights for women, or even curbing the Church's power, would be of enormous historical significance, if nothing else."

The look on the dowager's face conveyed her opinion of such a possibility. Wolf hoped to steer the conversation back on course and said, "So, based on this family story and something he'd found in an ancient book, Mr Truegood made this hypothesis. However, you rejected it for publication because of a lack of actual evidence?"

"In a nutshell, yes."

Mr Allen didn't have more to share, but before he left, he gave them the address of the fellow history enthusiast, Reverend Jonas Aldersham, with whom he was staying in Tenby. "I will likely stay for a week or so. Feel free to let me know if I can be of any more assistance."

After Mr Allen left, Wolf thought, "I wonder if that is why DIG was scratched in the dirt by the body. Perhaps his dying thought was to hope someone would continue to dig in the ruins to find this later copy of the Magna Carta." It made some sense, but didn't help them move the investigation forward at all.

CHAPTER 11

Almost from the moment they all sat down that evening, Wolf could feel how tense their dinner party was. After having been placed next to the dowager previously, it was clear from the scowl on Sir Jerome's face that he wasn't happy to find the situation repeated. For her part, the dowager might have accepted the necessity of sitting next to the man, but that didn't mean she had to pretend to be pleased about it. Her displeasure was exacerbated by having Cyril Hill on her other side. It hadn't taken her more than a few words to realise what a self-important, pompous prig the man was.

Clarice Hill seemed delighted to be sitting next to Wolf, but less so to have Squire Partridge to her right. Although given the way the disgusting older man was leering at her décolletage, Wolf could hardly blame the young woman.

Because of the odd numbers, Tabitha had placed Langley next to Mr Hill, hoping he might get the measure of the man. Tabitha was seated next to Langley, but also to the right of the squire, and when he wasn't staring lasciviously at Clarice, he turned his lecherous glances in her direction. In an appalling but necessary breach of decorum, Lady Anna was placed to Wolf's left, which meant she was sitting next to her husband. This appeared to be a situation that pleased neither party of the married couple.

The atmosphere around the dining table was already uncomfortable, and then it grew worse. As the soup plates were being cleared, Squire Partridge called up the table to Wolf, "Any news on that Truegood murder?"

Given that the two men had spoken that morning, Wolf could not imagine how much progress the squire expected them to have made in the investigation. Furthermore, the fact that the squire, who was himself a local magistrate, believed it was suitable to shout across the table during dinner with other people present was truly unbelievable.

Tabitha had much the same thought as her husband. However, since the squire had raised the subject of James Truegood's death, she was eager to use the opportunity to observe Clarice Hill's reaction. What was startling was how little she reacted. Indeed, no look of pain crossed her face at the mention of her deceased, supposed beloved. In fact, given that, at the very least, they knew she was acquainted with the man, there was minimal reaction.

It seemed safe to assume Clarice had already heard about the death, as her face showed no sign of surprise. Pembroke was a small town unlikely to have many murders, so it was not surprising that the news had spread. Perhaps Miss Hill had already cried herself to sleep and was now behaving stoically in her father's presence.

With this in mind, Tabitha continued to observe Clarice's face. Unless the woman was a superb actress, there were no signs of strong emotions being tightly controlled. In fact, no sooner had Wolf answered the squire with a vague response than Clarice was speaking to him in a lively manner and laughing at something he had said.

Given this reaction, or lack thereof, Tabitha felt it was even more important to find time to speak privately with Miss Hill. Her best opportunity would be after dinner, when the men stayed behind to drink their port and the women retired to the drawing room for tea and coffee. Although the dowager usually held strong opinions against this custom, she had been persuaded to set them aside to facilitate a conversation with Clarice Hill.

As the meal drew to a close, Tabitha stood up and invited the women to join her. For a moment, she worried the dowager had forgotten her promise and was about to cause trouble, but she caught the woman's eye and raised her eyebrows in a silent reminder.

The plan was for the dowager to engage Lady Anna in conversation while Tabitha spoke with Clarice. As they returned to the drawing room, the dowager invited Lady Anna to sit beside her as she forced herself to endure at least thirty minutes of petty local gossip.

Tabitha seized this opportunity to ask Clarice, "Miss Hill, have you ever visited Glanwyddan Hall before?" Of course, there was little reason to believe she had; indeed, Clarice indicated in the negative. "Then perhaps you would enjoy a tour? In particular, we have a charming conservatory with a delightful view over the gardens."

While it was possible that Miss Hill might decline the invitation, it would be a significant breach of etiquette. Given this, Tabitha was unsurprised when the woman replied, "That would be delightful, your ladyship."

In order to maintain the illusion, Tabitha endeavoured to give the tour some substance. She did her best to remember who the portraits were of that lined the walls and what history she could recall surrounding the various suits of armour and weapons on display. Miss Hill appeared no more interested in hearing these titbits than Tabitha was in telling them.

Finally, they arrived at the conservatory, also known as the Green Room. True to its name, the Green Room was decorated in various shades of green. Thanks to its glass roof and walls, it was the warmest part of the house and especially pleasant to sit in during the winter months. It once was a genuine conservatory full of orchids, reflecting the old earl's passion for the flowers. However, it had long since lost its exotic collection. Still, a few hardy plants persisted, enhancing the greenness of the room. Despite neglect, the conservatory retained a quiet charm, sunlit and slightly overgrown with foliage. It was one of Tabitha's favourite spots to sit in the hall.

As she had promised, the ample glass offered a lovely view of the beautifully maintained gardens. The room's furniture was arranged to make the most of the vista. Now, Tabitha sat in one armchair and encouraged Clarice to take the nearest other one. Clarice's expression did not suggest that the younger woman wondered why she was being singled out for a cosy conversation with the countess. Though considering her father's inflated ego, it was perhaps not surprising that his daughter also believed this was simply what she deserved.

After Squire Partridge had conveniently, if inappropriately, raised the topic of James Truegood's death, Tabitha had spent the rest of dinner mulling how best to approach this conversation. She decided there was no point in beating around the bush. It was now out in the open that Wolf was investigating, and there was no longer any concern about shocking Clarice with the news.

Once both women were settled, Tabitha began. "Miss Hill, I admit there is another reason I wished to speak with you privately."

"Oh, really, Lady Pembroke. Whyever can that be?"

"As you heard from Squire Partridge, Lord Pembroke is acting as the Justice of the Peace in the investigation of Mr Truegood's murder." As she said these last words, Tabitha paid particular attention to Miss Hill's face. It was one thing to know of the death, quite another to hear it was being considered a murder. However, yet again, whatever she might be thinking, her countenance was as untroubled as if they were discussing something far more mundane.

Tabitha continued. "As part of the investigation, Lord Pembroke examined Mr Truegood's belongings." For the first time, a small frown appeared on Clarice's brow. Still, she said nothing. "Among his belongings, we found a rather extensive collection of letters," she paused briefly, "from you."

Clarice Hill said nothing for a few moments. However, a range of expressions flickered across her face. If Tabitha had to guess, Miss Hill was contemplating lying to her and deciding which particular falsehood to tell.

Tabitha decided to save time and effort, saying, "Let us speak plainly, Miss Hill. Those letters implied a rather close friendship between you and Mr Truegood."

Perhaps Clarice blushed slightly; it was hard to tell. Certainly, she didn't respond, prompting Tabitha to continue. "Having read all your letters, I can only conclude that there was an illicit romance between the two of you, of which your father would not have approved. Is that correct?"

It seemed as if Clarice Hill would have very much liked to deny any such romance, but now that she knew what Tabitha had read, she must have decided there would be little point. Instead, she said, "James was very much in love with me, and I was fond of him. However, not fond enough to throw away my life on a penniless assistant schoolmaster. And absolutely not fond enough to justify incurring my father's certain wrath."

Tabitha couldn't help but ask, "Then why encourage the romance?"

Clarice sighed. "Life in Pembroke is as predictable as pudding. I have lived here my entire life and know everyone. Every dance and gathering is attended by the same people having the same conversations. It is always exciting when someone new arrives in town, particularly if that person is a young and handsome man. When James first moved to Pembroke, perhaps a year and a half ago, every girl was wild about him, almost before we had laid eyes on him. I met him at a dance held in town. He was standing talking with that peculiar man, Hywel, who is always staring so intently and making me uncomfortable. James and I danced that night, and then he asked if we might meet one day. When he declared himself, it was just so thrilling to have something new happen. Then, the correspondence just seemed to continue. It gave me something to look forward to; a little secret all of my own."

Tabitha did understand what the young woman was saying and felt some sympathy. She remembered being a young girl, eager for life to offer some kind of adventure. And she had been the daughter of a marquis, about to make her debut rather than the middle-class daughter of a country solicitor.

Despite her empathy for Clarice Hill, she had to ask, "So you led Mr Truegood on and allowed him to believe that you wished to marry him, but that your father stood in the way?"

For the first time in this conversation, Clarice appeared uncomfortable. "Well, I wouldn't put it quite like that. Mr Truegood did wish for us to become betrothed. However, I never told him explicitly that I would if not for Papa."

"However, you did suggest so?" Tabitha added. Clarice hung her head and looked truly ashamed. Yet, Tabitha wondered how sincere her contrition was. It was clear that, even if they were not lovers, James Truegood was someone Clarice Hill had exchanged personal letters with for some time. Given that, her apparent lack of concern at his death suggested a chilling heartlessness.

Tabitha decided to switch subjects. "Can you think of anyone who might want to harm Mr Truegood in any way?"

"To be honest, I am not the best person to ask. His letters to me were almost entirely filled with rather poor poetry and excessively flowery prose. And of course, there were all his ramblings about the Magna Carta. There was little he wrote beyond that."

This comment caught Tabitha's attention. "We have reason to believe that Mr Truegood thought he was close to discovering a lost copy of the Magna Carta. Is that what he wrote to you about? Do you remember what he said about it?"

Clarice Hill looked bored just at the mention of James Truegood's great passion. "Oh, how do you expect me to remember all the details? It was all about ruins, and someone called William something. I always skipped those parts of his letters. To be honest, even if James had been wealthy and successful, he was so clueless as to how to woo me properly that I might not have been inclined to return his love anyway."

Given Clarice's lack of any sentimentality over her putative lover's death, Tabitha didn't feel guilty asking, "Do you still have his letters?"

"I have them. Sometimes, I take them out and read them over. While they are far too maudlin for the most part, and so boring in places, sometimes it is nice to read about how pretty I am and how someone cannot live without me."

"And are you willing to let me read them?"

It was impossible to misinterpret Clarice's lack of enthusiasm at this. Nonetheless, she replied grudgingly, "You may have them, if you wish. However, Papa cannot know about them."

"Let me worry about that. Before you leave, I will mention searching for some books to lend you and will say that I will send them over with a servant tomorrow. You can slip the letters to him in exchange for the books."

There was little more to say, and Tabitha worried the men would return to the drawing room soon and Mr Hill would notice his daughter's absence.

Tabitha stood. "Let us return to the others. However, if you do think of anything that might help us find Mr Truegood's killer, I hope you will find a way to let me know." Clarice Hill nodded noncommittally, and the two women returned to the drawing room.

The rest of the evening passed uneventfully enough. The investigative group had agreed to meet briefly before retiring to bed to discuss anything they might have learned. Given this, Tabitha was eager to encourage her guests to leave as early as possible, and there was no suggestion of music or cards. Eventually, everyone caught the hint and made their excuses.

Chapter 12

It was late, and everyone was exhausted, but Tabitha and Wolf wanted to record everyone's impressions of the Hills that evening while their thoughts were still fresh.

The dowager sank into an armchair in the parlour. "The things I do for this group! That I would have to spend an entire dinner pretending to find that odious little man both insightful and amusing was almost beyond the pale!"

Tabitha was exhausted and desired nothing more than to curl up in bed. She was sorely tempted to point out that the dowager was the one insisting on being part of the investigation and was free to withdraw at any time, but she thought better of it and stilled her tongue.

Instead of snapping at the dowager, Tabitha took some blank note-cards and a pen and settled herself. They had asked Talbot to send in a tray of tea and coffee, and it seemed as if everyone had chosen the latter beverage while they tried to be alert enough to share their memories and observations.

Before anything else was discussed, Tabitha recounted her conversation with Clarice Hill. "I believe she was telling the truth, at least about her relationship with James Truegood. I think she is a vain and self-absorbed young woman, who merely toyed with Mr Truegood's affections for her own entertainment."

The dowager interrupted her. "Why are you so certain Miss Hill is telling the truth about that?"

"Well, to begin with, her utter indifference to his death, which was quite shocking, if I am honest. One would expect someone to be upset even over someone they were merely friends with. Miss Hill's reaction to the death was such indifference that one might infer the man was a stranger to her. But it is not only her cold-hearted response. Even when I first read her letters to Mr Truegood, they did not feel like love letters. Remember, I commented then that she was as likely to complain about the servants as she was to mention any romance between them; perhaps more so, in fact."

"Fine," the dowager muttered irritably. "Then she is nothing more than a common flirt. How does that make her any less relevant to this investigation?"

Wolf could see how close to her breaking point his wife was, and he responded for her. "I believe that Tabitha's observations make two things very unlikely: if this murder was a crime of passion, it was not Miss Hill who stabbed him in a jealous rage. Moreover, if there was no genuine affection on her part, then it seems unlikely that Mr Hill is our culprit. He would have no reason to believe that murder was the only way to prevent a betrothal that it seemed his daughter had no intention of entering into anyway."

A sullen sniff from the dowager was the only reply to this. However, the woman's determination to make at least one of the Hills a suspect did give Wolf pause. "Lady Pembroke, what was your impression of Mr Hill from your conversation during dinner? Did he say anything that might contradict my thesis?"

"The man is a snob of the worst kind," was the dowager's terse answer.

Given that the dowager herself was a huge snob, everyone was curious to hear what the worst kind might be. Of course, if this undeniable example of the pot calling the kettle black were pointed out to her, there was little doubt the dowager would respond that she was not a snob, but merely aware and proud of her social status and properly concerned that others equally know their own place in life.

Of course, no one needed to ask her to elaborate; the dowager was more than willing to provide more details. "Well, to begin with, there is the dreadful man's certainty that an invitation to dine here is not only his right, but that he had been overlooked during our last soirée in a way that we should feel embarrassed about. Can you believe that this was a topic he alluded to multiple times during dinner?"

No one could argue with the dowager's assessment so far. She continued, "I would not expect to share my table with the finest solicitor in Lincoln's Inn, let alone a country bumpkin with delusions of his legal prowess."

While no one disagreed with the dowager's description of Mr Hill, everyone was too tired to endure any more of her snobbish judgement of the man's pretentiousness. Instead, Wolf said gently but firmly, "Was there anything else that might necessitate us keeping him on our list of suspects, Lady Pembroke?"

As much as she would have liked to say yes, the dowager couldn't think of a single good reason for it, and so, reluctantly, she admitted there was nothing else. Langley had nothing of importance to add.

"As for my conversation with Miss Hill," Wolf said. "To your assessment that she is vain and self-absorbed, I will add that the young woman is rather vapid. I have no idea why she believed that I would be interested in the petty quarrels amongst the young women of Pembroke, but that is what I had to listen to for the most part. Again, none of that suggests she is a murderer, just a rather dull, self-involved dinner companion."

Everyone agreed that, at least until any other evidence surfaced, Mr and Miss Hill were not suspects, merely people who wouldn't be invited to dine again.

Overall, they had learned little of use at their dinner. At least this meant that this conversation could be brief, and everyone could make their way to their beds soon enough.

The next morning, everyone, barring the dowager, assembled for breakfast.

"One thing I forgot to mention last night," Wolf confessed, "was that as he was leaving, Squire Partridge mentioned that the local doctor performed the autopsy yesterday, from what he heard. I do not know why he was made aware of this and not me; however, it seems the man will be calling on me this morning with his report."

Despite his words, Wolf wasn't truly annoyed at being overlooked. In fact, he wasn't surprised. He might have decided to fulfil his JP duties in this instance, but Squire Partridge was probably the person the local authorities were most accustomed to dealing with. It was reasonable that the squire was the one who was alerted.

"Something that was niggling at the edge of my thoughts as I fell asleep last night was whether we should consider Mr Goodge a suspect," Tabitha said after taking her first restorative sip of coffee. "After all, given what Mr Allen told us about the research Mr Truegood has been involved in, it seems unlikely that the man he both worked with on such matters and in whose house he lived had no idea. Yet, Mr Goodge claimed to know nothing of the article Mr Truegood had submitted for publication."

Then, Tabitha explained the fleeting look that had crossed Mr Goodge's face when they asked about the article. "I wondered at the time if he was telling the truth. After all, William Marshal is his passion. It seems implausible that the two men would not have discussed Mr Truegood's theory. After all, if he was correct, he was descended from one of Marshal's stewards. That seems like something Jeremiah Goodge would be fascinated to learn."

While everyone agreed with how unlikely it was that Mr Goodge had been entirely honest, it was still hard to see how this amounted to a motive for murder. Nonetheless, they had learnt throughout their investigations to record facts as they emerged and not to prejudge connections between them. Therefore, it was decided that Mr Goodge's name would be added to the corkboard as the first suspect.

The doctor arrived at ten o'clock and was shown into the drawing room where Tabitha, Wolf, and Langley were waiting. The dowager had still not emerged from her bedchamber, and there was some debate about whether to inform her of the doctor's visit or to deal with the inevitable wrath of excluding her. In the end, the decision was made that they would see the doctor without her, assuming she did not show herself before his arrival. Everyone knew the inevitable unpleasantness they were risking, but decided it was worth it to see the doctor in peace.

Dr Warren Lloyd was a mild-mannered man of middle years. He was rarely called to handle suspicious deaths and was quite excited to have something different to break up the monotony of dealing with broken bones and outbreaks of measles, diphtheria, and typhoid. While he was overwhelmed by being in the presence of aristocrats, the man was delighted not only to have conducted a post-mortem on a murder victim but also to be able to report such interesting findings to the Earl of Pembroke himself.

"Dr Lloyd, so good of you to come all the way from Pembroke for this," Wolf said. He had decided to strike a balance in his behaviour that was less than the aristocratic arrogance and dominance, reminiscent of his grandfather, that he sometimes felt compelled to assume, but more dignified and imposing than he was apt to be as Wolf Chesterton. He accepted, however grudgingly, that whatever actual authority the earldom granted him could be greatly enhanced merely by adopting an attitude that seemed to expect it as his birthright. Still, this meeting with the local doctor seemed to be an instance where he could relax this rule somewhat.

The good doctor seemed appropriately cowed just to be in the aristocratic presence and clutched his folio tightly to his chest as if it were a shield.

When the introductions had been made and cups of tea poured and shared, Wolf said, "I believe you have conducted the post-mortem and wish to relay the results to me directly rather than through the coroner."

"Indeed, milord. Knowing that you have personally taken on this investigation, I wanted to waste no time in sharing what I have learned. I should say that I find it a great relief to hear that this has not been left to Constable Tucker, a good and honest man, but not one suited to a task such as this. Indeed, we should all count ourselves fortunate to have you in Pembrokeshire, willing and able to undertake such a task. One can only hope..."

It seemed that the doctor had many more platitudes he wished to shower on the Earl of Pembroke, and they might continue all morning if Wolf didn't take firmer control of the conversation.

Interrupting him, Wolf modulated his voice to sound more like his grandfather's. "Doctor Lloyd, I am grateful that you took the initiative to come to me and am eager to hear your conclusions."

"Indeed, of course, your lordship. My apologies for not getting straight to the point. I can only imagine how many other demands on your attention a great man such as yourself must have. And let me again say how honoured we all are..."

"Doctor Lloyd! The report?"

"Certainly, certainly." Then, sitting up a little straighter and puffing out his chest, the doctor declared with the dramatic force of an actor delivering a Shakespearean soliloquy on stage in the West End, "By my estimates, Mr Truegood died a few hours before you found him. Furthermore, I believe that Mr Truegood did not die from the stab wound but was, in fact, already dead by the time the dagger was plunged into his body."

Tabitha, Wolf, and Langley looked at each other; this was intriguing and not what they expected to hear.

"And so, what do you believe was the cause of death, Doctor Lloyd?" Tabitha asked.

"Well, of course, I am only a lowly rural doctor and do not have the equipment that those fancy police surgeons have in London or Bangor. However, in my humble opinion, the heart's stopped clean with no sign of rupture. Even though he was a young and sturdy fellow, I'd say his heart gave out for some reason. However, I cannot be sure without testing the contents of his stomach, which I don't have the facilities to do."

While the man hadn't said so explicitly, Langley asked, "So you believe he was poisoned?"

"I would hate to speculate. I am a man of science and merely go where the facts lead me," the doctor intoned solemnly.

Wolf attempted to conceal his irritation. "And we truly appreciate that. However, in your professional opinion, what else might have caused this death?"

"Of course, I have not had the pleasure of treating Mr Truegood as his personal physician, so I cannot say whether he might have had an underlying medical condition. While he seems to have been young and strong, it is possible that he was unwell, and that was what caused his death."

Taking a deep breath before replying, Wolf pointed out, "Yet, someone did thrust a dagger into his body, so one would assume that it is unlikely that James Truegood visited the Wogan Cavern, suddenly experienced an illness that caused him to expire on the spot, and was then stumbled across by someone who chose to stab a dead body. Can we all agree on this?"

For a moment, it seemed as if Doctor Lloyd was about to declare that this was still speculation and not within his remit as a scientist to comment on. However, the doctor nodded, perhaps noticing the clenching of his host's jaw and sensing that he was in danger of inviting aristocratic wrath. "Yes, that seems unlikely."

"Excellent. Then, I would assume that the more probable explanation is that Mr Truegood was poisoned and then stabbed by someone who, in all likelihood, knew he was already deceased."

"Indeed. However, without a chemical analysis of his stomach contents, I cannot confirm this scenario or speculate as to what poison might be involved."

"And how might we obtain such an analysis?" Tabitha asked.

The doctor shook his head sadly. "I would imagine that Scotland Yard has those capabilities, but it is hardly for a humble country doctor such as myself to speculate. Of course, I am sure that a man of your standing, your lordship," then perhaps remembering who else was in the room, "well, of both your lordships' standing, might be better able to command such an inquiry."

Wolf considered the man's words. In truth, his only real police contact was Bruiser, a somewhat ethically compromised police detective inspector in Whitechapel. Although he knew Langley had a good working relationship with the Home Secretary, using that connection seemed somewhat extreme, at least based on what they knew of Mr Truegood and his murder so far.

Finally, Tabitha had a thought. "What about asking Patrick Morgan?" Wolf considered the suggestion; it had a lot of merit. Dr Morgan was the police surgeon they had encountered during their recent visit to Anglesey. He was a young and well-educated man who had been surprisingly conversant with modern medical and dental practices, at least for someone working in rural Wales. Perhaps he did have both the knowledge and equipment to perform such an analysis. It was certainly worth sending a telegram to ask.

"Yes, Dr Morgan. I will have Talbot send a telegram to him. If the answer is negative, then we may have to fall back on your government connections, Langley. But let us try Morgan to start with."

He rang the bell and instructed the butler to send a telegram immediately to Dr Patrick Morgan in Beaumaris.

Chapter 13

Dr Morgan's response arrived during luncheon. Wolf had requested that Talbot bring the telegram to him immediately, and now he read it and summarised it for the group as they were being served their fish course.

"It seems that while he has the knowledge to perform such an analysis, he doesn't have the equipment to hand but believes he can access it, and so we should send the sample as soon as possible." Turning to Bear, Wolf said, "Would you take it to him? While it is possible to send the sample alone, I wish to ensure it reaches him as soon as possible."

Bear indicated his willingness to make the journey north to Beaumaris and immediately rose to prepare for it. As he was about to leave the dining room, he turned and asked, "Do you want me to wait for the results or have Dr Morgan send a telegram?"

Wolf considered the question. "Just sending the telegram to Dr Morgan has probably been fodder for local gossip; in a town as small as Pembroke, there is a low probability of sending a telegram in total privacy. However, we do not need to fuel speculation any further, particularly if Dr Morgan can identify the poison in the stomach contents. Please wait for the results, that is, unless he believes it will take some time. If so, ask him to be as discreet as possible in his response. I am not sure how he might do that such that it would not cause speculation, but ask him to try." Bear nodded and left the room.

The group was now left with the dilemma of what to do while they waited for the results. They pondered this question for two more courses.

Finally, Tabitha said, "While we do need to get confirmation of the poisoning and what was used, the doctor seemed quite sure that the stabbing was not the cause of death. Given this, as we said earlier, it is hard to believe that a healthy young man falls down dead and that someone who wished him harm happened upon the body, conveniently, but nevertheless decided to make the death seem like a murder."

No one disagreed. "Therefore," Tabitha continued, "we can proceed on the premise that someone poisoned Mr Truegood somehow and then, anticipating when and where he would die, followed him and stabbed him after death. The question is, why? If he was going to die, why go that extra step? And if it was somehow important that the dagger be involved, why poison him first?"

"Well, that is easy enough to answer," the dowager said smugly. "It is far easier to poison someone than to stab them. Even with my proficiency in using my swordstick, I consider it to be a method of defence rather than attack. If I wished to murder someone, poison would be my chosen method, without a doubt." As she said this, the old woman looked around the table with a knowing glance, as if to put the group on notice about her willingness to slip something into their food if she chose to.

Her vague threat aside, it was hard to argue with the dowager's logic. There was a reason that poison was known as the murder weapon of choice for women; it was easily accessible and easily administered by a woman. And unlike other methods, it did not discriminate based on brute strength and size. So, did this mean their murderer was a woman? Tabitha asked the question, but no one had a suitable response.

Wolf sighed and expressed his other concern. "Usually, we can assume different personas in an investigation in order to ferret out information, but that option is not open to us here; everyone knows who we are, and I am sure that word of my investigation will be all around the country soon enough. So, what do we do?"

Langley was the first to answer. "While you are correct that we do not have that option open to us, perhaps we can turn this seeming disadvantage to our favour."

"What on earth do you mean by that, Maxwell?" the dowager snapped. "Stop talking in riddles and speak plainly."

"I was just getting to that, Lady Pembroke," Langley said patiently. "As I was about to say, you command enormous respect in this county, Wolf, and wield an authority even beyond what you do in London. By our association with the earldom, none of us will need to explain who we are or justify our presence anywhere. If we want to talk with people, we will not need to conjure up fanciful reasons and stories; we will just command them to wait on us and ask what we need to."

Wolf considered Langley's words; on their face, they made sense. However, he still felt as if they had lost a valuable tool in being unable to slip into other personas. Perhaps the other man was right, and they would find that loss to bring unforeseen benefits. Regardless, this was the situation they found themselves in, so there was nothing to do but to embrace it as best they could.

"I do not disagree, Langley," Tabitha said. "However, that does not answer the question of who we should question and about what." She couldn't hide her frustration.

Shockingly, it was the dowager who seemed unfazed by the conundrum they were faced with. "Really, do I have to provide the solution to every apparent problem? It is astounding to what lengths you seem to go to exclude me from investigations, given how lost you are without me. Perhaps you will all finally recognise this fact in time to acknowledge it to me on my deathbed."

"Mama, if you have an idea, we would all appreciate hearing it," Tabitha said, hoping to deflect the woman from her slide into melodrama.

Smugness evident in her voice, the dowager said, "We know very little about this James Truegood. In any village or small town, there are always those women of a certain age who know everything there is to know about everyone. We need to find our local gossip. Even better if we can find a group of them."

"And how do we do that?" Wolf asked.

"Tomorrow is Sunday. We will attend church in Pembroke."

Wolf didn't know what the woman was talking about. During the more than a year he had known the dowager, she had never expressed any interest in attending church services. Instead, she usually said that she could converse with her maker from her bed if she felt it necessary.

However, Tabitha immediately realised what the dowager was suggesting. "Mama, what a brilliant idea." The dowager smiled like the Cheshire Cat.

Wolf shot her a look of confusion. Laughing, Tabitha explained, "As we have discussed, it is likely that most people in Pembroke know by now that you have taken on this investigation. Moreover, we are figures of curiosity to begin with in the county. If we turn up to church tomorrow, we will have every head turning and tongue wagging. We will remain behind after the service to speak to the vicar and other notables. It will be shocking if the local lace-curtain brigade does not approach us, offering their help."

Neither Langley nor Wolf shared the women's confidence, but as neither had a better idea, they saw no reason not to try.

"If we are going to do this, we should have Talbot send a man to Pembroke to warn the vicar. The man will want to polish his sermon and ensure that the best pews are reserved for us," the dowager said knowingly. Surprisingly, this was both insightful and sensible, and so they rang the bell to summon the butler and explain their plans.

With the expedition scheduled for the following morning, everyone felt somewhat at a loose end. They couldn't expect to hear from Dr Morgan for at least a day, maybe longer, and they had no leads to pursue.

"I am going to spend the afternoon in the nursery with the children," Tabitha announced. She knew from experience that once they were deeply engaged in an investigation, she would struggle to spend time with Melody, and she was determined to make up for that as much as she could until that moment came.

Wolf had estate business to manage, and Langley was eager to spend time with Rat on his studies. That left only the dowager, who decided to meet with her lady's maid, Withers, to determine what jewels and other finery the good people of Pembroke most deserved to see her adorned in.

Before she visited the nursery, Tabitha remembered she had told Miss Hill she would send a footman to bring her a book and, in return, secretly be given Mr Truegood's side of their correspondence. She went to find Talbot to ask him to have a man visit the Hill household.

When Tabitha finally left the children to their nursemaids almost two hours later, she went to find Talbot and collect the letters from Miss Hill. "I am sorry, but it seems no one was at home, and so Charlie left the book and returned empty-handed."

That was unfortunate, Tabitha thought. She would have to find some other way to get the letters.

CHAPTER 14

The following morning, Tabitha, Wolf, and Langley gathered for a leisurely breakfast. The dowager had not been seen yet that morning. Talbot had informed them that the service began at eleven o'clock, and it was already ten. Under normal circumstances, Tabitha might have secretly hoped that the woman had chosen not to accompany them, but, for once, she hoped the dowager hadn't changed her mind. Although she wasn't essential for their success, the dowager possessed certain skills that might prove very useful. In particular, the dowager's ability to cow a populace was unmatched. Well, perhaps Queen Victoria surpassed her, but perhaps not.

The group wanted to enter St Mary's the Virgin with full pomp and circumstance so that no one would be in any doubt about who they were or that they were in attendance. This required them to time their arrival just before the start of the service, ensuring the rest of the congregation would already be seated.

Wolf had inherited the earldom just over a year earlier and had visited Pembroke only once. Most people probably did not know what he looked like, and Tabitha had never visited the Pembroke Estate during her brief marriage to Jonathan. However, despite her dislike for Glanwyddan Hall, especially when her husband was alive, the dowager had visited many times over the years. There was a chance that some of the congregation would recognise her. Even if they did not, she always made certain that no one doubted her status and rank.

Just as Tabitha was starting to worry they might have to leave without her, the dowager swept into the breakfast room. If Tabitha had expected her to dress as if she were visiting Buckingham Palace, she wasn't disappointed. It seemed the conference with Withers the previous day had resulted in an outfit that would leave no doubt among the people of Pembroke about who was amongst them. The dowager was dressed with unmistakable intent: every detail of her clothes and jewels conveyed rank, history, and unwavering confidence in her superiority. She had not dressed to blend in.

Usually, such ostentatious pomposity would irritate Tabitha and Wolf, but this time, it served their purpose. The silks, diamonds, and peacock feathers would be all the congregation needed to recognise who was listening to the service that morning. Tabitha did not doubt that human nature would do the rest, at least when it came to the chattering magpies of Pembroke.

St Mary's was off the main Pembroke thoroughfare, just a few steps from the castle. Its grey stone walls, weathered and worn smooth in places by time, rose solemnly above the slate-roofed houses nearby. The squat, square tower, featuring a simple clock and lacking a spire but topped with a modest battlement, was typical of many medieval churches in south Wales. Ivy clung to the western wall. The churchyard was enclosed by a low wall, within which lay a scatter of old gravestones, some standing upright, many leaning, and a few sunken completely.

The warmth of the morning promised another hot August day, but inside, the air was cooler. The nave was long and narrow, with light filtering through stained glass that cast only the faintest colours on the stone floor. Rows of dark wooden pews stretched towards the chancel. Their ends were simply carved, with minimal decoration: a cross here, a vine there. Some bore small brass plaques bearing family names. The pews reserved for local dignitaries were close to the chancel arch and were slightly larger than the others, with padded seats and a small rail in front.

By the time their group entered through the solid, ancient oak door, the congregation was seated and waiting for the service to start. As Wolf led the way down the centre of the church, all eyes turned to witness the spectacle of the local toffs finally condescending to join the local populace in worship.

Tabitha was right in thinking that many older residents of Pembroke remembered the dowager and would recognise her now, though not necessarily for the best reasons. To be fair, neither her husband Philip nor his father before him had been good stewards of their land and titles. Philip preferred to spend his time at Glanwyddan Hall rather than in London, mainly because of his love for hunting, horses, and dogs, rather than any sense of duty to his tenants or neighbours. The fact that the dowager was tarred with the same brush as her irresponsible husband wasn't entirely justified. However, her well-known disdain for the estate and Wales in general might have coloured people's perceptions.

Whether the dowager knew or cared how she was viewed in Pembroke, she walked through the church with regal grace, her diamonds sparkling. The rhythmic tapping of her swordstick walking cane on the worn stone floors echoed with the steady beat of a regimental drummer, each strike deliberate and unmistakable, the perfect accompaniment to her sense of self-importance.

As the family made their way to the pews, Reverend Thomas Llewelyn, a Welsh-born, Oxford-educated clergyman who had ministered to this flock for more than thirty years, inclined his head in greeting. "This morning, we are honoured to have among us his lordship, the Earl of Pembroke, accompanied by the Countess and Dowager Countesses of Pembroke and the Earl of Langley. Welcome to you all to our humble church."

The stunned silence that had initially greeted their entrance into the church now turned into whispers along the pews, growing so loud that the vicar had to shush everyone before asking them to stand for the first hymn.

The service proceeded through the customary Anglican liturgy that Tabitha remembered so clearly from her weekly attendance at Sunday services during her childhood.

When he reached his sermon, it seemed that Reverend Llewelyn had decided, perhaps not so subtly, to genuflect towards his most esteemed parishioners that morning. "Today, I will read from Peter 2:13," he intoned solemnly. "Submit yourselves to every ordinance of man for the

Lord's sake: whether it be the king, as supreme; or unto governors, as unto them that are sent by him for the punishment of evildoers, and for the praise of them that do well. For so is the will of God, that with well doing ye may put to silence the ignorance of foolish men: As free, and not using your liberty for a cloak of maliciousness, but as the servants of God. Honour all men. Love the brotherhood. Fear God. Honour the king."

As if concerned that the reading might be too subtle, the vicar repeatedly turned his eyes towards Wolf with a gentle nod of his head as he read. Regardless of what the rest of his congregation thought about the vicar's choice of biblical passages, there was no doubt that the dowager approved; Tabitha could see the woman smiling beatifically at the vicar.

However, by the time he finished the final prayers and blessing and told the congregation to rise for the last hymn, the vicar appeared to have lost favour with the dowager, who whispered, far too loudly to Tabitha, "Did this really need to last quite so long? I have always believed that the mark of an excellent member of the clergy is a propensity for brevity."

Once the hymn was sung, the vicar descended from the pulpit, but instead of leading the way out of the church as he usually did, he deferred to his noble visitors. This was the moment they had been waiting for. Following Wolf's lead again, the group proceeded back through the church and exited the building.

Certainly, if the family regularly attended St Mary's, it would be expected that they would wait outside as the rest of the congregation exited, allowing the people of Pembroke to doff their caps and curtsey to their betters. However, given that this was their first visit, no one would have been surprised if they had returned to their carriage immediately and hurried home for their Sunday roast.

Since this was likely the general expectation, the good people of Pembroke were more than a little surprised to leave church that Sunday and find the aristocrats standing to the side of the paved path, under the shade of a yew tree.

Reverend Llewelyn seemed just as surprised as anyone else that their distinguished visitors had lingered, and appeared somewhat confused about what was expected of him.

Wolf noticed the vicar's hesitancy and began a conversation with him. If nothing else, considering his many years as vicar at St Mary's, the man might be a good source of information about their victim. He had only just started speaking with the vicar when he saw Jeremiah Goodge leaving the church. Wolf had a feeling that the man was hoping to slip away unnoticed, but once Wolf caught his eye, Mr Goodge had no choice but to come over and pay his respects.

"Your lordship, what an unexpected pleasure," Mr Goodge said, his tone suggesting he found it anything but that.

"Good to see you again, Mr Goodge. We did not get the chance to attend local services at Christmas, and I thought it important to show myself to the people of Pembroke," Wolf explained.

The vicar appeared momentarily puzzled. Then, he shook his head as the realisation sank in. "Oh yes, your lordship, I believe I did hear that you were on one of Mr Goodge's tours when you stumbled across the body of the unfortunate Mr Truegood."

"Indeed," Wolf agreed. "Poor Mr Truegood, so young and full of promise."

"And I hear you are to serve as the JP on the investigation, milord," the Reverend Llewelyn continued.

If nothing else, this conversation confirmed their belief that everyone in town was aware of the death and their involvement in the case.

As Wolf and Langley conversed with the vicar and Mr Goodge, Tabitha and the dowager stood slightly apart, observing the people of Pembroke file out of church. As the passersby simply bowed or curtseyed respectfully and continued walking, Tabitha began to worry that their plan might not succeed.

"Perhaps we were mistaken in the assumptions we made," she said quietly.

"Tabitha, why do you continue to doubt me?" the dowager grumbled. Before Tabitha could point out that this wasn't about doubting her, but rather the facts as they were unfolding before them, the dowager elbowed her sharply in the ribs. "And here they come, as I predicted."

Tabitha might have been inclined to question how the dowager could be so sure about the three women approaching them. Still, she had to admit that all three women had a certain gleam in their eyes that spoke of gossip-mongers eager for new tattle who believed they had caught sight of prey. One in particular, a sturdy-looking woman with a ruddy complexion, had an air about her that suggested she was the ringleader of this group of clucking hens.

While other people had exhibited humility in their shy acknowledgements of the great ladies in their midst, this woman marched up boldly and, after the merest hint of a bobbed curtsey, introduced herself. "Your ladyships, I am Mrs Chivers, the branch president of the Parish Mothers' Union. What an honour it is for us to have you join our service this morning."

Yes, thought Tabitha, as she looked the woman over, she could easily imagine this woman imperiously presiding over a group that lectured the rest of the town on moral purity, family values, and domestic responsibility. This was also just the kind of group that was most conducive to gossip if the wrong people oversaw it.

Immediately, Tabitha made a decision. Holding out her hand, she said, "How lovely to meet you, Mrs Chivers. What a worthwhile organisation the Mothers' Union is. I was just telling Lady Pembroke the other day that I would like us to get involved in a local group so that we can give our time and energy to the community, at least while we are staying in Pembrokeshire."

For a moment, the dowager looked confused, then irritated, and shot Tabitha a sharp look. When Tabitha slightly raised her eyebrows in response, the dowager realised her plan and smiled condescendingly. "Indeed, Mrs Chivers. We would like nothing more than to attend your next meeting and help you save the souls of the good people of Pembroke."

Tabitha hoped the other woman hadn't discerned the sarcasm in the dowager's voice. Fortunately, she seemed neither to have noticed nor to care.

Mrs Chivers clapped her hands together gleefully. "How serendipitous for you that we are holding our next meeting tomorrow morning, in the church parish hall at eleven o'clock. I hope you can join us."

"Lady Pembroke and I would be glad to join you," Tabitha assured the woman.

Chapter 15

By the time the group returned to the hall for the traditional Sunday roast, Bear was already home. As everyone gathered in the dining room, including Bear, Wolf remarked, “I am glad you were able to make it back. I was not sure how frequently the trains would run to Lamphey.”

“Well, there are only two on a Sunday, so I had to catch the very first one from Beaumaris this morning. I thought about trying to return last night, but Dr Morgan was worried I might miss the last train from Bangor and was kind enough to offer me a bed for the night.”

“Does he think he will have an answer for us soon?” Langley asked.

“He is hopeful that he will sometime tomorrow, Tuesday at the very latest. Which is why I didn’t stay,” Bear offered, “I asked him to be as discreet with his response in a telegram as possible.”

As they tucked into their roast beef, potatoes, two vegetables, and plenty of gravy, they discussed their morning outing.

“I have high hopes for Mrs Chivers and her chattering magpies,” the dowager announced cheerfully. “It has long been my opinion that those who set themselves up as worthy to police the morality of others are the most likely both to relish news of impropriety and tattle on it to others.”

No one could argue with her observation.

“I do agree that they are just the kind of women from whom we will learn everything there is to know about the good people of Pembroke and their peccadillos and secrets," Tabitha conceded.

As she speared a crispy roast potato, the dowager said triumphantly, "Really, what would you all do without me?"

"I did get the feeling that Mr Goodge was not particularly happy to see us," Wolf said.

"Yes, I felt that too," Langley agreed. "It was quite subtle, and perhaps unrelated to our appearance and was rather to do with something else. Nevertheless, the man seemed rather put out."

Tabitha and the dowager knew what they were doing the next day, and Wolf felt he couldn't sit around, twiddling his thumbs, waiting for their report and Dr Morgan's telegram.

As he pondered how to spend his time productively, he reflected on what they had been told about their victim. "We know James Truegood was an assistant schoolmaster, which suggests there was a more senior schoolmaster. I think I will visit the school tomorrow to speak with him. If the men worked closely together, he might be a valuable source of information. Langley, would you care to join me?"

The rest of the afternoon and evening were spent in leisurely activities appropriate to the day of rest. By the following morning, everyone was eager to return to more productive pursuits.

Tabitha dressed very carefully for their visit with the Mothers' Union. She wanted to seem friendly enough for the women to relax and start gossiping. She hoped the dowager would think the same and not wear her diamonds to breakfast.

When the elderly woman finally appeared, Tabitha sighed but recognised how much worse her outfit could have been. Although she had forsaken her diamonds, the dowager was wearing a rather ostentatious ruby choker. Nevertheless, her dress, though clearly of the highest quality, was quite simple, and for that, Tabitha could only be thankful.

"Is that what you are wearing?" the dowager said.

Tabitha sighed once more. In truth, her dress was an elegant grey silk Worth gown, complemented by a simple pearl necklace.

Stating what she hoped would be obvious, Tabitha said, "We do not want to overawe these women. Our aim is to lull them into a feeling of ease, such that they talk openly."

"That is our aim, is it?" Despite this, the dowager said. "Do not worry yourself, Tabitha. I know how to manage the Mrs Chivers of this world. Every village and town has one, not to mention many Mayfair drawing rooms. There is little, besides a title, separating her from Lady Hartley." Tabitha was only loosely acquainted with Lady Hartley but did know that she was an inveterate gossip, something the dowager was happy to use for her own purposes when it suited her.

Soon enough, they had finished eating and needed to be on their way if they were to reach St Mary's by eleven o'clock. The carriage pulled up outside the church just before the meeting was due to begin. The two women wandered back down the path towards the church's large oak door, hoping it would become clear where the parish hall was.

Luckily, just as they were standing under the yew tree, wondering where to go, they heard a voice. "Halloo. Lady Pembroke. Over here."

They turned towards the voice and saw Mrs Chivers waving to them from outside a more modern-looking building next to the church that they hadn't noticed before.

As they crossed the churchyard to the building, the dowager sniffed. "Halloo? What are we, a bunch of fishwives hawking today's catch? She will be calling out oi next!" Luckily, they had reached Mrs Chivers before Tabitha had to reply.

"Mrs Chivers, so good to see you again," Tabitha said. "Lady Pembroke and I are so looking forward to the meeting."

Mrs Chivers led them into the parish hall. The room smelt somewhat musty, but also of beeswax polish, as if someone had hoped the latter would mask the smell of the former. Rows of wooden chairs had been arranged neatly, many already occupied by sensible-looking women in quite severe clothes, their hats placed firmly on their laps. At the front, a table was draped with a clean cloth and held a small vase of wilting wild-flowers and a jug of water.

As Tabitha and the dowager entered the room, all the other women stood, many of them appearing quite overawed by their newest members. Mrs Chivers, relishing her role as the one who had introduced quality into their group, bustled to the front of the room where she had reserved two chairs in the middle for their guests. Tabitha and the dowager took their designated seats, and then all the other women settled in. Mrs Chivers moved to stand behind the table at the front, and another woman, who Tabitha believed had been part of the group they met yesterday, joined her. With her notebook at the ready, it appeared the woman was acting as the group's secretary.

"Good morning, ladies. As you can see, we are honoured to be joined this morning by the Countess and Dowager Countess of Pembroke, who were kind enough to accept the invitation I extended to them yesterday." She placed a strong emphasis on the 'I' to ensure everyone knew who was responsible for this honour.

"Now, let us begin with a prayer." Then Mrs Chivers intoned, "Lord, we thank Thee for placing woman in her proper sphere: to be a comfort to her husband, a guide to her children, and a keeper of the home. Grant us strength to uphold the virtues of modesty, humility, and diligence in all our labours. May we never be led astray by idle fancies or modern temptations, but remain steadfast in Thy commandments and the blessed pattern set forth in Holy Scripture. Endow us with the patience of Hannah, the wisdom of Deborah, and the quiet industry of the virtuous woman. Let no mother among us fail in her sacred charge. Amen."

As all the other women said amen, the dowager whispered, "Really? Is that my proper place? To be a comfort to my husband? Perhaps if she had met the late earl, even Mrs Chivers might rethink that plea."

The prayer was followed by a reading from the Book of Proverbs about the duties of a virtuous woman, which was met with polite nods and the occasional "Amen".

Tabitha could feel the dowager's restlessness and hoped the meeting would soon shift to more practical matters. Fortunately, it seemed it would. The next topic of the day was introduced: Miss Pritchard, a missionary's daughter returning from Ceylon, gave a soft-spoken, though fascinating account of Christian motherhood abroad. A few members fidgeted in their seats, uncertain whether the mention of elephants had any moral significance, but they applauded warmly at the end.

Finally, Mrs Chivers addressed the practical matters of the Mothers' Union: a new rota for visiting the confinement cases, repairs to the church kneelers, and a reminder about next month's bake sale to raise funds for the orphanage. She ended with the announcement that tea and a Victoria sponge were being laid out at the side of the room for those who wished to stay.

Of course, there was little doubt that everyone would stay to meet the Ladies Pembroke.

For the most part, the ladies of the Mothers' Union were well-meaning, charitable members of the community who cared deeply about the various causes the group championed. However, it quickly became evident that some of the women considered they had achieved a perch of moral superiority from which to dispense judgement to their less worthy neighbours. There was little doubt Mrs Chivers fell into this group.

Everyone seemed quite shy of the aristocrats in their midst, and most women hung back, talking in little groups as they sipped their tea, while never forgetting that two countesses were among them. This reticence suited Mrs Chivers, who had always intended to control with a tight fist who had access to the aristocrats.

As Mrs Chivers delivered cups of tea to Tabitha and the dowager, she gave a subtle nod of her head that Tabitha almost missed. The nod appeared to be directed towards a mousy-looking woman who Tabitha thought was another woman from church the day before. As the woman scampered across to join them, Tabitha noticed her wide eyes and a nose that seemed to twitch nervously.

"Your ladyships, I would like to present Mrs Adele Markham," Mrs Chivers announced as if she were introducing debutantes to the Queen. "Mrs Markham is my right-hand woman in all matters relating to the Mothers' Union."

Mrs Markham seemed an odd choice of woman to be considered so essential. Though Tabitha reflected that perhaps complete deference to Mrs Chivers was the primary requirement for the role. Mrs Markham was so overwhelmed that she could scarcely whisper a greeting.

"Adele, you need to speak up so that their ladyships can hear you," Mrs Chivers scolded.

Although the dowager usually had no time for incapacitating shyness, ironically, she had even less patience for bullies. "There is nothing wrong with my hearing, madam," she informed Mrs Chivers tartly. "Leave the woman be."

For a moment, it seemed as if Mrs Chivers might retort with something equally acid, but then she remembered who she was with and simply shook her head as if to dismiss poor Adele Markham.

Tabitha worried the dowager had offended the woman and that they might learn nothing useful. Eager to soothe Mrs Chivers's wounded pride, she said, "It seems you do admirable work here. The group is to be commended, and of course, its leader in particular."

Her words of praise had their intended effect; Mrs Chivers swelled with pride and looked around in the hope that others had heard.

Tabitha decided to take that opportunity to fish for the information they needed. "Yes, it feels very soothing to be here today after our terrible experience at the castle."

From the gleam in Mrs Chivers's eye, Tabitha guessed the woman had been hoping for just such an opportunity. For those who made gossiping almost a professional pursuit, gathering information was as important as relaying it, perhaps even more so.

"Yes, what a sad state of affairs," Mrs Chivers said in a tone of eager anticipation that was at odds with her actual words. "Poor, poor Mr True-good. And such a charming young man. Whoever would want to hurt such an inoffensive gentleman?"

Tabitha nodded in agreement. "Yes, it was quite shocking. I assume you know that Lord Pembroke has personally taken on this case in his capacity as Justice of the Peace."

"I may have heard something to that effect," Mrs Chivers demurred. Then, after looking around to make sure no one was near, she added, "In fact, I had hoped to have a word with your ladyship. Perhaps we might talk somewhere less public?"

What would best flatter Mrs Chivers? Tabitha wondered. An invitation to the hall, or having the Pembroke carriage stationed outside her door.

Tabitha chose to let the woman herself decide. "Would you like to come back with us to Glanwyddan Hall, or maybe we could go to your home?"

The gleam in Mrs Chivers's eyes grew even brighter, but she appeared conflicted about which option would grant her the greater bragging rights.

Finally, she said rather too loudly, "I would be delighted to join you at Glanwyddan Hall, your ladyship. Please lead the way to your carriage."

Chapter 16

Mrs Chivers strutted out of the parish hall like a peacock. She made sure to tell each woman she passed, "I am so sorry to leave early, but her ladyship has invited me to Glanwyddan Hall."

They'd better extract some useful information from the woman after all this, Tabitha thought. From the look on the dowager's face, her thoughts were heading in a rather more threatening direction.

As they left the church grounds, Mrs Chivers appeared to be searching for people to witness her moment of greatness. She walked as slowly as she could towards the carriage and seemed hesitant to get in.

While the dowager was entirely certain why the woman was dawdling, she had no patience for it. "Is there a problem, Mrs Chivers?" she snapped irritably. "If now is inconvenient, you have only to say."

"No, no, not at all," the woman replied anxiously. With that, she abandoned her hopes for a larger audience and stepped into the carriage.

The conversation during the journey was mainly small talk. They learned that Mrs Chivers had a son who was an apprentice to the apothecary and that her husband had died many years earlier. The more the woman talked, the less enthusiastic Tabitha and the dowager became about the idea of spending more time with her. Only after it was too late to rescind the invitation did Tabitha realise there was no way to avoid extending it to include lunch. By the time they arrived at Glanwyddan Hall, it would be past one o'clock, and not making the offer would be very rude.

Deciding she might as well get this out of the way, Tabitha extended the invitation then and there. She wouldn't have thought Mrs Chivers could be more puffed up by the outing than she already was, but it seemed she was wrong.

"Oh, Lady Pembroke," the woman gushed. "How gracious you are. It would be my honour to break bread with you and the earl."

Tabitha was unsure if Wolf had returned from his outing that morning, but she decided to say nothing. She could only hope to save him and Langley from this woman's company.

As they pulled up outside the hall, Mrs Chivers's mouth dropped open. She climbed the front steps in a kind of trance, and at the sight of the footman, in his Pembroke livery, opening the door for her, it seemed as if she could now die happy, having reached this pinnacle of social success.

In fact, the woman seemed so overawed that Tabitha hoped she would still be as eager a gossip as she might usually be. She needn't have worried. While Mrs Chivers was relatively quiet during the first few minutes of her visit, by the time they were seated at the dining table, she seemed to have overcome at least some of her intimidation at the grandeur she found herself in.

As they took their seats, the dowager whispered to Tabitha, "Let us make this as quick as possible."

Tabitha couldn't really argue with that. As the first course was served, she forced her face into its brightest smile and asked, "Now we are settled, what was it you wished to discuss, Mrs Chivers?"

"Well, perhaps it isn't my place to say," the woman began.

The dowager snapped, her patience at an end. "If it is not your place to say, then why did you accept our invitation? You said you had something to tell us, so no more dillydallying."

Tabitha suspected that few people dared to speak to Mrs Chivers in this way and that there were even fewer from whom she would tolerate it. The self-control needed to avoid answering as she would normally was evident in the tight line of her mouth and the tension with which she held herself.

After a moment, Mrs Chivers responded in a somewhat colder tone. "Milly, the woman who does for me is friendly with Mr Goodge's housekeeper. Apparently, everything wasn't as companionable in that household as you may have been led to believe." This was said with a very knowing look.

Was that all? Was that everything the woman had to offer?

It seemed the dowager had much the same feeling as Tabitha. She said in an even sharper tone than before, "Madam, do you have anything of substance to share that might be useful in his lordship's investigation, or is it merely idle tittle-tattle? If it is the former, please speak plainly. I am an old woman and do not have the time left on this earth for gentle allusions."

Tabitha was accustomed to this rhetorical device of the dowager, which she often used to excuse her impatience. Mrs Chivers's immediate alarm suggested she took the elderly woman quite literally and feared she was about to be confronted by her impending expiration before they had even finished their meal.

Answering as quickly as possible, Mrs Chivers elaborated. "They argued about some nonsense concerning the castle. Even though the castle is of historic importance, I still can't understand why grown men would be so fixated on it. After all, it isn't much more than a pile of rocks these days. Nevertheless, according to Mrs Wallace, their housekeeper, there were several disagreements, and the last one became quite heated." Mrs Chivers was becoming quite engrossed in her own storytelling by this point, and she lowered her voice for dramatic effect before adding, "I heard that Mr Goodge said that Mr Truegood wouldn't get to take credit for this, no matter what lengths he had to go to."

This was interesting, Tabitha thought. While they had suspected that the seemingly mild-mannered antiquarian had not told them the whole story, if Mrs Chivers was correct, there was hostility between him and his tenant that could be a motive for murder.

"Did Mrs Wallace say exactly what the men were fighting about?"

It was indisputable that Mrs Chivers relished every moment of her moment in the limelight and would have loved to have more details to titillate her audience.

Casting around for something else to add to her story, she finally said,

"Well, while Mrs Wallace did not give any more details to my woman about the tension in that house, she did mention something about Sir Christopher and that she guessed there was also something of an unusual relationship there."

Tabitha didn't know who Sir Christopher was, but rather than getting bogged down in an explanation, she simply asked, "Unusual how?"

Once again, Mrs Chivers seemed visibly disappointed with her inability to embellish more fully. All she could say was, "Well, why would a lowly assistant schoolteacher be sneaking around town with the local gentry?"

"What do you mean by sneaking around?"

Now, Mrs Chivers seemed to have found a subject she could really sink her teeth into. "Well, Mrs Wallace heard from Mrs Green, Sir Christopher's housekeeper, that Mr Truegood had been to Ashling House meeting with Sir Christopher three times in the last few weeks, and the last time was the day before he died. Now, what would those two men have to discuss that they needed to meet three times?"

Tabitha could think of all sorts of things, as it happened. "Perhaps Sir Christopher has need of a tutor. Does he have children?"

"Hah! As if that man should be carrying on his bloodline! No, thankfully, he has never been so blessed. Mrs Green said those meetings were very secretive, and she had a hard time hearing what they discussed." Mrs Chivers seemed to realise too late that she was condoning servants listening at doors. However, it was too late now, and so she said only, "But she did hear the word treasure, more than once."

As unpleasant as Mrs Chivers's company was, the luncheon had provided them with some interesting information, if it was true. Unfortunately, they were given everything pertinent to the investigation before the fish course was finished. They then had at least three other courses to suffer through. Tabitha made a mental note to indicate to Talbot that they would not be retiring to the drawing room for coffee. If she could have cut the meal short before dessert, she would have.

Mrs Chivers seemed not at all fazed by the situation. Instead, she prattled on about all the women in the Mothers' Union, spewing various bits of gossip. When she finished with her sisters in morality, she turned to Reverend Llewelyn, whom Mrs Chivers believed was past his prime and needed to retire. Under normal circumstances, Tabitha would have tried her best to dissuade their guest from her scandalmongering. However, since that was why they had invited her to dine with them, and they had openly encouraged her gossiping when it suited their interests, she couldn't think of any excuse to discourage her now.

Finally, they were served syllabub to end their meal, and even Mrs Chivers seemed to be running out of spiteful stories to tell her about her neighbours. If Tabitha was worried about how they would ever get rid of the woman without being bluntly rude, she needn't have had any concerns; she was not the person who would take the reins.

Almost before Mrs Chivers had savoured her last taste of the delicate lemon dessert, the dowager stood and said in a tone that brooked no dissent, "Well, as delightful as this visit has been, we will not keep you any longer, Mrs Chivers. I am sure you have a busy afternoon ahead of you, keeping the entire parish morally upright on nothing but weak tea and stronger opinions."

It seemed as if Mrs Chivers wanted to reassure them that she did not need to hurry away, but the dowager was already gesturing towards the door.

As Talbot gently but firmly guided Mrs Chivers out of the hall a few minutes later, the dowager remarked, "Let us hope we can find a motive for murder out of that torrent of idle gossip. At least then I will not feel that I have wasted an hour and a half of my life for no good reason." Tabitha couldn't disagree.

The dowager retired to her bedchamber for a nap to compensate her for two early mornings. Tabitha moved to the parlour to write up note-cards on what they'd learned during their excruciating luncheon.

Chapter 17

The carriage came to a halt outside a low stone building. The schoolhouse sat just off the main street, tucked behind a narrow strip of railings and a weathered wooden gate that hung slightly ajar. Wolf and Langley stepped down from the carriage, and the two men walked up the short path. Langley knocked, then pushed open the door without waiting for a reply.

The smell inside immediately transported Wolf back to his school days. What was that seemingly universal scent inherent to such establishments? Perhaps a mix of chalk dust, musty books, and carbolic acid? It was summer, and so there were no children in the schoolroom, but there was a man painting the walls.

"Excuse us. We are looking for the schoolmaster," Wolf said.

The man continued painting, but nodded towards a door at the back. "Mr Wells' office is just through there."

Wolf gave a quick nod and moved towards the door; Langley followed. A short knock on the door elicited a gruff, "Enter!"

From the look on the schoolmaster's face when they opened the door, it seemed he was expecting to see the painter, perhaps with a new excuse for why he hadn't finished the work yet. He had formed his already craggy features into a rather intimidating scowl, ready to berate the man for interrupting his work planning the autumn timetable.

When he found two very well-dressed men instead of a lazy workman, the schoolmaster looked rather confused. "I'm sorry. Can I help you?"

Wolf introduced himself and Langley, which only heightened the schoolmaster's consternation. He rose from his chair but then appeared unsure of the proper protocol for such a meeting.

Finally, he gestured to the two chairs in front of his desk. "Your lordships, may I offer you some tea, perhaps?"

Wolf assured Mr Wells that they needed no refreshments. The man retook his seat but was visibly nervous and couldn't keep his hands still as he gently tapped his fingertips on the desk.

"Mr Wells, I will get straight to the point," Wolf said. "As you may have heard, I am acting as the magistrate in the unfortunate death of your colleague, Mr James Truegood."

The schoolmaster shook his head sorrowfully. "What a dreadful affair, your lordship. James was a fine young man and an excellent teacher."

"How long did Mr Truegood work here?" Langley asked.

"It must have been about a year, perhaps a little more," Mr Wells said after contemplating the question for a moment. "His mother had died a few years ago, followed shortly afterwards by his father. He did not speak much about his life before moving here, but he hinted that he'd had some expectations of an inheritance which did not come to pass. I believe his father left him debts to settle, in fact. James moved to Pembroke for a fresh start."

The man shook his head again. "I had every expectation that James would take over as schoolmaster from me, in time." Given that Mr Wells didn't look much over forty, Wolf couldn't imagine that it was a prospect that gave James Truegood much cause for hope for his immediate future.

Turning to other matters, Wolf asked, "Did he talk much about his antiquarian interests?"

Mr Wells smiled fondly. "James spoke of little else, particularly over the last few months. I intuited that, while James was always interested in history, his true passion, especially for William Marshal and that period in Pembroke, was very much ignited by his association with Jeremiah Goodge. I do not know exactly how the two men came to know each other, but once James took a room with Mr Goodge, he became increasingly engrossed in the research interests they shared."

Wolf pondered how to ask the next question. Something had been niggling at the edge of his mind for days, but Wolf couldn't quite find the right way to phrase it.

Finally, he abandoned his attempts to find a more diplomatic way of expressing himself and asked, "Did you ever get the feeling that there was a professional rivalry between Mr Goodge and Mr Truegood?"

"Heavens, no! James looked up to Jeremiah as a mentor. I know he was thrilled when he was first asked to help with research on the book Jeremiah is writing." Wolf remembered that Mr Goodge himself had mentioned Truegood's work on his book.

Wolf decided to let this go, at least for the moment, and indeed, asked about the article James Truegood had submitted for publication. "Did he ever speak with you about his claim that he was a descendant of a steward of William Marshal's?

Mr Wells laughed. "Speak to me about it? He has spoken of little else lately. Based on some family lore and something he discovered in an ancient tome, he was sure that Marshal had hidden a later copy of the Magna Carta somewhere in Pembroke. In fact, I believe that was at least part of the reason he moved to the area; his family's long history in the region."

The schoolmaster's words echoed something Mr Allen had said. Langley asked, "You say 'somewhere in Pembroke'. Did Mr Truegood think that this document might be hidden somewhere other than the castle?"

"James seemed to be mainly focused on the castle for some time, but then he started talking about other possible sites, maybe some other ruins. Honestly, I didn't pay much attention when James started talking about this topic. He did get quite carried away."

Wolf pondered the man's words. He recalled Squire Partridge mentioning some ancient ruins that Mr Truegood had written to him about. Were these ruins the possible hiding place of the later Magna Carta?

It seemed that Mr Wells had nothing more of importance to share, but he promised to contact them if he remembered anything else.

As they returned to the carriage, Wolf said, "I think we need to return to Mr Goodge's residence and find the paper that James Truegood submitted for publication. We did not think to look for it previously, but now I wonder if that might tell us more than we realised."

Langley agreed, and they instructed Madison, their driver, to return to Mr Goodge's house.

While the antiquarian was surprised to see them again, he welcomed them into his home. "I was just finishing a fascinating book on Henry V," he explained as he offered them some tea.

"We will not disturb you, Mr Goodge. We merely wish to take another look at Mr Truegood's room." Wolf didn't go into detail about what they were looking for. If he had been pressed on why, he would have said that he had a gut instinct to keep his own counsel when it came to Mr Goodge. He couldn't quite put his finger on what it was, but he didn't believe the man was being entirely honest with them.

If Jeremiah Goodge was worried about what they might be searching for, he did not show it in his words or gestures. Instead, he said with an unconcerned air, "Do you need me to show you up, or do you remember which way to go? It is just that I'm at a particularly exciting point in this book and cannot tear myself away."

Wolf assured him they remembered the way and allowed the man to return to his book. Entering James Truegood's room, Wolf was again taken aback by the sheer number of books and papers.

"I worry about what else we might have missed the other day. I am not sure how long it might take to go through everything in here, but I suspect it is not the work of an hour or two," Wolf admitted to Langley, who agreed.

"I believe we should concentrate on the papers and set aside the books and periodicals for now. Fortunately, the man was very organised and appeared to have categorised his correspondence very systematically. I suggest we take all the papers, or at least everything that seems relevant, instead of trying to sort through them here. If we take everything back to the hall, we can enlist Mrs O'Leary and Bear to assist us in going through them."

It was a good suggestion, and Wolf wondered why they hadn't taken everything when they were here before. However, at that time, they had no particular reason to believe that James Truegood's death might be connected to his research. "Let us just be careful to keep each category of letter and note as clearly separated as Mr Truegood has them."

The men worked swiftly but carefully. They checked every drawer, looked in the cupboards, and even searched under the bed. They created separate piles for each group of papers, at least as far as James Truegood had categorised them. When they finished, there were ten different piles stacked in the room. Then, they began to take them downstairs and out to the carriage, taking care not to disturb the filing system.

If Mr Goodge wondered why they were coming and going from his house, he never reappeared to question the two earls.

When all the papers had been carefully taken out to the carriage, they returned to James Truegood's room one last time. Even with every loose paper and notebook removed, the room still appeared cluttered.

"Are any of these books worth taking?" Wolf asked, as much to himself as to Langley.

"I tried to glance at them while searching for papers, and based on that, I do not believe so," the other man replied. "We can always come back. From what I can tell, it does not seem as if Mr Goodge or anyone else had been in here and disturbed anything since we first visited."

"Do you truly believe we could tell?" Wolf asked with a laugh. Langley acknowledged it wasn't possible to be certain.

Chapter 18

Although Wolf and Langley had been absent for some time, it appeared that the luncheon with Mrs Chivers had not yet concluded. Thanks to a whispered request from Tabitha just before she had sat down with their guest, Talbot suggested to the two men that they dine in the breakfast room and save themselves from the town gossip. After the exhaustion of sorting through Mr Truegood's papers, both Wolf and Langley were happy to accept the suggestion. They were nearly finished with their meal when Talbot returned to tell them that Mrs Chivers had left and that Tabitha had gone to the parlour and had suggested they meet her there when they were ready.

"We will take our coffee in the parlour with her ladyship," Wolf told the butler, who nodded. "Oh, and Talbot, can you find Mrs O'Leary and Mr Caruthers and send them in to us when they are free? Where did the footmen take all the papers?"

"They are in the library, milord. I told them to bring in some extra tables to maintain the integrity of the piles."

Wolf thanked Talbot, and then he and Langley rose to find Tabitha. Upon entering the parlour, they saw her standing in front of the cork-board, staring at it intently. Wolf noticed new notecards pinned to it and assumed the ladies' morning had been fruitful.

Tabitha heard them enter and turned around. “You have a very intense look on your face,” Wolf observed as he bent to pour himself a cup of the coffee Talbot had brought in. “Did you learn something useful this morning?”

Laughing darkly, Tabitha said, “Let us hope so, given what we had to endure during our luncheon. I am surprised Mama was able to keep her comments to herself as well as she did.”

Mention of the dowager caused Langley to notice her absence and inquire about her. “She has retired for a nap. I believe that rising before noon for two days in a row has exhausted her, not to mention the physical strain her relative self-control this morning must have caused.” Tabitha then gave the two men an account of their conversation with Mrs Chivers.

When she had finished, Wolf said, “Those are both interesting pieces of information. We returned to Mr Goodge’s house and retrieved all of Mr Truegood’s papers, and yet again, I had the feeling he was not being entirely transparent about the nature of their relationship. This insight from the housekeeper would seem to confirm my instinct.”

“And who is this Sir Christopher?” Langley asked. “That relationship certainly seems like something we should look into more closely.”

The two men then conveyed their conversation with Mr Wells.

“For the most part, he simply echoed and confirmed what others have told us,” Wolf explained. “I believe the only new piece of information was that Mr Truegood seemed to think that whatever this thing is that he sought might be buried somewhere other than Pembroke Castle. Or at least that it is a possibility.”

As Wolf said this, the door opened, and Bear and Mrs O’Leary entered. Wolf explained the piles of papers laid out in the library and what they needed the two to assist with. “I know it will take some time, but I worry that this investigation has so many possible threads at this point, and that we may miss a connection if we do not scour every piece of paper. It may be that there is nothing more to be gleaned, but I would appreciate you looking through them anyway.”

Both private secretaries assured him that they didn’t mind searching the piles for possible clues. Tabitha caught sight of a quick glance passing between them and had to hide a smile; perhaps the idea of being compelled to spend hours in each other's company was less of a burden than it might be with a different accomplice.

Just before Bear and Mrs O'Leary left, Wolf added, "One thing we are searching for is the paper we believe James Truegood submitted to *Archaeologia Cambrensis.* However, please set aside any other materials you find that might be of interest. Specifically, Lady Pembroke learnt over lunch that our victim had been spending quite a lot of time with a Sir Christopher. If you find any reference of any kind to him, I would like to see it."

When Bear and Mrs O'Leary left to begin their work of sorting through the papers, the group resumed contemplating the new notecards.

"While I do not know who Sir Christopher is, I would assume he is a local landowner," Wolf mused.

Tabitha confirmed that Mrs Chivers had referred to him as local gentry. "She also said that Mr Goodge's housekeeper had mentioned that Sir Christopher's housekeeper had overheard the word 'treasure'."

Wolf considered how to swiftly learn more about this local landowner. Then, he had an idea and rang the bell for Talbot.

When the butler entered a few minutes later, Wolf said, "Talbot, please ask Mrs Budgers to come up when she has a moment."

Under normal circumstances, an earl requesting an audience with his cook would have caused even the most inscrutable butler to raise a well-controlled eyebrow. However, everyone at Glanwyddan Hall knew about Wolf's very special relationship with Mrs Budgers, going back to his days as a lonely young boy visiting his imperious grandfather.

Given that they had all just finished eating, Tabitha suspected that Mrs Budgers, who was getting on in age, was using the quiet before dinner preparations to enjoy a cup of tea and put her feet up. She felt terrible that they were interrupting the woman's rare moment of relaxation.

Within ten minutes, Mrs Budgers had appeared at the parlour door. When Wolf had returned to Glanwyddan Hall as the new earl after decades away, he had insisted that his beloved Budgie not stand on ceremony with him and still call him her Wolfie. Now, she entered the room and gave him a loving look that reminded Wolf of the kindness and warmth she had enveloped him with as a little boy.

"Budgie! I am so sorry to have disturbed your free time."

The woman beamed and looked as if she wanted nothing more than to sit and pull the tall, broad-shouldered earl onto her lap for a cuddle.

Instead, she said, "Wolfie, you know that you can never disturb your Budgie. What do you need, my love?"

It was fortunate the dowager was still napping, Tabitha thought. She knew the woman cringed every time the cook spoke to the Earl of Pembroke so familiarly.

"Will you come and take a seat, Budgie, and let me pour you a cup of tea?"

Again, under normal circumstances, the idea of a servant sitting in the company of her betters, let alone sipping tea with them, was unheard of. Tabitha suspected that if the dowager had been present, Mrs Budgers might have been more hesitant. However, the loving woman could deny her Wolfie nothing, and so took a seat and accepted the cup of tea.

When she was settled, Wolf asked, "Budgie, I know that you have been with the estate for a very long time. Do you know who Sir Christopher is who lives at Ashling House?"

"A long time, indeed," Mrs Budgers agreed. "Why, I came here as a scullery maid more than forty years ago, if you can believe it. Now, let me think on that name for a moment, my love."

The cook sipped her tea as she pondered the question. Finally, she said, "I haven't heard that name for many a year. I think the last time I heard it was when your grandfather, the old earl, was alive. He wasn't much for entertaining, you know, and didn't hold much truck with most of the local gentry. But he would sometimes have a Sir Christopher for dinner. I don't know for sure that it's the one you're asking about, though."

"What do you remember about this gentleman, Mrs Budgers?" asked Tabitha.

"Well, m'lady, of course I was in the kitchen so had nowt to do with the guests. But I do remember that the maids and footmen weren't so fond of him. A bit handsy with the women and rude to the men, from what I remember."

Tabitha thought wryly that Sir Christopher sounded like quite the charmer. "Do you know where Ashling House is located?" she asked.

"Well, now. I think it's not far outside Lamphey. Near the ruins over there. In fact, now I come to think about it, I had a niece who worked there for a while many years ago."

"The ruins?" Wolf asked. "Do you mean the Bishop's Summer Palace, Budgie?"

"Yes. That's it. His place is right by there."

"Given how close this Sir Christopher lives to here, I am rather surprised Roberts omitted him from the list of neighbours he invited to the hall at Christmas," Wolf observed.

Mrs Budgers laughed. "Well, perhaps not so surprising. The gentleman had a falling out with the old earl. I only heard bits and bobs, of course, but from what did trickle down to the kitchen, there had been some business dealings, and his lordship had lost money and thought he'd been swindled."

Well, that would explain it. Given that his grandfather was both incredibly astute and notoriously close-fisted, Wolf wondered what sort of man was able to defraud him of money. What he wasn't surprised about was that having done so, or even been perceived to have done so, Sir Christopher would be barred from the Pembroke Estate by future generations of earls.

It seemed Mrs Budgers had nothing more to say about Sir Christopher, and once she had finished her tea, she returned to her kitchen. The group sat contemplating what they had heard.

"If I have learned one thing today from our conversations with Mrs Chivers and then Mrs Budgers, it is how much gossip is spread by servants," Tabitha observed.

Of course, this wasn't new information. However, while Tabitha felt reasonably sure that her loyal, close-knit group of servants at Chesterton House could be trusted, what about those at Glanwyddan Hall? While they had brought some servants from London to bolster the hall's usual staff, she knew that her housekeeper further increased the numbers by hiring locally from villages and towns. Those individuals had no reason to feel any loyalty to the family.

"I do not think it is wise to leave this corkboard out when we are not using it," she decided. "We are forming hypotheses about local people, and I would hate for any of our musings to reach those people's ears, particularly before we have formed any conclusions," she said.

Wolf didn't need to ask what had prompted her thoughts to run in that direction; he'd been pondering something similar himself. "I will ask Talbot to lock it away securely when we are not in the parlour," he decided.

He was about to ring for Talbot to make this request when the man himself appeared in the doorway. "A telegram arrived for you, milord. I believe it is from Dr Morgan."

Wolf took the telegram, but before reading it he made the request about the corkboard of Talbot.

After scanning the telegram, he told the others, "Digitalis. He says that it mimics heart failure. While it is commonly used as a treatment for various heart conditions, if the dose is dramatically increased, it will cause death in a matter of hours. He confirms that the amount found was a quantity consistent with a dangerous or fatal dose."

This was interesting, but it still didn't answer why someone would poison James Truegood and then stab him. "Is it possible that he accidentally took too much medication?" Wolf suggested. Even as he said the words, he knew what Tabitha's answer would be.

"And then entirely coincidentally, someone stabbed him?" Tabitha replied, as Wolf knew she would. "Does that seem like the simplest answer?"

"No, no. I know how unlikely that scenario is. However, what also seems improbable is that someone would poison our victim with a substance that's nearly undetectable by the local police and mimics a natural death, but then stab James Truegood, thereby alerting the authorities that it was murder."

None of them had a satisfactory answer to this.

Wolf wrote a note to be delivered to Dr Lloyd, informing him of Dr Morgan's conclusion, and rang the bell to ask Talbot to have it delivered as soon as possible.

"Digitalis," Wolf repeated. "I wonder if that is what the victim meant when he wrote DIG in the dirt?" It certainly seemed plausible.

Chapter 19

While their investigation seemed to have more questions than answers so far, there was one clear gap in their knowledge: James Truegood's side of the correspondence with Clarice Hill. While Tabitha wasn't certain that the letters would help them identify the killer directly, she hoped they would shed light on their victim's character and state of mind. Perhaps, buried in those details that Clarice found so boring, there might even be more information about Mr Truegood's research or about his meetings with Sir Christopher.

Tabitha had spoken to the footman who had taken the book to Miss Hill and was supposed to retrieve the letters in return. He believed that he was turned away even though the mistress of the house was at home. It seemed the maid who answered the door was flustered and had not lied convincingly.

As Tabitha mulled this over, she remembered that Clarice had agreed to share the letters quite grudgingly and wondered why the young woman wouldn't want to hand them over. Then she asked the question out loud.

"Are we certain that she was at home?" Langley asked.

"Charlie, the footman, seemed quite certain that the maid was lying."

"Well, then," Wolf replied. "Let us visit the Hill household this afternoon. Turning away a footman is one thing, but dealing with the Earl and

Countess of Pembroke is quite another. If I am present, I might be able to distract Mr Hill while you receive the letters from his daughter."

It seemed like a reasonable plan, and within the hour, the Pembroke carriage was pulling up outside a modest yet charming house on what looked to be one of the better streets in Pembroke. It was exactly the sort of place Tabitha would expect a prosperous local solicitor to live in.

While it would have been very unusual for Tabitha and Wolf to have paid a social call on the Hills before the dinner party, now it would not be as remarkable. Nevertheless, it was surprising enough to cause the maid who opened the door to become tongue-tied and wide-eyed at the sight of the grand carriage and the liveried servant announcing the arrival of the Earl of Pembroke. As expected, the girl had no option but to welcome them, settle them in the grandest room of the house, and assure them she would alert her master and mistress.

In the carriage, Tabitha and Wolf discussed how they might separate the girl from her father. Wolf suggested that he ask to speak privately with the solicitor about an estate matter. There were a few issues that had recently arisen, which he planned to have his solicitor in London handle, but Mr Hill didn't need to know about that. The prospect of aristocratic patronage would surely be too tempting for the man, prompting him to grant Wolf an immediate audience in his study.

They were shown into a pleasant, sunny room by a maid, who left to inform her master of his illustrious guests. They were not waiting for long before Mr and Miss Hill hurried into the room, followed by the maid bearing a tea tray. Cyril Hill looked delighted to have his recent hosts honour him so soon after the dinner. Clarice Hill seemed less happy to see them. She couldn't meet Tabitha's eye and, once they were all seated, fidgeted with the lace on her dress and chewed her lip.

Tabitha wondered what the young woman thought would happen after she dismissed the footman. Did she believe Tabitha would give up trying to retrieve the letters? The group made small talk as they sipped tea and nibbled on rather dry fruitcake.

Finally, Wolf said, "After our conversations the other night at dinner, it occurred to me that you might be able to help me with some local legal matters. Would we be able to speak privately? I am sure the ladies do not want to be bored with estate matters."

As expected, Mr Hill could hardly contain his enthusiasm at the prospect and leapt out of his chair to lead Wolf out of the room and into his study.

When they had left and Wolf had ensured the door was closed behind him, Tabitha folded her hands in her lap and spoke in a clear, firm voice. "I assume you know why I am here, Miss Hill."

The younger woman still could not meet her eye and merely stammered something inaudible in reply.

Tabitha could see that Clarice would not make this easy. She decided she didn't have time to waste playing these games. "Miss Hill, I have done my best to conduct this business in a way that will not expose your behaviour to your father. However, if necessary, I will ask him directly to have you hand over the letters. Is that your preference?"

At this threat, Clarice Hill's eyes widened in terror. "Please, your ladyship, no!"

In a somewhat gentler but still firm voice, Tabitha said, "It is not my intention to expose you in such a manner. However, when you turn away my man, and now seem unwilling to hand the letters over to me, I fear I have no choice."

It seemed that this threat was finally sufficient. Clarice Hill stood and said in a dejected voice, "I will get them for you."

Tabitha suddenly thought of a new concern. "And Miss Hill, please do not attempt to remove any letters. Remember, we already possess Mr Truegood's side of the correspondence. It will be apparent if there are gaps in the communications."

As it happened, Tabitha wasn't certain it would be. Nevertheless, this appeared to be a reasonable threat to make. Indeed, Miss Hill nodded her head in apparent compliance. She left the room and, no more than a few minutes later, returned with a bundle of letters tied with a pink ribbon. She handed them over, and Tabitha placed them in the larger-than-usual handbag she had brought for the outing.

Once that transaction was finished, the tense silence between the two women became almost unbearable. Tabitha was so relieved when the door finally opened and Wolf and Mr Hill came in that she immediately stood up.

There you are, my dear," she said, casting Wolf a look she hoped he would interpret correctly. "We have taken up enough of these good people's time, do you not think? Let us make our farewells."

Wolf fully understood his wife's hint, and a few minutes later, they were back in the carriage, heading to Glanwyddan Hall.

"Did you get the letters?" Wolf asked.

"I did," Tabitha replied, pulling them out of her bag. "I will say, Clarice Hill did not make it easy, and I am afraid I had to resort to threats. I also told her that we would know if she removed any of the letters."

"Would we?" Wolf asked, echoing Tabitha's own concerns.

"Perhaps," she said with a shrug. "In any case, I hope the threat of it was enough to put paid to any thoughts she might have had about editing the selection she shared." They could only hope she was right.

As soon as they returned home, Tabitha removed her hat and settled into an armchair in the parlour to read through the letters. Wolf sat nearby, reading a book. Once she had finished reading them, Tabitha reread them to be certain she hadn't missed anything.

Wolf noticed her beginning again and asked, "You are reading them twice?"

"I just want to make sure." She put the letters aside. "We already knew that, whatever her feelings, James Truegood was in love with Clarice Hill. Her letters suggested that she encouraged his feelings. His letters confirm beyond doubt how much she encouraged them, particularly on the occasions they met at social gatherings. I suspect that there may be no more to Miss Hill's unwillingness to share these letters than that they simply reveal how much she led him a merry dance. Certainly, this is not a correspondence a young woman would wish to be made public, especially when she was neither betrothed to the man nor had any intention of being so."

"Is there nothing of use to us in them?" Wolf asked hopefully.

"Only one thing. Mr Truegood mentions his visits to Sir Christopher and says he has high hopes of convincing the man not only to allow him to survey the ruins but potentially to fund the fieldwork."

Wolf considered her words. "Well, I suppose that explains the multiple visits to Ashling Hall. Is there anything else that should make us in any way suspicious of Sir Christopher?"

"Not specifically," Tabitha admitted. "However, there was one line that gave me pause. Wait, let me read it to you." She searched through the letters until she found the one she wanted to quote. "James writes: 'My only concern is that Sir Christopher may have latched onto something I mentioned in passing: that there may be other treasures buried there. I do not wish to mislead anyone, yet I cannot deny definitively that it is a possibility.'"

Returning the letter to the pile of others, she asked, "What do you make of that?"

"Well, we heard from Budgie that even in my grandfather's day, Sir Christopher engaged in questionable business deals, or at least so the old earl claimed. Is it so hard to believe that such a man, upon hearing the word treasure even once, might fixate on that?"

Tabitha couldn't argue with his words, but they made her think of something. "What happened to the knife used to stab James Truegood?"

"I assume the constable has kept it as evidence. Why?"

"I believe we should examine it, or more precisely, have someone knowledgeable look at it. Perhaps it is part of the so-called treasure."

Wolf agreed, but couldn't imagine where they would find such a person. The only local person they knew who might have knowledge about a possible antiquity was Mr Goodge, and Wolf would prefer to avoid involving him until they were certain of his motives.

"What about Mr Allen?" Tabitha suggested. "He mentioned he would be staying in Tenby for at least a week. At the very least, he might know someone locally who knows something about the possible provenance of such a weapon."

As she spoke these words, the dowager entered the room. "Weapon? What weapon? What have I missed? Has someone else been killed? Really, Tabitha, I would expect you to wake me from my nap if there was another corpse."

Tabitha heaved a sigh and proceeded to recount everything they had learned that day.

When she arrived at their decision to seek out John Romilly Allen's help in identifying the dagger, the dowager said quite unexpectedly, "I will go and talk with him?"

Before she could think better of it, Tabitha asked, in surprise, "Really, Mama?"

"Why are you so shocked, Tabitha? Do you not believe I am up to the journey of a mere few miles? Or is it rather that you do not believe I can be trusted to conduct such an interview?"

Rather than admit that it was a bit of both, Tabitha said, "Of course, if you feel you can step away from the main path of the investigation for a day, your help would be very welcome."

"Step away from the path? Is that what you are claiming I will be doing? Given how much investigating you seem to do while I am conveniently sleeping, I doubt I will miss much!

And so, that was that. All that remained was for Wolf to send a man to retrieve the dagger from Constable Tucker.

Chapter 20

At a surprisingly early hour the next morning, the dowager was ready to depart for Tenby.

When faced with the choice between a one-and-a-half-hour carriage ride each way or a twenty-minute train journey plus the additional need to hire a carriage at the station, the dowager declared, "I would rather spend longer travelling as befits a countess, than save time and be mistaken for a charwoman."

While Tabitha and Wolf both raised their eyebrows at the idea that the imperious woman in silk and furs would ever be mistaken for anything other than a great lady of means, they kept their thoughts to themselves.

The constable had sent the faux murder weapon to Wolf, and now he handed it to the dowager. She turned it over, examining it. The blade seemed long for a dagger at just over ten inches. It was slender, triangular, and tapered to a sharp point. The metal bore the darkened sheen of age, and the hilt was wrapped in faded red leather, bound in a criss-cross pattern. The crossguard was plain but well-proportioned and marked with a shallow engraving of a lion rampant.

"I do not claim to know much about such matters, I admit, but it looks as if it could be very old," the dowager said as she slipped it into an oversized reticule she was carrying for the purpose.

"Hopefully, Mr Allen will know more than we do," Wolf said optimistically. As the dowager turned to leave, he added, "Regardless of what he thinks about this dagger, ask him what he thinks of the possibility that actual ancient treasures might be buried somewhere around here." The dowager nodded her assent and left.

The truth about the journey was that the dowager believed she could nap much more easily during an uninterrupted carriage ride than on the train. Her lady's maid, Withers, accompanied her and sat quietly reading on the opposite bench, pretending not to notice her mistress' gentle snoring.

When the carriage finally stopped in Tenby, the dowager still hadn't woken from her sleep. If it weren't for the ongoing snores, Withers might have worried that the woman had passed away. As it was, she gently tapped the dowager's arm until she finally awoke with a start.

"Where are we?" she demanded groggily.

"We have arrived in Tenby, milady."

The dowager peered out of the carriage window at the rather small, slightly crumbling vicarage they had stopped in front of. The gate was hanging off, and it looked as if at least one chimney was in danger of falling. She had volunteered for this expedition out of a fit of pique, but now the dowager wondered if she had been too quick to offer. Was she expected to take tea in a common parsonage?

Although the dowager was tempted to signal the driver to return immediately to Glanwyddan Hall, she steeled herself and signalled that Withers should help her out of the carriage and then go and knock on the door.

The maid did so and then waited a few moments before knocking again. Finally, she heard a voice mumbling, "Yes, yes. Coming." The door was opened by an elderly man whose white hair seemed to stand up in every direction. His spectacles, which were askew, perched on the end of a rather long nose.

From his dog collar, it appeared this was Reverend Aldersham. The dowager harboured a rather low opinion of members of the clergy in general, but had a particular distaste for those like the man before her, who appeared to be a woolly-headed old fool.

"May I help you, madam?" he asked Withers, not noticing the grand lady standing by what was left of his garden gate.

"We are hoping to find Mr Allen. Her ladyship was told he is staying with you," Withers said with all the hauteur of one who served a countess.

"Yes, yes. John is here. Although he didn't say he was expecting anyone. I will have to see if he can take a break from his research for visitors."

From her position, the dowager could hear enough to be quite irritated. "You may tell Mr Allen that the Dowager Countess of Pembroke has come a long way to speak with him and does not intend to leave without an audience!"

Now, the vicar noticed the petite, yet somewhat terrifying-looking, elderly woman at the end of his garden path. He looked up in astonishment at the dowager's words.

"Oh, my," was all he could manage before gathering himself and saying, "You'd better come in then."

Reverend Aldersham led the way and walked into a cosy, if rather cluttered, parlour. Every surface was covered with books, papers, forgotten cups of tea, and, just peeking out from beneath a discarded tea cosy, some buttered toast that the vicar had started eating that morning before being distracted.

Although the vicar was not usually one to care about social niceties and certainly did not stand on ceremony in ordinary circumstances, upon entering his front room, even he could see that it might not be an appropriate place to entertain a dowager countess.

Before the dowager and Withers could even follow him in, Reverend Aldersham turned and said, "Perhaps I should take you straight to John. He is in my study."

Luckily, Mr John Romilly Allen was a very tidy man. As much as he enjoyed the company of his fellow historian, he always found the vicar's high tolerance for mess challenging. Because of this, the very first thing he did on each visit was to claim the study, tidy it up, and insist it be his domain during his stay. Consequently, it was a place the dowager could be taken to where she might not be appalled by clutter and discarded food.

When he heard the door open, Mr Allen looked up, expecting only to see his host. When he saw the two women in his wake, his bespectacled eyes widened in surprise.

The man stood looking confused. The elder of the two women appeared familiar for some reason, though he couldn't quite place why. His curiosity was satisfied when Reverend Aldersham announced the visitor's identity.

"Ah, yes! Of course, I remember Lady Pembroke from my tour of Lamphey Bishop's Summer Palace the other day. Although I believe you didn't join us for the entire lecture." Even as he said this, Mr Allen recalled his relief when the loudly critical elderly woman decided to return to her carriage. What on earth could she want with him now?

The dowager seated herself in one of the chairs in front of the desk, while Withers moved herself into a darker corner. Without any preamble, the dowager pulled the dagger out of the larger-than-normal reticule she was carrying and placed it on the desk.

"Oh, my!" Reverend Aldersham gasped.

Mr Allen leant across the desk and picked up the weapon, turning it over and then back again, examining every inch of it.

"Might I inquire where you acquired this, your ladyship?" he asked.

"In due time. First, what can you tell me about it?" Looking up from the dagger, Mr Allen explained, "I am not an expert in such things. However, fortunately for you, my host is. Jonas, would you care to take a look?"

It was clear from the sceptical look on the dowager's face what she thought of the idea that the vicar, whom she had already mentally dismissed as a doddering old fool, was the person whose expert advice she needed. It was probably for the best that the vicar was standing just behind her left shoulder and so couldn't see her face. Now, he came forward and took the dagger from his friend.

After only a few seconds of examination, he declared, "This is a fake, and not a very convincing one at that."

"How can you be so certain, sir?" the dowager demanded irritably. "I have examined a hangnail for longer than you looked at the weapon."

Either Jonas Aldersham didn't hear the criticism implied by the dowager's words, or he didn't care. Whichever it was, he answered her in a mild tone that suggested no offence. "Your ladyship, there are so many reasons to be sure this is not genuine that I am spoilt for where to start. However, let me give you the reasons that jumped out at me as soon as I saw this dagger."

Until that moment, the vicar had not been particularly animated in his speech. However, now, his face lit up as he began to lecture on his favourite subject. "Let us begin with the blade." He held out the dagger to illustrate his point. "While it does look like a misericorde, the kind of weapon used to deliver a knight's final mercy blow, where the metal appears to have the dark sheen of age, close inspection reveals the patina to be uneven, perhaps even painted in places, as though someone has tried to simulate corrosion."

Then, pointing with his free hand to the red leather handle, he said, "While this was the fashion with knightly blades, the wrapping is suspiciously unworn. Likewise, the crossguard is too smooth to be hand-forged, and the engraving on it, a lion rampant, while vaguely similar to the Marshal arms, is not an exact match."

Finally, in a tone that suggested he believed he was delivering the final coup de grace, the vicar pronounced, "This disc-shaped pommel at the end of the grip is clearly polished brass masquerading as aged bronze and is far too bright in its crevices." He shrugged and added, "Honestly, I doubt this was even made with the intention of being taken seriously as the genuine article. The issues I just enumerated are unsubtle. My guess is that whoever sold this did so, making little effort to pretend this was a real historic find, but rather being quite open about this being merely a souvenir."

The dowager wanted to argue with the man simply because of her personal distaste for his slovenly ways, but even she realised the futility of such a debate. Instead, she asked, "And where might one buy such souvenirs?"

"It isn't unusual to find curiosity shops, sometimes even bookstores, near historic sites, selling such items. In fact, we have one such shop here in Tenby. I have spoken with the proprietor over the years about any confusion there might be in customers' minds regarding the authenticity of his items. He swears he is entirely transparent about the true nature of the items he sells. However, I remain doubtful."

"Nevertheless, you have no such doubts about the historical provenance of this dagger?" the dowager asked, still not entirely convinced that the man was the expert he claimed to be.

"Absolutely none. If you still need to be persuaded, I am happy to show you examples from my personal collection of genuine daggers from the period and demonstrate exactly how each compares to this one."

The thought of enduring any longer listening to this man drone on about old pieces of metal was more than the dowager could bear, so she decided she had been persuaded. As far as she was concerned, she had accomplished what she set out to do, and there was no reason to stay even a moment longer in this dingy little cottage.

The dowager was about to stand to leave when she remembered Wolf's other request. Turning to Mr Allen, she asked, "Lord Pembroke had one more question: is there any reason to believe there might be actual valuable relics, treasure as you might say, connected to William Marshal, but buried in or around the Summer Palace in Lamphey or nearby?"

The historian stroked his chin as he considered the question. Finally, he answered, "On the face of it, it sounds like folklore," Mr Allen said, adjusting his spectacles. "But we must consider the context. William Marshal was more than a warlord; he was a statesman with deep ties to both the Crown and the Church. In 1218, the year after the First Barons' War ended, the kingdom was still unstable. Marshal was ageing. He'd served as regent for the young Henry III and would have known that not everything could be trusted to parchment sent through royal channels. We know the bishops used Lamphey as their summer residence. While there's no record of Marshal staying there, it would have been neutral ground. For a man who had to balance baronial loyalty, ecclesiastical influence, and royal suspicion, it might have been a sensible spot to keep certain items."

The dowager was tempted to remark that she'd already had one history lesson that week and didn't need another. However, even she realised that she was a guest in this house and had asked for Mr Allen's help, and so she did no more than purse her lips a little.

Having finished his explanation, John Allen then shook his head and said, "But this is all mere speculation. Jonas, what do you think of the idea?"

The vicar chuckled. "Oh, that old chestnut again? Every few years, someone has the idea that there's a hidden stash of treasure somewhere around Lamphey. The myth, I believe, started from a misreading of a particular 14th-century monastic chronicle that seemed to mention a concealed deposit near Lamphey. It doesn't seem to matter how many times it's debunked, it keeps rearing its head again." And that seemed to be that.

Just as the dowager was preparing to take her leave, Mr Allen said, "I will be returning to the Pembroke area the day after tomorrow, if you have any more questions. This time, I will be staying for a night or two at The Old Kings Arms. Jeremiah Goodge has some findings at Pembroke Castle, particularly Wogan Cavern, which he wishes to show me. He has also suggested that we sketch the rock formations and structural remains for an article in *Archaeologia Cambrensis*."

Chapter 21

With the dowager off on her errand for most of the day, Tabitha and Wolf considered how best to spend their time. They had retired to the parlour and now sat reviewing what they had so far on the corkboard.

"I would guess that whoever murdered James Truegood, stabbed him with that dagger to encourage the local constabulary to make a connection to the treasure hunting it seems he may have been involved with," Tabitha theorised, tapping a pen against her chin absentmindedly.

Wolf agreed with his wife's hypothesis and considered its implications. "If you are correct, then whoever killed Mr Truegood had some knowledge of whatever was happening with Sir Christopher, or at least the expectations that had been created about possible treasure."

"Of course, by that logic, this Sir Christopher is then the least likely suspect, if only for the effort the murderer made to point the finger of guilt towards him." Tabitha then thought about what she'd said. "Although that would be quite the feint if, in fact, the killer is Sir Christopher: point the clues so clearly towards himself that it becomes more believable that it is not."

"Just following that logic is giving me a headache," Wolf said, laughing. "What we need to do is to find a way to talk to this Sir Christopher. I do not think we can just turn up on his doorstep or indeed invite him to ours, at least with no good reason. It is quite likely that he has heard that I am the magistrate on the case, and will immediately be suspicious and on his guard."

Tabitha agreed and considered what their next move might be. She pondered the problem for some minutes before clapping her hands together and saying, "I have an idea. Today is August 9th, is it not?"

Wolf tended to lose track of time when they were in Pembrokeshire, but that seemed a reasonable assumption.

"Then, we should host a Glorious Twelfth event."

"What on earth is the Glorious Twelfth?" Wolf asked, mystified.

Tabitha laughed. "I forget that you did not grow up on a great estate. Still, you visited your grandfather during the summers. I am surprised he did not do something even though Pembrokeshire does not have suitable moorland habitat for red grouse."

"My love, I have absolutely no idea what you are talking about."

"The Glorious Twelfth marks the start of red grouse shooting in Britain. Of course, it is most celebrated in the northern moors of England and Scotland, where grouse are plentiful. Nevertheless, even in Cambridgeshire, my father still marked the date and usually hosted a partridge shoot."

"And you are suggesting I do likewise?"

"Well, of course, it is not the official start to partridge season, but my father never let that stop him. I believe we have sufficient managed covers of hedgerows, fallow fields, and stubble for a decent shoot."

Wolf shook his head, not in challenge at her words, but rather at his own lack of knowledge about such things. Usually, he had few regrets about his upbringing, at least so far as it lacked so many of the affectations and experiences common to an aristocrat. However, there were times when he felt no more prepared to be an earl than if he had been a chimney sweep suddenly elevated far beyond his appropriate sphere. This was one of those times.

"I will take your word for it," was his only reply. Then, he considered another aspect of Tabitha's suggestion. "However, this plan means that we will not meet someone who is suddenly one of our prime suspects for another three days."

Tabitha smiled. "Ah, but that is the real genius of this idea; it will give you the perfect excuse to visit the man today!"

When she saw the blank look on her husband's face, Tabitha elaborated. "You can send invitations to Sir Jerome and Squire Partridge today. I will ask Roberts who else might be invited. However, given the bad blood between Sir Christopher and your grandfather, it would be quite bizarre for you to send him an invitation out of nowhere. What does make much more sense is for you to visit him in person, perhaps even this afternoon, and offer to let bygones be bygones."

"Then, Friday can be a follow-up if I am not able to get any relevant information out of him today! Tabitha, that is a wonderful idea."

Tabitha blushed with pleasure. "If nothing else, we can include a lavish luncheon in the fields. The hunt should start around half-past nine, so a break for lunch is perfect. I will make sure there is sufficient claret involved, and that should lubricate conversation perfectly. Partridge is usually hunted walked-up rather than formally this time of year, so the hunt will lend itself perfectly to small, casual conversations."

"I will take your word for it." Wolf checked his pocket watch. "Is it too early to pay the visit now?"

"Perhaps wait an hour," Tabitha suggested. "You can use that time to change your clothes," she said with a pointed look.

When it seemed as if Wolf was going to argue that he was dressed well enough for such a visit, Tabitha said, "Just tell Thompson the nature of your social call and he will know what to do."

Wolf shrugged and gave up the argument, instead going to seek out his valet to be dressed appropriately. Tabitha went to seek out the estate steward to pull the guest list together and work out the details of the hunt, and then Mrs Jenkins to plan for the luncheon.

Though she hadn't admitted it to Wolf, Tabitha was excited at the thought of the hunt. While she didn't care one way or another for the shooting part of such an event, the traditions around such a day were something she had fond memories of from her childhood and which she hadn't had a chance to participate in since before her marriage to Jonathan.

Forty-five minutes later, Wolf was dressed in what Thompson considered appropriate attire for an earl making a visit to a country neighbour.

As far as Wolf was concerned, he looked absurd. He didn't even know he owned such attire, but apparently Thompson had prepared for every eventuality and had been positively gleeful about the opportunity to dress his master in one such outfit. When he was told about the planned shoot, he almost vibrated with excitement.

Wolf was dressed in a well-tailored tweed suit of moss-green check. The white shirt bore a high, starched collar, fastened with a dark silk tie knotted neatly at the throat. Brown leather boots showed a careful polish, and he wore a soft grey felt trilby, the brim slightly turned down against the afternoon sun. Over Wolf's strong objections, Thompson insisted he carry brown gloves and a walking stick, more for appearance than necessity.

"Your lordship, you radiate understated authority and appear as a man at ease with both his rank and his setting," his valet assured him, after Wolf had tried one more time to leave the walking stick behind.

"Are you saying that I rarely appear as such?" Wolf asked.

Thompson clasped his hands in front of him and pursed his lips. "How would you like me to answer that, milord?"

Wolf rolled his eyes but said nothing more; he was very aware of what a gem Thompson was and that the man would always win such battles. Instead, he went downstairs to present himself to his wife for inspection. After her conversations with Roberts, the steward, and Mrs Jenkins, Tabitha had returned to the parlour.

When Wolf first entered the room, Tabitha had to work hard to keep her face straight and not smirk. It wasn't that her husband looked bad; quite the contrary. It was rather that Tabitha could only imagine how Wolf felt about his outfit and how much arguing there had been with his valet.

It seemed she had not controlled her smirk as well as she'd hoped. "I look ridiculous, do I not?" Wolf said sullenly.

Tabitha rose and approached him, taking his hands. "You look very dapper and quite the country gentleman. I would not be surprised if you find Sir Christopher dressed quite similarly." Wolf didn't seem placated by her words, so Tabitha tried again. "You want to put this man at his ease, do you not? So, you are better off looking the part of a landowner familiar with hosting shooting parties rather than raising any questions about why a man who seems to have never even shot a clay pigeon might suddenly have chosen to traipse his property to shoot partridge."

Although Wolf knew her words made sense, he continued to pout. Tabitha's mouth twitched with suppressed laughter, but she said nothing further. Instead, she kissed her husband and sent him on his way. Only after he had closed the parlour door behind him did she let out a chuckle. She wished she could join him, but this was a visit best made man-to-man. She would only be a distraction.

Perhaps it wasn't such a bad thing that she couldn't join him, Tabitha thought as she settled back into her armchair and yawned. She was exhausted for no reason she could think of. She had a book on the table next to her she'd intended to read, but before she knew it, Tabitha had drifted off to sleep.

Chapter 22

Wolf wasn't sure what he had expected from his visit with Sir Christopher. If he had to guess, he imagined an old man sitting by his fireplace, a blanket over his knees, perhaps smoking a pipe. After all, the man had been friends with Wolf's grandfather, who had died eighteen years earlier. What he hadn't expected was to be shown out to a lawn at the back of the house, where a vigorous-looking man was shooting clay pigeons.

On closer inspection, it was clear the man wasn't young, but he didn't seem decrepit. His hair barely had any grey in it, though Wolf wondered how much was natural. He didn't know any men of high birth who dyed their hair, but he knew it was quite common among theatre folks and certain dandies. Did Sir Christopher dye his hair?

The butler stood silent for a moment to allow his master to take his shot, then he cleared his throat and announced, "The Earl of Pembroke, sir."

Sir Christopher spun around in surprise and lowered his gun. "Pembroke, heh? Are you the new earl? The grandson of that wily old fox, Jeremiah?"

Wily old fox was probably one of the nicer things his grandfather had ever been called. "Yes, I am Jeremy Chesterton, the Earl of Pembroke."

Looking Wolf up and down, Sir Christopher said, "I can see something of your grandfather in you. I hope you are not the dastard he was."

WHAT WAS THE APPROPRIATE RESPONSE TO SUCH A sentiment? Wolf couldn't imagine, but it did offer a convenient prompt to explain his appearance. "Sir Christopher, I have heard that you and my grandfather did not part on the best of terms, and that is why I am here. I wish to mend the breach. I do not want to be at odds with such a close neighbour, and to that end, I would like to invite you to a partridge shoot on Friday."

"In honour of the Glorious Twelfth, is it?" Sir Christopher asked. Apparently, everyone but Wolf knew what the day was.

"Indeed. It will be an intimate gathering of neighbouring landowners."

"Including that awful bore, Jerome, I supposed."

Wolf couldn't deny this fact, but added, "And Squire Partridge, I hope."

Sir Christopher chuckled. "Well, old Partridge certainly livens up any event. Just keep any pretty maids out of his sight." Then, after a pause, he added, "Or even ugly ones, if half of what I have heard is true." Given what Budgie had said about Sir Christopher, this seemed to be the thief crying, 'Stop thief!'

Wolf had no desire to discuss the unfortunate predilections of the local gentry. Fortunately, Sir Christopher appeared to have other ideas.

Handing his gun to a servant, he approached Wolf with his hand extended. "Well, it is jolly good of you, old chap, to make the offer. I have no wish to continue the feud. To be honest, I can't quite remember what we even argued about. It was so long ago. Let us go into the house and celebrate with a drink or two." And with that, he patted Wolf's back and chuckled again.

Wolf hadn't paid much attention to the house's interior on his way through to the lawn, but now, re-entering it, he noticed how dilapidated everything looked. The paint was peeling, and there was a distinct smell of damp. Overall, the place appeared as if no one had bothered to spend a penny on it for many years. While Sir Christopher seemed able to afford at least some servants, their uniforms looked old and, upon closer inspection, showed signs of extensive darning and other repairs. It appeared that Sir Christopher was clinging to gentility by the skin of his teeth.

Sir Christopher led Wolf into a library-study where the dust was so thick that Wolf concluded the house might not have any maids. Perhaps the entire staff was just the man who had answered the door and whoever was releasing his targets on the lawn. And of course, he remembered that Mrs Chivers had heard her gossip through the housekeeper, a Mrs Green, if Wolf's memory was correct.

Although Wolf did his best not to react to the obvious lack of housekeeping, something of his thoughts must have shown on his face.

"Apologies for the mess," Sir Christopher said, waving his hand to take in the room. "I have had a bit of trouble keeping staff lately. You know how it is." Wolf did not know how it was, but was polite enough not to comment.

Sir Christopher poured them each a drink. The man's brandy confirmed that he was all crest and no coin, as Wolf's father had often said about himself. As Wolf forced himself to sip the rotgut, he wondered how far Sir Christopher would go to restore his fortune. Certainly, the prospect of finding treasures on his land must have thrilled him. Once that possibility was dangled before him, how might he have reacted if those riches were not found?

One thing Wolf couldn't decide was whether to bring up the topic of James Truegood's killing now or wait until Friday.

The decision was settled for him when Sir Christopher sank into a very saggy-looking old armchair and said nonchalantly, "I hear you are the magistrate on this murder in Pembroke."

Where was the man planning to go with this? Wolf wondered. Determined to give away as little as possible, he replied, "I am. I feel I have been somewhat negligent in such duties since inheriting. How did you hear?"

Even as he asked, he wondered how surprising it was. While Lamphey was a few miles from Pembroke, he was sure gossip had no trouble travelling that distance.

"It was in The Herald on Friday. The Pembrokeshire Herald. You are not a reader?"

Wolf wasn't and made a mental note to rectify that immediately.

Sir Christopher rose and approached a table where newspapers were piled up haphazardly. He rifled through them before pulling out an issue and handing it to Wolf.

Well-known Antiquary Found Dead in Ruins

Considerable local interest has been stirred by the sudden death of Mr James Truegood, Pembroke Assistant Schoolmaster and a gentleman of scholarly reputation.

Mr Truegood's body was discovered late Tuesday afternoon in Wogan Cavern at Pembroke Castle. The circumstances attending the discovery have led the local constabulary to initiate further inquiries. A post-mortem examination has been ordered.

The inquest will be opened at an as-yet indeterminate date at the Pembroke Town Hall, where it is expected that the Earl of Pembroke, serving as Acting Magistrate, will be in attendance.

Wolf looked up from the article as Sir Christopher asked with an almost studied casualness, "So, what have you determined so far? I hear he was stabbed with a dagger."

For a moment, Wolf wondered how Sir Christopher knew that, given that it wasn't mentioned in the newspaper, but then, again, he considered how quickly gossip spread in small communities. It wasn't hard to believe that Constable Tucker had mentioned it to someone, maybe his wife, and that word had spread out from there.

Adopting as neutral a tone as possible, Wolf replied, "Yes. Mr Truegood was stabbed." It appeared that the actual cause of death, poison, was not yet common knowledge. Wolf had no intention of fuelling rumours about the death by confirming anything that was not already known.

As much as he had no intention of fanning the flames of local chatter, Wolf was curious to see where Sir Christopher tried to take the conversation. "Did you know the deceased at all?" In the normal course of events, why would a member of the local gentry know a poor assistant schoolmaster in a neighbouring town?

Sir Christopher paused for a moment before replying. Because of the angle at which they sat, Wolf couldn't get a clear view of the other man's face and therefore couldn't read his expression. Yet the brief pause, combined with the seemingly forced casualness when he spoke, led Wolf to believe he was about to be lied to.

"James Truegood? Well, of course, he was not part of my social circle; that is a given." Another pause. "But yes, I had met the man briefly, once or twice."

"Did you share his enthusiasm for local history?"

"In a fashion, you might say that." Was Sir Christopher going to say more? Wolf waited. He didn't want to seem overly suspicious, particularly as there would be an opportunity to pick the conversation back up at the partridge hunt.

Luckily, Sir Christopher elaborated without being pressed. "Actually, he had an interest in some ruins on my land and wanted my permission to work on the site."

"Did you give permission? And if so, did he find anything?"

"I believe I granted permission. As for what he might have discovered, I have no idea."

Wolf didn't point out that this all sounded like more than a couple of brief interactions. The conversation made him even more eager to hear what the dowager had to report about the dagger pulled out of James Truegood.

He did have one more question. "Do you know who else might have known about Mr Truegood's interest in the ruins on your land?"

This question appeared to pique Sir Christopher's interest. He asked sharply, "Why? Do you think it is related to his death?"

Worried that he might have revealed his hand too obviously, Wolf leaned back in his chair, took a sip of the nearly undrinkable brandy, and said, "No reason. I was just curious. I am trying to learn all I can about the man and his final days."

"Well, there's nothing worth fussing over here."

As soon as it seemed polite to do so, Wolf made his excuses and left Ashling House.

Chapter 23

Withers had the foresight to bring a hamper of food in the carriage, so there was no need to stop for a meal on the return to Lamphey. As the dowager nibbled on a cucumber sandwich, she reflected on what she had learned. It appeared the killer hadn't gone to great lengths to ensure the dagger used to stab the corpse could pass as authentic. Instead, they had relied on Constable Tucker's incompetence and laziness.

Of course, she thought, reaching for another triangle of sandwich, if their group hadn't been visiting Pembroke Castle that day and Rat hadn't ventured down to Wogan Cavern, the killer might have achieved their goal. This thought led her to another: was Wogan Cavern the intended site of James Truegood's death? After all, it was just a coincidence that they came across the body. If the dagger was meant as misdirection, it probably meant the murderer expected the body to be found while still identifiable. How likely was that in such a place?

Was there a reason the killer was certain the body would be discovered sooner rather than later? Then, she recalled Mr Allen's parting words about his return to Pembroke and the plan to visit the castle with Mr Goodge. Had the plan been that he would find the body? If so, who else knew about his visit?

The dowager was so elated by her insight that, for a moment, she wished she had taken the train after all and could return more swiftly. She also wished she had something to jot her thoughts down on; she didn't want to forget them before she returned to the hall.

Then, she had a thought. "Withers, do you still waste your time scribbling in that journal of yours?"

"I do, milady."

"And do you have it with you?"

The lady's maid looked at her mistress with curiosity. She had served the dowager for nearly forty years, yet the woman still had the ability to confound her at times.

"I always bring my journal on long carriage rides. I find that writing in it is a pleasant way to pass the time." In fact, Withers had spent most of the journey to Tenby writing in her journal while the dowager napped.

"Excellent. I need a pen and something to write on. Your journal will do nicely."

Usually, Withers was able to maintain an inscrutability worthy of a butler. She hadn't lasted as long with the dowager as she had by showing her emotions. However, now, when ordered to hand over her personal journal, where she recorded her innermost thoughts, the woman showed a moment of shock and horror on her face.

Even the dowager, not usually particularly perceptive about other people's feelings, couldn't help but notice her maid's expression. "There is no need to panic, woman. I have no interest in reading your ramblings. I merely wish to have a blank piece of paper, something to lean on, and a pen. I will flick to an empty page at the back and promise not to even glance at whatever petty grievances you have written against me."

Her words did not sufficiently placate Withers, but the woman realised she had no choice and reached into her ample carpetbag, pulled out her journal, and handed it over with a pen. It occurred to the dowager that it might be amusing to tease her maid just a little more, perhaps by opening to a random page and reading what was written. Although the idea was tempting, she was too excited to write down her thoughts while they were fresh, and so she resisted the urge. Instead, she scribbled for thirty minutes, occasionally crossing out something and replacing it with a new thought.

What never crossed the dowager's mind was that this leather-bound notepad, with its high-quality paper, probably hadn't been cheap, at least for a servant. She used several pages without any regard for her maid's purse. Withers watched her journal pages dwindle with an inward sigh.

Finally, the dowager looked up and said, "I think I have captured everything I learned today and all the thoughts I have had. Do you have any scissors on you to cut the pages out?"

As it happened, Withers was always prepared for hours with little to do while she waited for her mistress somewhere, and so usually carried her embroidery with her. Today was no exception, and she rummaged through her carpetbag once more, pulling out some scissors. She then carefully cut out the pages from her journal and handed them to the dowager.

By the time the carriage returned to Glanwyddan Hall, the dowager was so thrilled by what she believed to be her great insights that she hardly waited for help to get out. She eagerly bounded into the house, at least as much as was possible for a septuagenarian with a bad hip. A rather startled footman informed the dowager that Lord and Lady Pembroke were finishing their luncheon, and so the dowager, barely pausing to hand him her hat and gloves, made her way to the dining room, her notes clutched in her hand as if brandishing a world-changing discovery.

Over luncheon, Wolf had been detailing his visit to Sir Christopher to Langley, Bear, and Mrs O'Leary. Rose O'Leary usually chose not to dine with her employers when the dowager was present, and so had only agreed to join them that day after being assured she had gone to Tenby and wouldn't be back for some time. Upon seeing the terrifying dowager countess enter the dining room, eyes blazing, Mrs O'Leary dropped her fork in shock and appeared as if she wanted to bolt from the room. Tabitha understood and offered her a supportive smile. The woman stayed, but looked very uncomfortable.

"Mama! You are back sooner than we expected," Tabitha said.

"Am I? I went there, spoke with the historian and returned. What else did you expect me to do? Quite frankly, I could not get out of that dilapidated pile of stones quickly enough. I certainly was not going to risk my life by drinking tea out of a cup that likely has not been washed properly in a long time."

Tabitha caught Wolf's eye; it seemed as if there was a story there, but no one wanted to encourage the dowager's rant. Instead, Wolf asked, "And what did you learn?"

The dowager took an empty chair and told Talbot to bring her a cup of tea. "I am quite parched." Then, she fanned the papers in her hand out on the table in front of her unnecessarily dramatically. "While the trip was long and unpleasant, I believe that what I have learned and the insights I have noted will cast this entire investigation in a new light." This was quite the claim, but no one was rash enough to question it.

Instead, Tabitha replied, "Perhaps you might hold off for a few minutes, and we can retire to the parlour and you can have your tea there. Wolf has had an interesting morning as well, and I would like to write everything up on notecards while it is fresh in our minds."

While the idea of sitting in the more comfortable parlour while quenching her thirst was appealing, the dowager worried that the change of venue would diminish some of the drama of her announcements or, worse, that whatever Wolf had to report might steal her thunder. Begrudgingly, she agreed to wait a few minutes while everyone apart from Rose O'Leary moved to the parlour.

No sooner had they all settled themselves and Tabitha collected blank notecards than Talbot entered and announced that Dr Lloyd had returned. Although the parlour was not normally a place where they received visitors, the dowager announced that she was not moving again, and so Wolf asked Talbot to send the doctor in.

Dr Lloyd entered the room bright-eyed, with a broad smile on his face. He was very excited to have news to share with the earl and had hurried to Glanwyddan Hall as quickly as he could.

Once the greetings were finished and tea was poured, Wolf asked, "We were not expecting you, Dr Lloyd. Can I assume that you bring information about the investigation?"

"Indeed, I do, indeed I do, your lordship. And I hurried here as soon as I learned the news, not wishing to keep such an important detail from you for even an hour."

Wolf recalled how trying the doctor could be. Doing his best to keep his voice calm yet assertive, he asked, "And what is this news, Dr Lloyd?"

"Well, I received your note yesterday and pondered on it for some time. It is certainly fascinating to see the great strides that modern science has made, allowing us to detect such things. Of course, it will be quite some time before a humble country doctor like myself has access to such diagnostic tools, but still, it remains a modern marvel."

Just as Wolf was taking a calming breath before urging the doctor to make his revelation more swiftly, the dowager, feeling she had already had her moment to shine dulled by the delay in leaving the dining room, snapped. "Dr Lloyd, if you have something to say, then say it. Some of us have been waiting far too long to give our input, and do not appreciate you taking the scenic route to get to your point. Some of us are not getting any younger!"

For a change, Wolf couldn't really argue with the woman's brusqueness.

Dr Lloyd looked stunned for a moment, but then recovered and got to the point of his story. "When I read that Mr Truegood was a victim of poisoning from digitalis, it occurred to me to wonder if he had been using it for medicinal purposes. While I had not treated him, he also hadn't been in Pembroke long. Anyway, I took it upon myself to speak to the apothecary, Mr Davies. And..."

Pausing for dramatic effect, Dr Lloyd looked around the room at his audience, caught sight of the dowager's face, and hurried to finish his sentence. "Mr Davies informed me that James Truegood had a weak heart and took digitalis for it."

The doctor leant back with a self-satisfied smile; it was rare for him to be the star performer in such an exciting drama.

Everyone considered the doctor's words. Langley was the first to speak. "Is it possible that he took a higher dose than usual and that was what caused his death?"

"I had the same thought," Dr Lloyd said, puffed out with pride at his pre-emptive consideration of the question. "However, Mr Davies assured me that James Truegood told him he had been taking the same dose of digitalis since he was a boy. It is very unlikely that he would have accidentally taken too much. Mr Davies said that Mr Truegood took ten minims three times a day. Digitalis accumulates in the body over time, so taking even a double dose could be dangerous. However, he believes that while a double dose might trigger dangerous symptoms, a triple dose would ensure death."

"Dr Tucker confirmed that the amount found in the victim's stomach would have been a fatal dose even before we knew this," Wolf said, considering what they had just learned.

Dr Lloyd had nothing more to add and left after another cup of tea.

No sooner had the doctor left the room than the dowager launched into an explanation of her day's discoveries and her subsequent insights. Everyone had to acknowledge that the news about the dagger was significant.

The dowager concluded with the news that Mr Allen would be returning to Pembroke shortly to work at Pembroke Castle. "And most importantly, I believe, in Wogan Cavern. So, someone would definitely be visiting the cavern barely a week after the murder. The question is, who knew this?"

Then, with a triumphant flourish, the dowager pronounced, "I believe we need to create both a timeline and start listing our suspects and recording who knew which particular elements of the crime. Let us start with who knew about Mr Allen's visit? Who knew about the purported buried treasure? Who knew about Mr Truegood's weak heart?"

It really was an excellent idea, and the dowager was gratified to receive almost as much agreement and praise as she felt was her due.

Chapter 24

As they reviewed everything they now knew, three main suspects were put on the corkboard: Jeremiah Goodge, Sir Christopher, and last, and probably least, Clarice Hill. The first two had the clearest motives possible: for Mr Goodge, something connected to stolen glory at the castle and William Marshal, and for Sir Christopher, the alleged treasure.

"Though if Mr Allen had already rejected Truegood's article, why would Jeremiah Goodge kill him?" Langley wondered.

"Perhaps James Truegood had submitted it for publication elsewhere," Tabitha suggested. "There is no doubt that Mr Goodge was hiding something from us. And why did he not mention that Mr Allen was not only in the neighbourhood, but touring the castle with him this week?"

While it was a reasonable question, no one could recall if they had asked a question so specific that it would have been unreasonable not to provide this information.

"It certainly is believable that Mr Goodge knew of his tenant's heart condition and use of digitalis. He also would have had access to Mr Truegood's room to swap the medication for a much higher dosage," Tabitha continued.

Then, she reflected on the day of their tour. "Mr Goodge seemed quite eager to dissuade us from touring the cavern. If he wanted the body discovered, why do that?"

Wolf could think of one reason. "Perhaps he did not wish to be present when the body was found and was unsure he could control his reaction sufficiently." It was a sound enough theory, especially if Mr Goodge knew the body would be found within days.

"I do not know a lot about digitalis," Langley said. "However, my father recovered from rheumatic fever in childhood and took it occasionally for what he would call his 'flutterings'. I do know that my mother was forever worried he would accidentally overdose. Apparently, it is an easy thing to do. Given this, why not merely increase the dosage and stop there? Why go to the dramatic extremes of the stabbing at all?"

This was the crucial question, wasn't it? Why bother?

Tabitha articulated another concern. "If our working theory is that the killer wanted the body to be found and the motive to be seen as linked to the treasure, then the person had to be quite certain of when and where Mr Truegood would collapse. After all, if it had happened on Pembroke's Main Street, there would have been little chance of plunging a dagger into his body unnoticed."

"I believe a trip into Pembroke is warranted," the dowager observed. "I think we need to talk with this apothecary and understand whether the stronger dose of digitalis was purchased from him. I assume the man keeps records."

It was yet another excellent idea. The dowager had been sweeping the board of late, Tabitha reflected. Whatever concerns she might have about the aged woman's frailty, there was little real reason to doubt her mental faculties. It was probably fortunate that the dowager didn't know any of this had even entered Tabitha's mind.

"We do not all need to descend upon the apothecary," Wolf said, knowing even as he uttered the words that the dowager would insist on being one of the party.

And she did. "As the person who came up with the idea, and in fact, seemingly every good one today, it goes without saying that I will be going."

"I would never suggest otherwise," Wolf said. The look he received in reply was all the dowager needed to say of her belief in the truth of that statement.

Tabitha glanced at the clock on the mantelpiece; it was past two o'clock. "I believe I will call on Mrs Chivers," she announced. "She was the person who told us about Sir Christopher and his meetings with the victim. I would like to press her to see if there is anything more she didn't divulge."

The dowager chuckled darkly. "I doubt that woman held back. Her tongue was dripping with such venom that she hardly seemed to be moderating what she said."

Tabitha agreed, but there might have been more that the town gossip had simply forgotten to mention. If nothing else, further prodding could reveal something. Moreover, Tabitha was pleased she didn't have to dissuade the dowager from joining her; this interview called for a gentler touch.

"Wolf, why do you not go with Mama and the carriage can drop me off at Mrs Chivers's home on the way. We can stop at the post office and ask where she lives." This plan was acceptable to everyone, even the dowager, who felt confident she had chosen the more interesting assignment.

Tabitha went to change into a dress more suitable for a social call, and thirty minutes later, the group set off for Pembroke. After stopping at the post office and easily obtaining Mrs Chivers's address, Wolf and the dowager drove Tabitha the quarter of a mile further to a pretty townhouse with roses around the door. They waited to see if the lady of the house was home. On seeing Tabitha admitted into the house, they carried on to the apothecary shop, which was on Main Street, near The Old Kings Arms, where Mr Allen had mentioned he would be staying.

The apothecary's shop front was narrow but deep. Gold lettering on the gleaming glass window announced "H. Davies, Chemist & Druggist", flanked by painted mortar-and-pestle symbols.

The dowager and Wolf stepped inside, breathing in air that was pleasantly cool after the heat of the carriage, but also faintly medicinal. There were shelves around most of the shop, climbing almost to the ceiling. Some were stacked with neat rows of glass jars in greens, ambers, and deep cobalt, some filled with powders, others with liquids that caught the afternoon light. One area of the shelves held brown-paper parcels and tins. A counter ran along the back, behind which scales sat ready beside a brass cash till. Small drawers with porcelain knobs were labelled in neat handwriting. Everything about this shop suggested it was run with the level of attention to detail and care one would expect in a chemist.

Standing behind the counter was a short, lean man with a trim moustache and kind eyes that gleamed behind round spectacles. Upon seeing the clearly upper-class gentleman and elderly lady who had entered his shop, Mr Henry Davies straightened slightly, throwing his shoulders back. He had always taken great pride in his shop being renowned far and wide for its quality and service, and these new customers were proof of just how extensive that reputation was.

"Good afternoon," Mr Davies said. "How may I assist you today?"

Wolf introduced himself and the dowager, explaining that he was there in his magisterial capacity. There was no one else in the shop, but even so, Wolf kept his voice low.

"Ah yes, I heard from Dr Lloyd that you had taken a personal interest in the investigation, your lordship."

"Indeed. In fact, it is because of Dr Lloyd that we are here. He relayed his conversation with you about Mr Truegood's heart complaint, and I had some additional questions."

"Whatever I can do to help," Mr Davies assured them.

Even though no one was in the shop, Wolf still felt uneasy about having the conversation so publicly. "Is there somewhere we might speak privately?" he asked.

"Certainly. Let me just get my assistant out here." Then, Mr Davies turned and called, "Hywel, can you watch out front please?"

There was a muffled sound from the back, and then a sullen-looking young man with lank, greasy hair and a face covered in spots entered from behind a curtain that separated the front of the shop from the back.

"Hywel, there you are. Can you please keep watch at the front while I take my visitors through to the back?"

The young man nodded sulkily. Mr Davies gestured for Wolf and the dowager to follow him through the curtain into the back of the shop. The curtain led into a short corridor that ended in a door, which opened into a room that seemed to be a cross between a kitchen and a workshop. The room at the back of the shop was as tidy and well-organised as the shelves in the front. There were some additional scales out and a jar containing powder. It looked as if they had interrupted Hywel while he was measuring out medicine.

"Can I get you a cup of tea?" Mr Davies asked.

The dowager had no intention of imbibing anything made in the same room where pills and powders were prepared. Luckily, instead of saying that, she simply indicated no. Wolf refused the offer as well, but not with the same concern.

Mr Davies indicated that they should sit around the small table in the middle of the room.

Once everyone was settled, Wolf returned to his earlier statement. "As I said, Dr Lloyd relayed that you have been providing James Truegood with digitalis for a heart condition."

"INDEED. SOON AFTER MR TRUEGOOD MOVED TO PEMBROKE, he came in and asked for a tincture of digitalis. It seemed he had been taking it for many years and knew the exact dosage required. He became a regular customer from then onwards. Of course, I warned him about the dangers of overdosing, but he appeared very aware and assured me that he always exercised great caution."

"And when was the last time Mr Truegood came in for his medication?"

Mr Davies pursed his lips and squinted as he considered the question. "Well, I know it was last week. I remember he was quite frantic. He seemed to believe he had more left than he actually did, and he was worried about missing his daily dose. But which day was it now? I do remember it was quite early in the morning because I had just opened the shop, and he was the first customer through the door. So, it must have been at eight o'clock, perhaps on Tuesday?"

"Are you sure, sir?" the dowager asked sharply. "I would hope that man in your profession prides himself on accuracy!"

The imperious old woman's implication struck Mr Davies to his core; if there was anything he took pride in, it was his attention to detail. "Excuse me a moment," he said, rising and leaving the room, only to return with a ledger in his arms.

"This is my poison register. The sale will be recorded here." The man opened the ledger, flicked through a few pages, then ran his finger down the paper until he found what he was looking for. "Ah, here it is. I misspoke. He came in on Thursday, 4th August and bought his usual dosage of digitalis tincture, 1 oz, for a weak heart."

"And you served him?" Wolf asked.

"I was there when he first came in, but then Hywel took over, which is why I was initially mistaken about the day. The two young men have become somewhat friendly over the time Mr Truegood had been getting his medicine from us, so I left Hywel serving him and talking about whatever it is that young men speak of these days and stepped out of the shop to run an errand."

While the dagger appeared to be sufficient evidence that the death was not accidental, Wolf felt he had to ask. "Is there any chance Mr Truegood might have been given a higher dose by mistake?"

Mr Davies' expression clearly showed his indignation at such a suggestion. However, to be clear, he said in a huffy tone, "Lord Pembroke, I have run this shop for forty years and apprenticed under my father before that. I prepare every tincture myself and have never made a mistake. I can assure you that if the ledger states Mr Truegood was given one ounce, that is what he was given."

Chapter 25

Mrs Chivers herself had opened the front door. The woman appeared quite flustered upon seeing the Countess of Pembroke on her doorstep. "Oh, your ladyship, do excuse me for opening the door myself. I can't imagine where that Milly has gone. I only opened it because I thought it might be Mrs Evans from next door returning the knitting pattern I lent her last week. When I ran into her this morning, she mentioned she was finished with it and would drop it off."

All this was said as Tabitha stood in the hallway. Suddenly realising this, Mrs Chivers became even more flustered. "But what am I about keeping your ladyship standing here? Please, excuse me."

With that, Mrs Chivers led the way into the front room of the house, which was decorated much as Tabitha might have expected: over-furnished, over-embroidered, and over-moral, with almost every inch covered in lace and badly painted holy pictures. As she took a seat and looked around, Tabitha felt even more relieved that the dowager had decided to accompany Wolf; she could only imagine what the snobbish woman would have thought of these furnishings.

"I will just go and find Milly and have her bring in some tea, milady. Please excuse me for a moment."

While Mrs Chivers went to find Milly, Tabitha surveyed the room.

There was no doubt this was the home of someone eager to project profound piety. While religious iconography of all types lined the walls, there was nothing designed to lift the spirit. A large, garish painting of *The Last Supper* in vivid colours showed figures with odd proportions, framed by a gilt border shaped with grapes and vines. On a sideboard, there was a particularly ugly gilded plaster crucifix adorned with cheap-looking artificial flowers, sitting on a crocheted doily. The whole effect was overly pious in intention but gaudy in execution.

Even as she caught herself thinking this, Tabitha realised how much her observations resembled something the dowager might say. Feeling ashamed of her harsh judgement of Mrs Chivers's expression of faith, Tabitha tried to view the room more kindly. Fortunately, she was prevented from undertaking this almost herculean task by the woman's re-entry, followed by a young woman she presumed was Milly, carrying a tray.

"If I had known you were coming, I would have had Milly bake a cake, milady. Apologies, but we only have some biscuits."

"Please do not concern yourself, Mrs Chivers," Tabitha assured her, in a tone more soothing than perhaps it needed to be, but which was an attempt to compensate for her earlier harsh thoughts. "I ate not long ago. However, a cup of tea would be lovely."

The tea was poured, Milly left the room, and Tabitha was left alone with her hostess. She pondered the best way to start the conversation. While she didn't want to seem too obvious in her questions, her presence in the house uninvited and so soon after welcoming the woman to Glanwyddan Hall was unusual enough that there had to be a reason beyond a simple social visit.

As luck would have it, Tabitha was spared from having to navigate this delicate path of social etiquette when Mrs Chivers brought up the subject directly. "How is the investigation proceeding, your ladyship?"

While she was pleased not to have to force the topic artificially, Tabitha was very mindful of what an inveterate gossip Mrs Chivers was; she couldn't tell the woman anything she wasn't comfortable seeing spread all over town. On the other hand, could she turn this to their advantage? What if there was something they wanted her to gossip about? Tabitha felt the investigation wasn't progressing as quickly as it could.

They had suspects but weak motives. What if they could somehow force their murderer's hand?

Choosing her words carefully while trying to affect nonchalance, Tabitha confided, "Quite well. In fact, the dowager countess made quite a breakthrough yesterday. You may have heard that Mr Truegood was stabbed with quite an elaborate dagger."

Mrs Chivers seemed to be choosing her words just as carefully as she admitted, "I may have heard something about that." Then she added very quickly, "Not that I listen to gossip. It's the devil's mouthpiece as I always tell those keen to pass it on."

"Of course, of course," Tabitha reassured her. Then she paused deliberately, as if weighing whether to share something else.

Noticing the pause, Mrs Chivers added, "However, this isn't gossip. You are married to the magistrate and are merely sharing important information with me in my official capacity as the branch president of the Parish Mothers' Union."

Tabitha had no clue why the woman thought that was any kind of justification. Why would the Mothers' Union need this information? However, she didn't voice this question. Instead, she nodded at the sage observation.

Finally, after she believed she had sufficiently gone through the motions of a cautious deliberation, Tabitha said conspiratorially, "Well, the earl has learned two key pieces of information: James Truegood was poisoned with an overdose of digitalis, which was what killed him. We assume it was added to his food or drink at some point hours before his death. And, it seems the dagger was a cheap fake, probably purchased locally from a shop that traffics in such faux curiosities."

Mrs Chivers's hand shot to her mouth. "No! You don't say! Well, I never! And you have this dagger at the hall?"

"We do. His lordship's intention is to visit all the local stores that might sell such an item to see if anyone recognises it and remembers who they sold it to." Actually, this wasn't Wolf's intention, but now that Tabitha had said it, she wondered if it wasn't worth sending Bear around to do just that.

"I hope you have it somewhere safe, your ladyship. You would not want this murderer to get wind of your plan and attempt to steal it."

"Oh yes. No need to worry. His lordship has it under lock and key in his study. Really, it is the key piece of evidence we possess. Without it, I am not sure we would have any chance of tracking down this killer." Even Tabitha thought she was laying it on rather thick, but Mrs Chivers was clearly lapping all the information up to be disseminated later throughout Pembrokeshire.

Pivoting to the question she wished to ask, Tabitha said casually, "My husband called on Sir Christopher yesterday to invite him to a partridge hunt we are holding on Friday. I am not sure if you are aware of this, but it appears there has been bad blood between the two families for many years."

Tabitha could have sworn that Mrs Chivers licked her lips at the mention of this scandalous topic.

"Well, again, not that I am one to engage in tea-table talk, but yes, there was no love lost between the old earl, his lordship's grandfather, and Sir Christopher. It's said they fell out over a bad business deal." Then, looking around her as if someone might have sneaked into her house and was listening, she said, "And his lordship wasn't the only one from what I've heard."

Forcing her face into an expression of shock at the delicious tittle-tattle to come, Tabitha exclaimed, "Really?"

"Oh yes. I don't know all the details, of course. But I know that Sir Christopher was given the cut direct by many local gentry at the time and even for some years afterwards. That was the start of it all, I hear."

Genuinely confused, Tabitha asked, "Start of what?"

"Well, you said his lordship had visited Ashling Hall, so he must have seen. Barely any staff, from what I hear. Mrs Green has been taking on more and more over the last few years. Now, she's cook, cleaner, and housekeeper. I don't know why she stays, though, at her age, perhaps she worries about finding a new position. And I hear the place is crumbling about his ears, and the butcher never gets paid on time. Once, he had to refuse a delivery until he got paid some of what he was owed."

While Wolf had shared his observations about Ashling Hall, it was interesting to hear just how dire Sir Christopher's finances appeared to be. It made sense that he might have jumped at the promise of possible treasure. The question was, how upset might he have become if those hopes were dashed? Though that still left the question of why Sir Christopher would then make a point of suggesting the death had something to do with said treasure.

Tabitha had one more thing she wanted to ask about, but she was at a loss as to how to introduce it into the conversation without arousing Mrs Chivers's suspicions. Finally, attempting to make the latest pivot seem as natural as possible, Tabitha said, "We are meeting as many locals as we can on this visit. There is the hunt on Friday, and of course, last week we had Mr Cyril Hill and his charming daughter to dinner."

At the mention of the Hills, Mrs Chivers's face tightened as if she were sucking a lemon. It seemed completely unconscious, which was perhaps the most intriguing aspect of her reaction.

"I sense that the Hills are not amongst your favourite people, Mrs Chivers."

Realising how much she had given away by her expression, Mrs Chivers said, "I have nothing against the father, but that girl is no better than she ought to be."

That was quite the judgement to make against an unmarried young woman from a respectable family. Perhaps this was why Mrs Chivers felt compelled to say more. "I know this may seem harsh. But in my opinion, the young woman is a flirt of the worst kind." Mrs Chivers clamped her mouth shut and, for once, this seemed to be all she was willing to say.

In fact, after this, the woman's appetite for tittle-tattle seemed quite satiated, leaving Tabitha no reason to stay any longer than necessary.

The first thing Tabitha mentioned after she'd climbed into the carriage ten minutes later was her idea of finding the source of the dagger. "While we cannot be certain, it's probably that it was bought somewhere nearby. Can we ask Bear to tour the local towns looking for a shop that might sell such an item?"

Wolf considered the suggestion. "I am sure he will do so, I only question how useful it will really be. For all we know, that dagger was something the killer had in their house for quite some time."

"I agree. However, I do think it is worth doing, just in case." Reluctantly, Wolf agreed to ask Bear to spend the next day on the almost certainly pointless task.

Tabitha then shared the gossip she'd intentionally told Mrs Chivers, expecting it to be disseminated throughout the town.

"What are you expecting to happen if it is?" the dowager asked, rather dismissively.

"I do not know. However, if the murderer has believed up until now that the dagger was viewed as the murder weapon and now hears otherwise, perhaps they will panic and make a false move."

The dowager shot her a look of such withering contempt at such an idea that Tabitha might have defended her actions further if she weren't so exhausted from her afternoon. Perhaps she would take another nap before dinner.

Chapter 26

The following day, both Tabitha and Wolf had tasks to do in preparation for their Glorious Twelfth hunt.

Over breakfast, Tabitha, who had no appetite and was only sipping tea, wondered if they still needed to hold the event. "Do you believe there is anything more to learn from Sir Christopher? If not, it is merely a day taken away from the investigation."

Wolf considered her words. "We have not struck Sir Christopher off our list of suspects yet. And even if we had, what reason could we give for backing out of the invitation? If he turns out not to be a murderer, I would genuinely like to mend fences with one of our nearest neighbours, even if he is not the most pleasant person to be around."

After Wolf had recounted his time with Sir Christopher, Tabitha suspected that the old earl might have had more reasons for falling out with him than merely a bad business deal; the man sounded rather dreadful. When she added Mrs Budgers's comments about how he behaved around the female servants, Tabitha began to dread hosting him for the day. Nonetheless, Wolf's points were sensible, and so she resigned herself to enduring his company. Could his lechery be worse than Squire Partridge's?

Tabitha sipped her tea and mentally listed the things she needed to discuss with Mrs Jenkins for the hunt and luncheon. These thoughts were interrupted by Talbot, who announced that Constable Tucker was on the telephone for Wolf.

"I am surprised the police station has a telephone," Wolf observed as he wiped his mouth and stood.

"I believe the constable is calling from the post office. He seems quite concerned about the lack of privacy, and I had to ask him to repeat himself twice before I could hear who it was," Talbot replied.

A few minutes later, Wolf returned. By then, Langley had joined them for breakfast, and he and Tabitha were eager to hear what the constable wanted.

"Well, it seems that your strategically shared gossip may have had an effect," Wolf said, retaking his seat. "Mr Goodge had a break-in last night."

"That is interesting. Are we sure it is related to what I told Mrs Chivers?" As much as Tabitha wanted to believe she had managed to prompt their killer into acting, she was also reluctant to see causal links just because she wished to.

"Of course, there is no way to be certain. Constable Tucker was called there early this morning. Mr Goodge is not entirely sure when the break-in occurred. It seems he was out until quite late last night and did not notice anything until his housekeeper arrived this morning and found his study in disarray."

Tabitha sighed. Did this rule out Jeremiah Goodge as a suspect, or was it possible it was another deliberately placed red herring? She expressed this thought, then added, "I assume you are visiting Pembroke this morning?"

"You do not wish to join me?" Wolf asked. He had noticed that his wife had barely eaten anything that morning and that she had seemed out of sorts for some days now. Nothing was a clearer sign that she was not feeling herself than Tabitha voluntarily recusing herself from an investigation.

"It is not that, but rather that I feel I cannot abandon Mrs Jenkins after springing this hunting party on her at such short notice. I know that Mrs Budgers wanted me to review the final menu today, and there are decisions to be made regarding exactly when and where to serve luncheon."

While Tabitha's words made perfect sense, Wolf still suspected that her sudden interest in domestic matters was a pretext for not joining, which was unlike her. Usually, he might have insisted that all those details be handled by the housekeeper with input from Mrs O'Leary. However, he had no desire to push Tabitha if she wished to remain behind.

Instead, turning to Langley, Wolf asked, "Will you accompany me in that case? I would be grateful for the extra pair of eyes and ears."

Fifteen minutes later, the two men had left for Pembroke. Tabitha fully intended to go and find Mrs Jenkins immediately and start on the list of tasks she had outlined, but she just couldn't seem to bring herself to rise from the table. Finally, she switched from tea to coffee and managed to gather enough energy to begin her day. Whatever was going on with her, she wondered. Perhaps she would ask Dr Lloyd to visit if this lethargy persisted.

Wolf had instructed Constable Tucker to meet him at Mr Goodge's house. It appeared that Mr Goodge had sent Mrs Wallace, his housekeeper, to the Tucker police station that morning when she realised they had been burgled. The constable had then gone to the post office to put a telephone call through to Glanwyddan Hall and hadn't yet visited the Goodge residence.

He couldn't pretend to be sorry at this evidence of Constable Tucker's reluctance to take even a small step alone; Wolf was far from convinced that the man was capable of more than dealing with local drunks at closing time and managing escaped pigs. Perhaps he should just be grateful that Tucker had even bothered to let him know about the break-in.

By the time the carriage pulled up outside Jeremiah Goodge's house, a small crowd had gathered there. It appeared that word had spread about the break-in, and the sight of Constable Tucker, waiting outside patiently for the earl to arrive, was considered interesting enough to liven up what otherwise promised to be a rather dull Thursday morning.

As Wolf descended, he heard a woman in the crowd say, "First a murder and then this. Whatever is Pembroke coming to? I wouldn't be at all surprised if it was all down to gypsies. Mrs Smith at number ten told me that her Bobby saw some in Mr Morris' fields the other week. Mark my words, nine times out of ten, it's the gypsies." This announcement was met with murmurs of agreement from her neighbours.

Whatever interest the crowd had in watching Constable Tucker stand outside the house, refusing to answer questions, was nothing compared to the excitement caused by the appearance of the Pembroke Carriage.

When the handsome new earl appeared, the crowd could hardly have been more excited than if Marie Lloyd, queen of the music hall, were among them. There were audible gasps, and some oohs and aahs.

One voice was heard pronouncing, "Well, I never, tidy bit of a chap, look you!" While Wolf didn't know exactly what this local colloquialism meant, it was clear enough when it was followed by, "Looks like he's stepped out of a portrait, he does. Much better than that cousin of his, if you ask me."

Wolf could hear Langley chuckling behind him, but he tried not to let his embarrassment at the comments show on his face.

Constable Tucker looked very relieved at their appearance. "Your lordship, proper glad to see you, I am. It's a right circus out here, it is."

"Perhaps you should have waited indoors," Wolf suggested.

The constable shook his head violently. "Oh no. That wouldn't be right."

It was unclear what was wrong with that, but Wolf had no desire to talk any longer than necessary in front of their audience. Instead, he signalled that they should proceed to the front door.

The door was answered by a dour-looking woman, whose chatelaine indicated that this was Mrs Wallace, the housekeeper. Wolf wondered where she had been on their previous visits. Perhaps she didn't come in every day.

The woman took one look at Wolf, gave a stern nod, and said, "The master is waiting on you."

They followed her into the room they had been in previously and found an anxious-looking Jeremiah Goodge sitting in his armchair.

At their entry, he sprang up. "Your lordships, thank you so much for coming so quickly. I'm quite beside myself. What a violation. To think, I might have been murdered in my sleep!"

"Do you believe the intruder entered during the night? I was given to understand that it was more likely he broke in while you were out in the evening," Wolf began.

"Who knows? Mrs Wallace first noticed that things had been disturbed this morning."

Mrs Wallace had lingered in the doorway. Now, Wolf suggested that she stay and explain what she had discovered.

"Yes, yes. Mrs Wallace, why don't you bring in a fresh pot of tea and then his lordship can question you," Mr Goodge suggested. Wolf didn't feel the need for tea but realised it was the social lubricant that convention demanded.

While the housekeeper was in the kitchen, Wolf took the opportunity to question her master. "What time did you go out last night, and what time did you return, Mr Goodge?"

"Well, I went to the parish hall for the monthly meeting of the historical society. It always starts promptly at seven o'clock, and Mrs Chivers is such a stickler for punctuality."

Wolf started at the familiar name. "Mrs Chivers runs the historical society?"

A look of pure hatred washed over Mr Goodge's face. "She does now. I ran it for many years until that woman took control some months ago. Heaven help us, but she was single-minded once she fixed her sights on it. Until then, I had never thought she had any interests beyond moral censorship of the people of Pembroke."

"Do you have any idea why she became interested?" Wolf didn't think it relevant but was curious, nonetheless.

"I believe it started when we sponsored a series of talks on local smugglers and followed this up with a pageant featuring the children from the school, on the subject. It seems she thought, and I quote, 'It was an inappropriate topic for good Christians to glorify.' She then decided that my leadership was lacking in moral clarity and that she needed to intervene to ensure our projects were not unsuitable, unwholesome, or morally ambiguous."

While Wolf had not personally interacted with Mrs Chivers, he had heard enough from Tabitha to sympathise with the historian. Mr Goodge continued, "This year, she insisted the pageant be St George and the Dragon and that she direct it to ensure sufficient moral probity." He added quickly, "Not that I have a particular problem with St George. Rather, it is that there are many lesser-known stories that are particularly relevant to Pembrokeshire. And of course, she insisted that her son, Hywel, play St George, even though the boy has no talent for drama."

Wolf had no wish to spend his morning listening to this recitation of grievances against Mrs Chivers. Hoping to steer the conversation towards something more relevant to the investigation, Wolf asked, "And so you left just before seven and returned when?"

"Let me think now. I know the meeting went longer than usual. That dreadful woman insisted on revisiting all of our upcoming external speakers, even though I am sure we did that earlier in the year. Normally, our meeting finishes by nine o'clock at the latest. Still, thanks to Mrs Chivers's insistence on nitpicking every detail of matters that were agreed upon during my tenure as chairman, I believe we didn't leave the parish hall until past ten. Truly, I was so exhausted by the time I got home that I went straight upstairs to bed and fell asleep."

"So, you noticed nothing untoward when you returned?" Langley pressed.

"No. However, I cannot be certain that I would have, given my exhaustion."

Wolf decided to abandon this line of questioning for now. "Let us move to this morning, then. What time does Mrs Wallace arrive?"

"Let me see now. I am not quite sure, to be honest. I know she always has my breakfast ready by the time I rise."

Wolf was becoming very frustrated and was glad to see the housekeeper returning with tea. Now, he asked her the question directly.

Her face still set in a moue of distaste at the inconvenience to her day, the woman said, "I arrive at seven o'clock sharp, and I leave at half-past six, once the master has eaten his supper."

"And when did you first notice the intrusion?"

"Well, I noticed that a pane of glass in the back door was broken immediately. That's how the blackguard must have got in. Nothing was out of place in the kitchen, but then I went through to the master's study and papers and books were everywhere. It was like someone went in there and just threw stuff around willy-nilly."

"And was that the only room that was disturbed?"

"Well, I thought so at first. Then, I went upstairs, and it looked like someone had rifled through Mr Truegood's room as well. However, that room was already in such a state, who can really tell? Oh, and a few drawers were opened in the master's room."

Turning back to Jeremiah Goodge, Wolf asked, "Is there anything of particular value in the house that you think the intruder might have been looking for?"

"Well, I do have a very rare, first edition print of Fenton's *A Historical Tour through Pembrokeshire.* It is signed by Richard Fenton himself and contains a passage related to a local scandal that was subsequently removed." Suddenly puffed up with pride, Mr Goodge explained, "I've received multiple offers for it over the years, but I will never sell it at any price."

"And was this book stolen?"

"Heavens, no! Thank goodness, that remained untouched." Wolf had to take several deep breaths to keep his irritation in check. "So, what was stolen?"

Mr Goodge hesitated. "Well, nothing as far as I can tell. But who knows? The villain made such a mess that anything could have been taken, and I wouldn't realise for some time."

"I understand that, Mr Goodge. However, you know that your first edition book was not taken, so is there anything else of value you specifically checked that is also untouched?"

Mr Goodge had to admit that nothing had been taken from what he could see. He made a point of saying that he couldn't speak for Mr Truegood's room, though.

Just as they were about to look at the mess made by the intruder, Wolf realised he hadn't assigned a task to the constable. Should he? From what he could tell, Constable Tucker was happily ensconced in an armchair, drinking his tea and nibbling on a piece of ginger cake. The man seemed in no hurry to participate more fully in the investigation, so Wolf and Langley left him where he was.

"Thank is all very helpful, Mr Goodge. Langley, why do you not examine the study while I go up to the bedrooms to see if I can spot anything?" Thirty minutes later, back in the carriage, Wolf admitted, "I am not sure I would know if anything had been taken from James Truegood's room. I found a bottle labelled *Tincture of Digitalis*, but it was empty, and based on the worn ink of the label, it did not look as if it had been purchased only a few days ago. Overall, nothing stood out as having been removed besides the room being messier than before. What was our intruder searching for?"

"Perhaps the more recent bottle?" Langley suggested.

Chapter 27

After Tabitha had pushed herself up from the breakfast table and headed to the servants' quarters to meet with Mrs Jenkins, she felt completely exhausted. She longed to crawl back into bed, but it was only mid-morning. Instead, she chose to visit the children in the nursery to see if their lively spirits could help restore her energy.

The nursery at Glanwyddan Hall consisted of three interconnected rooms. One was arranged as a schoolroom, another was filled with toys and books, and the last featured comfy armchairs and a plush rug by the fireplace. It was a quiet place to take the children when they needed to calm down. This was where Tabitha found the nursemaids, Mary, her sister Kitty, and the newest member of staff, Missy Palmer.

The nursemaids sat on the rug, each with a child on her lap, while Mary read them all a story. Everyone was captivated by the tale, and even Dodo, the dog, appeared to be paying attention.

Tabitha had entered the room so quietly that no one noticed her in the doorway. She stood there for a while, watching the three children who were not related to her by blood but had become very dear to her. Of course, the twins, Willy and Liam, were Rose O'Leary's boys, and Tabitha's role was that of a loving aunt. However, Melody was now the beloved daughter she had never expected to have. She didn't believe she could love the little girl more, even if she had given birth to her, and she thanked the heavens every day that fate had brought Melody and her brother Rat into her life.

Dodo was the first to notice they had a visitor. She lifted her head off her paws and, once she realised the human was Tabitha, jumped up and ran across the room, eager for attention.

As Tabitha stroked the silky ears, she thought about how the spaniel was another big change that the past year or so had brought. Before Dodo's unexpected arrival in the household, Tabitha had never thought of herself as a dog person. When Lord Langley first handed them the puppy as a gift to Melody, Tabitha was angry and would have given the dog back if it hadn't been for the fact that it would have broken Melody's heart.

Tabitha couldn't say exactly when she realised how charmed she was by the dog; certainly, when Dodo helped save Tabitha's life, her heart softened a little toward the canine. But it was more than that. Maybe it was the dog's rich, chocolate-brown eyes. When Tabitha looked Dodo in the eyes, she sometimes felt the dog could see straight into her soul. Whatever it was, Tabitha had fallen in love with the animal somewhere along the way, and now she couldn't imagine life without her.

As soon as Dodo trotted over to Tabitha, the children all looked up. When they saw Tabitha standing there watching them, all three jumped up and joined Dodo in vying for attention.

Mary and the other nursemaids jumped to their feet and curtsied.

"I am so sorry to interrupt your quiet time, Mary," Tabitha said.

"We were almost at the end of the story, m'lady," Mary assured her. "Then, we were going to play until it's time for the children to eat."

"Then, please continue with your reading, and I will sit here and listen." Tabitha took a seat in one of the armchairs, and Melody insisted on sitting in her lap instead of returning to Mary's.

The little girl curled up, her head resting on Tabitha's shoulder. "I'm glad you came, Tabby Cat," Melody whispered before putting her thumb in her mouth.

Tabitha kissed the red-gold ringlets. "So am I, Melly."

Mary continued the story for another five minutes. Then, closing the book, she said, "We can finish Alice's story tomorrow, children." Tabitha smiled; another significant change over the past year was that Mary had become a very proficient reader. When Tabitha had hired a tutor for Melody, she had offered lessons for any servant who wanted to learn to read and write. It was gratifying to see how many had taken her up on the offer and were still working on their maths and reading.

Everyone moved into the large playroom, where Mary asked, "What shall we play?"

"Hide and seek!" one of the twins, Willy, yelled.

"I don't wanna play that," Liam declared. "I get scared."

"We will have a doll's tea party," Melody announced with an imperiousness worthy of the dowager.

"Don't wanna!" both boys yelled simultaneously.

As tempted as Tabitha was to step in and resolve the quarrel, she knew that Mary was more than capable of handling disagreements among the children, and she had no desire to undermine her authority.

After a nod of encouragement from Tabitha, Mary announced, "Why not play Oranges and Lemons? Kitty and I will be the arch."

At that moment, the nursery door opened, and Rat walked in. Melody's older brother was a great favourite of the twins, and all the children hurried to greet him. "Rat, will you play Oranges and Lemons with us?" Melody asked. Although the boy looked a bit embarrassed by all the attention, he assured the younger children he would be happy to play.

Kitty was the tallest of the nursemaids and almost as tall as Tabitha. "Why do Kitty and I not be the arch? Then everyone can play," Tabitha suggested.

Tabitha and Kitty stood facing each other, their arms raised to form an arch. Mary gathered the children into a line, with Rat leading. Then, everyone started singing. The nursery echoed with the sing-song chant of, "Oranges and lemons, say the bells of St. Clement's..." as the line of children moved beneath the raised arms. Starched pinafores swayed and boots softly thudded on the rug.

When they got to the line, *"Here comes a chopper to chop off your head!"* Mary and Kitty's arms dropped, trapping Liam. Giggling, he whispered his choice and darted to his new spot in the "lemon" camp as the game began anew.

Round and round the line wound, everyone's voices growing louder with each verse. One by one, the children and nursemaids were caught and claimed, the "oranges" and "lemons" ranks swelling until only Missy remained to be captured. At the last ringing "chop!" she shrieked in mock alarm and ran to join the oranges. Then, it was time for the final tug-of-war. With much laughter and shrieking, the lemons gave way. The oranges, led by Tabitha, collapsed in a heap of lace, curls, and giggles.

"We won!" Melody shrieked. For a moment, it looked as if Liam was going to cry in frustration at his loss.

Desperate to distract the little boy, Tabitha suggested, "Let us get the blocks out and build a fort."

This suggestion seemed satisfactory to everyone, and the next hour was spent building a large fort on the floor. The twins went to get their favourite tin soldiers and paraded them around the structure, singing, "The Grand Old Duke of York. He had ten thousand men. He marched them up to the top of the hill, and he marched them down again."

By the time two of the kitchen maids came in with trays of boiled eggs and toasted soldiers, Tabitha was worn out. She'd had a wonderful time with the children but wasn't upset to hand them back to their nursemaids and go downstairs for her midday meal. Not that she was hungry.

She entered the dining room to find the dowager already seated. "Finally!" the woman said in a snit. "I have been ready to eat for fifteen minutes. I was about to tell Talbot I would not wait for you and to serve the soup."

"I am sorry, Mama. I was with the children in the nursery, playing, and lost track of time."

"Playing? What on earth do you mean, playing?"

"We were playing Oranges and Lemons, then built a fort and sang The Grand Old Duke of York," Tabitha explained.

The dowager looked at the younger woman as if she were describing an utterly unfamiliar and baffling experience. "You were down on the floor playing with toys, Tabitha? Please remember that you are the Countess of Pembroke."

Tabitha was tired and irritable. Instead of ignoring the dowager's sniping, she replied, "Do you not play with Melody when she visits you?"

"We play chess! That is not at all the same thing."

Talbot entered the dining room with the soup tureen, followed closely by Wolf and Langley, who had just returned from Pembroke. Since the dowager hadn't been at breakfast, she was unaware of the break-in at Mr Goodge's home. Wolf explained everything they had heard and seen. "Do you think it was just a common thief, Jeremy?" the dowager asked between spoonfuls of fish soup.

"It does not seem as if anything valuable was stolen. If anything, I would say that the intruder was searching for something and tried to make it look like he was looking through belongings in the other rooms."

"What do you believe he was searching for?" Tabitha asked.

"I am not sure," Wolf admitted. "However, I believe it must have been something in James Truegood's bedchamber."

"Does Mr Goodge have any idea when this home intrusion occurred?"

"Well, his housekeeper did not notice anything until she arrived this morning," Langley chimed in. "However, we believe the break-in happened when Mr Goodge was at the meeting of the historical society yesterday evening. His bedchamber was one of the rooms rifled through, and I have to believe he would have woken if someone had entered during the night.

Tabitha shook her head in confusion. "Yet he did not notice this when he arrived home later in the evening?"

It was a good question, and Wolf merely shrugged his shoulders. "I do not disagree. However, he said that he was very tired and always uses only a candle when retiring to bed at night, and just did not notice until he was woken this morning by Mrs Wallace."

Wolf and Langley then told them that Mrs Chivers had taken over the historical society six months ago. With a wry chuckle, Wolf explained, "Apparently, she did not approve of the choice of topic for a pageant the society put in and took the group in hand to ensure they chose a more respectable theme this year. It seems Sir George and the Dragon was deemed sufficiently morally uplifting in her eyes."

Tabitha blinked, then put down her soup spoon. "Say that again."

"Which part?" Wolf asked.

"Mrs Chivers was in charge of a medieval pageant this year?" Wolf nodded, and Tabitha continued, "And Mrs Chivers ran the meeting last night, you said?" Again, Wolf nodded, unsure where his wife was going with this line of thought.

Chapter 28

"I need to go and look at the corkboard!" Tabitha announced, starting to rise from her chair.

She had barely touched her soup, and Wolf remembered how little breakfast his wife had eaten. "Tabitha, eat something first. Whatever it is can wait a few more minutes."

"I am not sure it will," Tabitha replied. "I have thoughts sitting just on the edge of my mind that I need to jostle. You do not have to join me," she assured the others.

"I am certainly not leaving," the dowager said with a sniff. "What has this dining room become? Victoria Station, with everyone coming and going as if they are catching the nine o'clock train to Brighton? Talbot, you may take the soup plates away and proceed with the next course."

It was tempting for Wolf to remind the woman that she was now the dowager countess and that the only people who gave such orders were he and Tabitha. However, Wolf knew this was one of those times when he needed to save his breath to cool his porridge.

Instead of reprimanding the dowager, Wolf spoke directly to the butler. "Talbot, many apologies to you and to Mrs Budgers, but her ladyship and I are moving to the parlour. Would it be possible to send some sandwiches through at your earliest convenience, please?"

"Sandwiches in the parlour? What are we, coal miners?" The dowager's horror had reached full-peak high dudgeon at this point. "I will be eating the rest of my meal at the table with a knife and fork, as my maker intended." Turning to Langley, she said, "I hope you are not planning to join this impromptu picnic, Maxwell."

Lord Langley had no desire to worsen the situation and agreed that he would continue through whatever courses remained. The dowager greeted this news with a look that suggested she would have expected nothing less, and heaven help Langley if he stood to leave before she finished her last spoonful of Charlotte Russe.

Throwing Langley a look of gratitude for his sacrifice, Wolf stood up, and he and Tabitha left the dining room. Tabitha said very little as they walked to the parlour. Wolf retrieved the corkboard from where Talbot now kept it safely, and Tabitha took a stack of blank notecards. She had Wolf repeat everything that had happened and what they had learned that morning while she took notes.

Tabitha stood to pin them to the corkboard, but then paused. "I need to do this as a timeline, and the board is too constrictive." Tabitha took all the notecards off the board and looked around the room for a surface large enough. She saw nothing, so she moved to an empty spot on the rug and sat on the floor, the cards in her lap.

"It's fortunate her ladyship did not join us. I worry she would see you sitting on the floor as the fall of civilisation," Wolf observed.

Tabitha laughed in agreement. "She may already believe that after I told her I played Oranges and Lemons in the nursery with the children. Apparently, joining in games with one's children is the kind of event that preceded the French Revolution."

She started laying the notecards out on the rug to reflect the timeline as they knew it. As she did so, Tabitha spoke her thoughts out loud. "We know that two weeks ago, James Truegood received a letter of rejection from Mr Allen regarding his article. This article talks about 'treasure' in Pembroke. We believe he meant a copy of the Magna Carta when he talked about treasure."

Wolf picked up her thread. "Yet, somehow, Sir Christopher seemed to believe there was actual treasure buried somewhere on his grounds. Are these two things connected?"

"Exactly. And we know that Mr Truegood's last conversation with Sir Christopher was the day before he was killed." Saying that, Tabitha placed the relevant notecard in its correct place in the timeline she was building.

Then, recalling what Wolf had mentioned earlier, Tabitha wrote a notecard that said, "Mrs Chivers directed a medieval pageant earlier this year," and placed it near the beginning of the timeline.

"Now, let us review the day of Mr Truegood's death. What do we know?" With that, Tabitha searched through the notecards until she found the ones she'd written after Wolf and the dowager's visit to Mr Davies' apothecary.

Tabitha retrieved each card, read what it said, and then placed it on the floor. "We know that Mr Truegood was unpleasantly surprised to find out that he had run out of digitalis."

"Oh, and I did find an empty bottle labelled digitalis in his room," Wolf suddenly remembered.

Tabitha continued. "We know that he was the first customer at the apothecary shop on the morning of August 4th at approximately eight o'clock in the morning."

Wolf added, "Where he was served by the apothecary assistant, Hywel Chivers."

Tabitha's head shot up. "Wait. You did not tell me his name at the time. Mrs Chivers's son, the apothecary assistant's name is Hywel?"

"Yes. I cannot believe I forgot to mention it. Though, why does it matter?"

"When I spoke to Clarice Hill the night of our dinner here, she mentioned that when she first met James Truegood, he was with, and let me think about how she put it... Right, she said, 'That peculiar man, Hywel, who is always staring at me so intently and makes me uncomfortable.' I did not realise at the time that this was Mrs Chivers's son."

"He certainly was a rather odd young man," Wolf admitted. "Very sullen, I might almost call him rather unwholesome in a way I cannot quite put my finger on."

"And this young man, Hywel Chivers, served our victim and gave him a new bottle of digitalis. Then, Mr Truegood left, and at some point, in the next two hours or so, went to Pembroke Castle, where he collapsed. Now, we arrived at Pembroke Castle at noon. However, we know that

Wogan Cavern can be accessed directly, without going through the castle grounds. What time would you say Rat went down there?"

"Well, I remember looking at my pocket watch about the time we went into the supposed birthplace of Henry VII, and it was half past one. So, it must have been around then."

"So, James Truegood leaves the apothecary not long after eight o'clock. We did not find the digitalis bottle on his body, so he must have gone home and then headed to the castle shortly after. Let's assume he reached the castle around nine o'clock in the morning. Within the next hour or two, he collapses and dies. Let's say around eleven o'clock. Two and a half hours later, Rat finds the body." Wolf continued, "Therefore, the dagger must have been plunged into the body between eleven and half past one."

"Correct. Now, let's jump forward to yesterday. I visit Mrs Chivers and tell her that we know the victim was poisoned with digitalis. Then, at some point last night, Mr Goodge's house was broken into by someone who seemed to be searching for something.

"You think the intruder was looking for the new bottle of digitalis?" Wolf asked.

"I do. And why would they do that if not because it contained evidence that the dosage was a much higher concentration than it should be? Because, of course, the additional digitalis that killed Mr Truegood could have been administered in another way. It could have been added to his food or drink. However, surely the simplest way was just to increase the concentration of the digitalis he was going to take that morning because he had run out and was frantic."

Tabitha suddenly had a thought and sat up straight, struck by its implications. "What if Hywel somehow orchestrated that James ran out of digitalis? Perhaps he broke in previously and emptied out the bottle, even. Or perhaps he gave him too little on a previous visit to the apothecary."

It made sense. In fact, the more Tabitha stared at the notecards before her, the more it all made sense. "Hywel must have known that Mr Goodge would be out of the house last night and that it would be the perfect time to break in. I would imagine that the combination of your visit to the apothecary and mine to his mother might have precipitated the attempt to retrieve the new, tainted bottle of digitalis."

Everything made sense, except for one thing: "But why? We know how, when, and where. What we do not have is any kind of motive." Tabitha chewed on her lip as she pondered what they knew and how none of it seemed to add up to a rational motive for murder.

Of course, they had encountered killers like Maureen Prescott, whose motives stemmed from insanity. Was that what they were dealing with here?

The lack of a clear motive indicated a larger issue. "Not only do we not know why, but we have no proof," Wolf pointed out. "If we assume Hywel found the digitalis bottle and disposed of it, then there's no evidence that was how the poison was administered."

"There is the dagger," Tabitha said. "I think it might be from the pageant Mrs Chivers organised."

"Even if it is, I doubt it is one-of-a-kind. I do not have high hopes of Bear turning up much of use today."

Tabitha considered Wolf's words. They seemed to have so many pieces of the puzzle, yet no way to prove any of it. "When I suggested sowing some seeds of rumour and putting the cat among the pigeons, I did not realise it would lead to a potentially crucial piece of evidence disappearing," she said rather despondently.

She reviewed the notecards with their possible suspects written on them. Of course, Hywel Chivers hadn't been one of those until minutes before. "Every other suspect has an obvious motive of some sort. Yet the person who has the means and the opportunity seems to have none. How perplexing!"

"Oh, there is a motive," Wolf assured her. "We just do not know what it is yet. I think we need to return to Pembroke and speak with Clarice Hill. She was the first person to tell us about James Truegood's friendship with Hywel, but she also made that comment about how he unnerved her. I want to understand more about what she meant by that. How soon could you be ready to leave?"

As he said these words, the door opened, and the dowager entered. It seemed she might have been more motivated to cut her meal short than she wanted to admit. "Where are we going?"

Tabitha and Wolf both sighed.

Chapter 29

In the carriage heading to Pembroke, Tabitha and Wolf caught the dowager up on their insights about Hywel Chivers.

The dowager chuckled somewhat maliciously. "How delicious! Mrs Chivers has always been so free with her tongue, spreading mischief wherever she goes. How fitting, then, that it be her offspring who committed this heinous crime!"

While Tabitha had no desire to encourage the dowager's unconcealed joy in the town gossip's downfall, it was difficult to argue with the sentiment.

Indeed, it seemed the dowager was not finished with her gleeful judgment. "While I do not usually approve of quoting the Germans, this may be the most perfect example of schadenfreude I have come across in quite some time, and so I believe I will grant myself license to say it now." Was she done now? It appeared not. "That woman scattered enough poison with her words. How poetic that actual poison was her son's choice of murder weapon!"

Finally, Wolf stepped in. "Lady Pembroke, this is only a hypothesis at the moment. A strong hypothesis with a high likelihood of being correct. Still, perhaps we should temper our response until we have definitive evidence that we are right."

Wolf's words were met with a haughty sniff, but the dowager said no more on the subject.

Casting about for a more productive conversational thread, Tabitha asked, "Is our plan to try to separate Clarice Hill from her father again?"

Wolf considered the question. "I believe that the time for artifice is over; Miss Hill and her father are no longer suspects, or at least are far down our list. It is time for plain speaking."

"Even if we expose Clarice's friendship with the victim?" Tabitha asked, reluctant to expose the young woman. Wolf acknowledged that it might come to that. However, he believed they could navigate the line of inquiry they wanted to pursue without being overly detailed about that aspect of it.

They decided that Wolf would take the lead and try to be as flexible as the situation at the Hill residence allowed. If they could speak with Clarice alone, that would be ideal. However, if her father insisted on joining them, Wolf would aim to give away as little as possible.

What they hadn't expected was the situation they found. Their first knock on the door went unanswered, as did the second and third. They knew the Hills had servants, so it was hard to believe no one was available to greet visitors. Wolf knocked once more, this time very loudly, and was about to suggest they give up when a very flustered-looking maid answered the door. Tabitha recognised the maid from their previous visit, and it seemed that after a moment, the maid recognised them as well.

The maid became even more flustered once she realised who the visitors were. The poor girl stood in the doorway, clearly unsure of what to do.

Finally, the dilemma was resolved when the dowager snapped, "Are you planning to invite us in or do you intend to leave the Earl and Countess of Pembroke, not to mention the Dowager Countess of Pembroke, standing on the doorstep like a common temperance zealot with pamphlets?"

The young maid's eyes widened, and she stammered, "I'm sorry, m'lady, m'lord, uh, can you follow me?"

The group was shown into the same room as during their previous visit. Of course, the dowager had not been one of the party then, and she now looked around the room with curiosity.

"So, this is what the home of a middling solicitor in a town beyond the reach of polite society looks like!" Luckily, they were spared any other snobbish remarks by the door opening.

Mr Hill entered the room, looking nearly as flustered as his maid. "Lord Pembroke, your ladyships, forgive me, but did we have an appointment I have forgotten?"

The man's face was ashen, and he seemed so distracted that Tabitha couldn't help but ask, "Is everything all right, Mr Hill? Has something happened?" The man entered the room, sank into an armchair, and lowered his head into his hands in despair. Cyril Hill sat like this for so long without speaking that Tabitha wondered if he was ever going to answer her.

Finally, as his visitors were starting to think it might be best to come back another time, Mr Hill said, "I am sorry to be such a terrible host, but you see, well, my darling Clarice seems to be missing."

"Missing? What do you mean, Mr Hill?" Wolf asked.

"She went to the Reading Room at ten o'clock this morning and hasn't returned home."

"Is it not possible she is merely delayed?" As she said this, Tabitha checked the clock on the mantel; it was now almost half past one. It was hard to imagine what could delay someone for so many hours, but it was possible.

"Clarice is a very responsible and reliable young woman. She was supposed to meet a friend at a local teahouse and would never be so rude as to not show up without sending a note. I was not expecting her home earlier because she was going to the tearoom directly from the Reading Room. However, when she did not arrive, her friend Martha called here to check on Clarice's well-being. That was when I was alerted to her disappearance."

Although they were well aware of how inept Constable Tucker was, Wolf still asked whether he had been alerted. It appeared that word had been sent to the police station, and Mr Hill was waiting for the constable to call.

"Can I ask the reason for your visit, Lord Pembroke?" Mr Hill inquired, though it seemed more out of politeness than genuine curiosity, and he appeared too worried about his daughter to care much.

"Actually, we wanted to talk to Miss Hill," Wolf admitted. He was worried Cyril Hill would ask why, but the anxious father was far too preoccupied for such a question.

Tabitha wanted to ask a question but was unsure how to phrase it delicately. Finally, she decided that such a line of questioning could only be so sensitive and simply asked, "Mr Hill, do you have any reason to believe that your daughter might have eloped?"

"Eloped? Why on earth would she elope?" the man asked in utter bemusement.

Again, Tabitha searched for the right words. "The first time your daughter's name came to our attention, there was a suggestion that you had high hopes for the kind of marriage your daughter might make."

It was evident that Mr Hill wanted to ask who they had been speaking with about Clarice. However, he said instead, "What father wouldn't want his daughter to make a good marriage? I do not believe I am any different from any loving father."

Treading as carefully as she could, Tabitha replied, "And of course, that is true. What is also true is that sometimes, young people view a potential spouse's value more highly than perhaps a parent does."

Now, Mr Hill seemed to understand her point. "Are you suggesting that my Clarice has fallen in love with someone I do not approve of or at least she believes I would not approve?"

"I am merely asking if it is possible," Tabitha said gently. "She would not be the first young woman to decide to take such matters into her own hands and head for Gretna Green."

It seemed as if Mr Hill was going to deny the very possibility of such a thing, but he didn't. Instead, he stood and left the room, returning a few minutes later with a young woman who appeared to be a lady's maid. He introduced her as Penny Jones, who was indeed Clarice Hill's maid.

"I do not believe that my daughter would leave without taking Penny with her," Mr Hill said confidently. "However, I think it's best if we ask Penny what she knows."

It seemed that Penny Jones was already aware that her mistress was missing and was quite distressed.

Speaking gently to the young woman, Tabitha asked, "Penny, do you know of any understanding between your mistress and a young man?"

The maid shook her head. Tabitha continued, "Do you know of any affection she might hold for a young man?" Again, the maid shook her head.

Was she telling the truth? It was Tabitha's experience that young women often entrusted a lot of their most private thoughts and secrets to their maids; certainly, she had with Ginny at Clarice's age. In fact, she still did. So, did Penny know something and was just unwilling to break her mistress's confidence?

"Penny. I understand you're very loyal to Miss Hill. However, she might be in danger, so we need to know whatever you know. Do you understand?"

Finally, the maid answered. "Yes, m'lady. I swear, I'm telling the truth. There are young men who want to court her, but Miss Clarice hasn't given her heart to anyone."

Despite this assurance, something about the maid's answer caught Tabitha's attention: young men, in the plural. Of course, they knew about James Truegood, but were there other young men throwing themselves at Clarice Hill's feet? And was that relevant either to her disappearance or to their investigation? Again, treading as carefully as possible, Tabitha posed the question.

The maid seemed visibly uncomfortable, and her eyes kept flicking between Tabitha's face and Mr Hill's profile.

Finally, Tabitha suggested, "Mr Hill, is there somewhere I might talk privately with Penny?" Looking shocked at the suggestion, Cyrill Hill asked why she needed to speak privately with his daughter's maid.

Tabitha had hoped it would be obvious. However, it seemed it wasn't. "Mr Hill, I remember being your daughter's age. In truth, I am not much older than she is. I would confide many of my hopes and dreams to my maid, Ginny, and I did so knowing those secrets would stay between us. Keeping her mistress's secrets safe is perhaps the most important job a lady's maid has. Far more so than curling hair and pressing dresses. I imagine that Penny is worried she might be speaking out of turn by sharing any of those secrets, even innocent ones, with Clarice's father. If she and I talk privately, I can assure her that I will only share information I consider essential for her mistress's safety, and nothing more."

For a moment, it looked as if Mr Hill was going to argue and insist that he had the right to know anything about his daughter that her maid knew. Then, despair washed over his face, and it appeared he realised that this might be the price he would have to pay if he had any hope of having his beloved daughter restored to him safely.

A few minutes later, Tabitha and Penny were seated in Mr Hill's study, the door closed firmly behind them.

"Now, Penny, you heard what I promised, did you not? I will not break Miss Clarice's confidence about anything you tell me unless I believe doing so is necessary to ensure her safe return." As Tabitha said this, she placed her hand over the maid's in what she hoped was a reassuring gesture. All Tabitha could think of was that if she'd known the situation they were walking into, she would have brought Ginny with her to have this conversation.

After a pause and a sigh, the maid relented. "Well, there was Mr Truegood."

"Yes, we know about his courtship, or attempted courtship. But who else was there?"

"Mr Truegood's friend."

It took Tabitha a moment to register who the maid was talking about. "Hywel Chivers? He was one of Miss Hill's suitors?"

"He wanted to be," the maid answered with a shake of her head. "Miss Clarice tried to be kind to begin with. But even when she dropped the hint like a ton of coal, it still seemed to go in one ear and out the other."

It took a moment for Tabitha to realise the implications of what she had heard: now they had a motive for James Truegood's murder.

Chapter 30

By the time Tabitha returned to the others, Constable Tucker had arrived. He was perched on the edge of a chair, clutching his helmet, and looked very uncomfortable. When Tabitha entered the room, the constable leapt to his feet, his face hopeful that she had learned something to spare him from having to exert himself to search for Clarice Hill.

On the short walk from the study to the front room, Tabitha had considered what she wanted to say in front of Cyrill Hill. Indeed, nothing was to be gained by suggesting that a murderer might have abducted his beloved daughter.

As much as Tabitha felt a little guilty about what she was about to say, she couldn't imagine Wolf would see much benefit in adding Constable Tucker to the next steps in their investigation. "Mr Hill, unfortunately, Penny did not have much to share that illuminated where your daughter might be. We will be on our way and will leave you to give all the relevant details to Constable Tucker. I am confident you are in excellent hands."

The expression on Mr Hill's face indicated he was not as confident. For his part, the constable shot her an anxious look. He had hoped the earl and his wife would get involved in this investigation as well. However, he had a sinking feeling that he would be left searching for Clarice Hill alone.

Wolf caught Tabitha's eye and realised she had learned something, but didn't wish to talk about it until they were out of the house. With this in mind, he stood and prepared to leave.

"But what of my daughter, milord?" Mr Hill sputtered as he realised his aristocratic visitors were leaving.

"As Lady Pembroke said, we will leave you in Constable Tucker's capable hands," Wolf said, adding to Tabitha's previous insincere endorsement of the police constable. The look he received in reply again spoke volumes about Mr Hill's opinion of the local police officer's ability. For a moment, it seemed as if the distraught father was going to protest and try to persuade them to stay. Then, his shoulders sank in resignation at his fate.

Just before they left the house, Mr Hill asked in a pleading tone, "If in the course of your investigation, you hear anything that might be pertinent to my daughter's disappearance, I beg you to let me and Constable Tucker know, milord." Wolf promised he would.

Tabitha's heart broke for the man. She almost wished she had told him what she'd learned from Penny, even if only to give him a crumb of hope that they might know something, maybe, about Clarice's disappearance. However, it was all conjecture so far. Even if Hywel Chivers was their murderer, and even if a romantic rivalry for the young woman's affections was his motive, it didn't follow necessarily that he had snatched Clarice.

Back in the carriage, the dowager grumbled, "Well, that was a waste of time, it seems."

Wolf wasn't so sure. "Did the lady's maid tell you anything of note, Tabitha?"

Tabitha nodded and shared the news about Hywel Chivers and her epiphany that this was his motive for murder.

"Well, well," the dowager exclaimed. "All this fuss over that chit of a girl!"

Ignoring the old woman's asperity, Tabitha continued, "I believe the first thing to do is to see whether Mr Chivers can be found at his place of employment. If he cannot, then we will know it is likely he has something to do with Clarice's disappearance."

This seemed a sensible next step, and so Wolf directed Madison to drive them back to Mr Davies' apothecary.

Tabitha hadn't been with them during the last visit, and now she looked around the shop with interest. There was no one behind the counter when they entered, but the dowager rang the bell impatiently and, moments later, Mr Davies scurried out from behind the curtain.

"Apologies, apologies. I am rather short-handed today, so I'm trying to do everything myself," he told them. That answered their central question: clearly, Hywel Chivers was not at work.

Trying to appear as nonchalant as possible, Wolf asked, "Where is your assistant?"

"His mother came this morning and said that Hywel had taken to his bed with a terrible head cold. Of course, it isn't good for business to have customers served by someone sneezing and coughing, so I sent her home with some Friar's Balsam and some cough syrup and said I hope he is feeling better by tomorrow."

Tabitha had one more question for the apothecary: "Mr Davies, on the day that James Truegood came in for his digitalis, do you remember Mr Chivers leaving the shop at all?"

The apothecary stared down at his counter and stroked his chin as he considered the question. "Now, let me think. Last Thursday feels so long ago now." Finally, he looked up and answered, "While both Hywel and I usually take our midday meal in the back, in shifts, now that you ask, I remember he said he'd forgotten to bring his food from home."

"What time would that have been?"

"While I cannot remember the exact time, I do recall that I had suggested he take his turn to eat because the shop was quiet. He went into the back, then returned and asked if he could run home to retrieve the food he'd forgotten there."

"Was this unusual?" Wolf asked.

"Very unusual. Mr Chivers is normally a very precise and organised young man; that's why I hired him in the first place. However, he mentioned that he had been distracted by something that morning and had forgotten. Of course, I let him go."

"And how long was he gone for?"

"I don't remember the exact amount of time. But I do recall thinking he'd been gone longer than I would have expected. I mentioned it when he came back, and he said his mother had asked him to do a quick errand for her while he was there. Well, who am I to criticise someone for being a devoted son?"

Mr Davies looked at them in confusion. "Can I ask why you are asking these questions, milord?"

"I am merely attempting to build a timeline of the day of Mr Truegood's death and the whereabouts of everyone he came into contact with that day." Wolf realised this was a rather flimsy excuse, but Mr Davies seemed to accept it.

As they left the apothecary shop, the dowager pronounced, in rather too loud a voice, "Well, I believe that settles it: this Chivers boy is both a murderer and a kidnapper."

Tabitha tried to shush the dowager, who ignored her and continued, "Though, perhaps he is a double murderer by now. I have to say, this investigation has become much more interesting than I had anticipated."

Luckily, this last sentence was spoken from within the carriage. Even so, Tabitha felt compelled to say, "Mama, we do not know anything for certain yet. This is all circumstantial evidence so far."

"Tabitha, when someone reaches my age, they are able to say certain things with more certainty that might be less justified in someone as relatively young as you are. There is no mistaking a rose when you are pricked by its thorns."

There was little point in arguing. Besides, Tabitha agreed with the dowager's main argument: it was hard to believe that Hywel Chivers wouldn't turn out to be their villain. The question was: where to go next? The dowager was eager to storm into Hywel Chivers's home, her sword-stick in hand, and confront Mrs Chivers about her son's misdeeds.

"It may come to that, or a version of that," Wolf conceded. "However, let us hold off on such a dramatic encounter for now."

The dowager huffed. "You really have become increasingly dull since your marriage to Tabitha, Jeremy! I had hoped that some of your previous swashbuckling ways would have rubbed off on her, and am disconcerted to see the influence going in the opposite, unfortunate direction."

Wolf was tempted to rush to defend his wife, but a quick shake of Tabitha's head told him to hold back. Of course, his level-headed wife was right; what was to be gained?

Instead, Wolf suggested they go to the Reading Room. "Let us gather more information about what time Clarice arrived and left and whether she seemed to be alone."

It was a sensible suggestion, and even the dowager agreed to it, however reluctantly. "Just be aware, I brought my swordstick with me today and I intend to use it on someone, even if it is just to poke you, Jeremy." Wolf considered himself warned. As it happened, he and Tabitha had also armed themselves before leaving for Pembroke, if only as a precaution.

As they drove to the Reading Room, the group talked about what they had learned. "While it would be easy to jump to conclusions, I believe that it is still possible that Hywel had nothing to do with Clarice's disappearance," Wolf insisted.

Tabitha shook her head in disagreement. "I believe the maid, Penny, was telling the truth. And I find it unbelievable that a young woman would have a romance even her maid knows nothing about. Not that I was ever inclined to run off to Gretna Green, but if I ever had, I would have taken Ginny with me. Of that, I have no doubt."

Chapter 31

The Reading Room was on Main Street, just a short walk from the apothecary shop. Once they arrived, Tabitha realised they might as well have walked. Though since this was likely a quick stop before heading to the Chivers home, it was probably best to keep the carriage nearby. The Reading Room, a subscription-based library and gathering place, was a simple stone-fronted building with tall sash windows and a modest brass plate at the door.

The group got out of the carriage and headed inside. The main room was long and narrow, illuminated by two sputtering gas lamps. A pair of tall windows faced the street and let in some much-needed natural light to the otherwise quite dark space. At one end was a heavy oak table covered with newspapers, including The Times, the Western Mail, and the Pembrokeshire Herald.

Tabitha looked around the room, whose walls were lined with floor-to-ceiling shelves that held neat rows of books in sober covers. Based on other such libraries she'd visited, Tabitha assumed these books were mainly histories, sermons, inspiring biographies, and the occasional set of Scott or Dickens for lighter reading.

There weren't many patrons in the room. A few older men sat with unlit pipes, frowning over newspapers, and two younger women were poring over books very intently. The librarian, a schoolmasterly man in a black coat, kept a close watch on the room from behind a tall desk, where the lending register was open for members to sign out their books.

Wolf made his way over to the librarian, followed by Tabitha and the dowager. The librarian watched them approach, his expression showing his surprise. Whether he recognised the Earl of Pembroke or not, there was little doubt these people were quality and not the library's usual patrons.

"Good morning," the librarian said in a low voice. "How might I be of assistance?"

"Is there somewhere we might speak privately?" Wolf asked.

It was evident from the look of surprise on the man's face that this was not what the librarian had been expecting. "I am sorry, sir, but I need to remain here to serve the patrons."

The dowager pushed forward. "This is the Earl of Pembroke, and I am the Dowager Countess of Pembroke, and this is regarding a matter of the highest importance. It is not a request but rather a directive: we need to speak with you privately. Now, do you have a room we can move to or not?"

The librarian, Mr Spall, had lived in Pembroke for most of his life. As soon as the dowager revealed her identity, he remembered being a young boy on a day when the old earl came into town with his son and his daughter-in-law. He couldn't recall the reason for the visit, but he had a very clear memory of this woman, only younger, but no less intimidating.

"I do have an office, milady. Perhaps we can move into there," Mr Spall stuttered.

The man got off his stool and pointed toward a door behind him. He led the way into a small, neat office that had only two chairs. The librarian seemed briefly stumped about what to do and looked around as if an extra chair might somehow appear out of thin air.

Wolf understood the man's dilemma and assured him, "I am perfectly happy to stand while the ladies sit." Mr Spall didn't seem entirely convinced of this statement's truth, but he was not a man who would contradict the word of an earl. Tabitha and the dowager each took a seat, while Wolf stood behind Tabitha's chair and Mr Spall nervously hopped from foot to foot, unsure of where he should position himself.

Finally, the dowager could take no more of it. "Stand still, man, for goodness' sake." Out of sheer terror, Mr Spall was then rooted to the spot for the rest of the conversation.

Tabitha was eager to start the conversation. They had no clue what kind of danger Clarice Hill might be in.

"Mr… I am sorry, what is your name?"

"Spall, your ladyship. Martin Spall."

"Excellent. Now, Mr Spall, do you know Miss Clarice Hill?"

The librarian was so happy that he could answer this question affirmatively and hopefully end this uncomfortable conversation soon that he nodded his head quite vigorously.

"A simple yes or no will suffice," the dowager scolded him. "There is no need for melodramatic responses."

Suitably chagrined, Mr Spall responded, "Yes, I know Miss Hill. She is a regular visitor to the Reading Room."

Shooting the dowager a sharp look to prevent her from further interruptions, Tabitha continued, "Did she visit this morning or indeed any time today?" Mr Spall considered the question. "Well, let me think now. I remember seeing her recently because we discussed *Bleak House* at some length. But was that today or yesterday?"

Out of the corner of her eye, Tabitha saw the dowager about to jump in and impatiently scold the man. She turned and shot a glare at the woman, who responded with a quick, innocent-looking smile.

Tabitha continued, "Please try to remember, Mr Spall. It is very important."

"No, no, it was definitely yesterday. I remember because I commented that it was a rather overcast morning, and Miss Hill wondered if it would rain later."

"And you have been here all day, and she has definitely not returned?"

"I have been here all day, and she hasn't been in yet."

They thanked the librarian and were about to leave when Tabitha had one last thought. "Do you know Hywel Chivers?"

At the mention of Hywel's name, a very odd expression appeared on Mr Spall's face. If Tabitha had been forced to describe it, she would have called it disgust.

"Yes, I know Hywel," Mr Spall admitted. "I know Mrs Chivers has done her best over the years, since Mr Chivers passed. But I must admit I don't like the lad, never have. When he was a boy, he would catch frogs and torture them. If rumour is to be believed, Mr Franks, the butcher, once caught him with a kitten he was trying to drown, just for the fun of it. If you ask me, there is something a bit off with that one. I know that my daughter says that he makes all the young women uncomfortable at dances."

Wolf reflected on when they met Hywel at the apothecary. He seemed rather sullen, but nothing more than that. Though their interaction had been brief, so there was probably insufficient time to make an accurate assessment.

Now that he was on a roll, Mr Spall seemed eager to keep going. "I never understood why Mr Davies took him on as an apprentice. Though Mrs Spall thinks that it might be because he has an interest in making Mrs Chivers the next Mrs Davies, if you know what I mean."

Tabitha assured him she understood what he meant. It seemed the librarian had nothing else to add, so they said their goodbyes.

They sat in the carriage, thinking over what they had learned that morning. Tabitha was the first to speak. "We know Clarice Hill left her house just before ten o'clock to walk to the Reading Room. But it looks like she never made it there. Did she go somewhere else instead, or was she taken?"

"How long do you think it would take to walk from the Hill house to Main Street?" Wolf mused.

"No more than ten minutes, I would say," Tabitha replied. Then, picking up Wolf's train of thought, she added, "Someone must have seen her at some point during that walk. Maybe they also saw Hywel."

The dowager felt compelled to be the voice of reason. Sighing at the need for her to point out something so obvious, she said, "I cannot imagine that Mr Hill will thank us for broadcasting to all of his neighbours that his daughter is missing. On the off chance that this is merely a misunderstanding, it will have unnecessarily set tongues wagging."

Tabitha had to admit that the woman had a point. While it may end up being necessary to trace the exact point Clarice had deviated from her intended path, perhaps it wasn't the most urgent thing to do at that moment.

"Mama is right. I think the next thing to do is to pay a visit to the

Chivers residence. Perhaps we will find Hywel in bed with his mother, spreading mustard paste on his chest."

No one thought that was likely.

Tabitha had one more thought: "It is possible that Mrs Chivers's involvement goes beyond providing an excuse for her son to miss a day of work. Perhaps she even purposefully delayed the historical society meeting to facilitate the break-in."

Again, no one disagreed with Tabitha. How involved was Mrs Chivers in her son's crimes?

Chapter 32

If there had been any doubt that Mrs Chivers shared some culpability for her son's actions, it was quickly dispelled by the expression on her face when she entered her parlour and found Tabitha, Wolf, and the dowager waiting for her. The expression was so fleeting and so quickly replaced by an insincere smile that Tabitha could have easily missed it if she hadn't been paying attention at that instance. As it was, she saw it for long enough to put a name to it: guilt mixed with a heavy dose of fear.

"Milord, miladies, what a surprise," Mrs Chivers said. Tabitha suspected this would be the last truthful statement the woman would say during that visit.

During the brief journey from the library, Tabitha had made a shocking suggestion: that the dowager take the lead in this conversation. The woman was primed and ready to engage in hand-to-hand combat with someone, and the time for kid gloves was over as far as Mrs Chivers was concerned. The dowager carried herself with imperious assurance, her tongue as sharp as her judgement was keen, and, at least in the woman's own opinion, unerring. Mrs Chivers would be no match for the dowager in full battle mode.

While Tabitha didn't express her thoughts in quite these terms, the dowager needed little convincing. Now, the woman leapt into the fray with the enthusiastic aggression of a hungry predator with its next kill in sight. "Yes, Mrs Chivers, I am sure it is somewhat of a surprise to see us. I am sure you had hoped that you had thrown us sufficiently off the scent with your stories." Tabitha could have sworn the dowager licked her lips as she said this.

"I am sorry, your ladyship, but I do not understand what you mean," Mrs Chivers said with a nervous twitch.

"We would like to speak with your son, if you would be so kind as to call him down." The dowager said this with such relish that Tabitha almost felt sorry for her prey.

Looking for all the world like a rabbit caught in a snare, Mrs Chivers said, "Unfortunately, Hywel is unwell and has taken to his bed. He is far too poorly to come downstairs."

"Then I will go to him," the dowager declared.

Mrs Chivers tried to block the door with her body, saying, "I would not like your ladyship to expose herself to whatever deadly plague he might have come down with. I would be happy to carry a message up to him."

"Deadly plague? The apothecary said it was a head cold! Which is it, woman?"

"Well, of course, many a weakened body has been carried away by what seemed to be a head cold at first. I am just taking all necessary precautions to protect you, Lady Pembroke."

"Are you calling me old and feeble?"

"No, no. Nothing of the sort. I am merely exercising appropriate precaution."

There were various ways this situation might have been handled. They might have told Mrs Chivers what they suspected about her son. Perhaps they would have demanded he present himself and thereby force her into an admission. However, none of those would have provided the high drama the dowager was itching for.

Instead, she unsheathed her swordstick and waved it in front of her. "Stand back, woman! I will go and see for myself."

It was unclear what shocked Mrs Chivers the most: the sword being brandished in her front room, or the prospect of the Dowager Countess of Pembroke charging up her stairs and making her way through the bedrooms.

Tabitha decided that of the two separate crimes they wished to hold Hywel Chivers accountable for, Clarice Hill's abduction was the more urgent. Ensuring the young woman's safety was of paramount importance. Once that was secured, they could piece together Hywel's involvement in James Truegood's murder.

"Mrs Chivers," Tabitha began, her voice calm but firm. "Your son has not been at the apothecary shop today. Meanwhile, Clarice Hill has disappeared, and we have reason to believe your son is responsible. Do you know where he has gone?"

The woman pressed her lips together thinly. "Hywel's poorly. I told Mr Davies so. He's a good boy, always has been. People talk too much in this town."

Wolf's tone was sharp. "We have little time for evasions. If Miss Hill comes to harm..."

At that moment, the woman appeared to make a decision. Whether it was Wolf's veiled threat or the still-outstretched weapon, she visibly wilted and admitted, "He is not here. Hywel is not here."

The dowager, somewhat hesitantly, lowered her swordstick.

"Mrs Chivers, if your son isn't here, where is he?" Wolf asked.

"I don't know," the woman answered with a trembling voice.

"Does he have Clarice Hill with him?" Tabitha asked.

Mrs Chivers's eyes grew wide with alarm. "Don't you dare put wickedness on him. Hywel's no villain. When he was a lad, he never harmed a soul, despite what they said. Oh, I know what people have always thought of my boy. My poor, sweet boy. No wonder if he gets angry sometimes."

"We have no wish to hurt your son or blame him for anything he has not done," Tabitha assured Mrs Chivers. It seemed unproductive to terrorise the woman any further, at least for now. Better to let her believe she was helping to improve the situation for her son. "You are correct; this is probably a big misunderstanding."

Mrs Chivers hadn't said this, but she nodded along, relieved to be given a way out. "Yes. That's what it is, a misunderstanding. I'm sure

Hywel just wanted to talk to the girl. Nothing more. He just wants a bit of peace and quiet to talk to her."

"Did he bring Clarice here?" Wolf demanded. "And if so, where has he taken her now?"

Torn between trying to defend her beloved son and terrified of what might happen to both of them if she didn't help the magistrate, Mrs Chivers said, "He stopped here. To get some food."

"Food? What do you mean, get some food? Speak plainly, woman," the dowager said, raising her swordstick again and waving it in Mrs Chivers's face.

Mrs Chivers sighed. "He told me this morning that he wasn't feeling well and that he wanted me to tell Mr Davies he wouldn't be at work. I did as he asked, but when I returned, he was up and dressed. He wouldn't tell me much, but he said he had to speak to someone. He said he had to speak to her and that he had to explain some things. And then he left. He never told me who 'her' was."

"And then what?"

"Then, sometime later, he burst in and said he needed food. I looked outside and saw a cart sitting outside the house. I asked him what he was doing with the cart, and he told me to mind my own business. Then, he stormed into the kitchen, grabbed some bread, cheese, and a few other things, and left."

Tabitha considered what Mrs Chivers had told them. Turning to Wolf, she said, "If he has a cart, then he must have planned to go somewhere outside of Pembroke, and if he took food, then he must be expecting to be gone for some time at least."

Turning back to face Mrs Chivers, she asked, "Did he take anything else?"

"He grabbed a blanket and muttered something about 'her catching a chill'."

Given that it was a particularly warm August, what did this suggest about where he might have taken Clarice?

"Mrs Chivers, is there somewhere around here that holds a special connection for Hywel?"

The woman hesitated for a moment, and in that moment, Tabitha was sure Mrs Chivers had some idea where her son and Miss Hill might be.

Tabitha tried again, but this time, the gentleness and compassion were absent from her voice. "Mrs Chivers, at this moment, your son may be guilty of abduction. If we do not find him in time, he may become guilty of murder." She didn't mention that they believed he was already guilty of another murder. "If you do not tell me all you know, I will be forced to summon Constable Tucker, and we will continue this conversation at the police station."

The thought of being dragged in cuffs for all her neighbours to see seemed sufficient motivation, finally. "The coast. He might have gone to the cliffs. He always loved the caves at Stackpole. His father would take him there when he was a boy, gathering limpets and fishing. He did mutter something as he left. I heard him say under his breath that no one would think to look for him somewhere so wet and lonely."

"Thank you, Mrs Chivers. How far is the drive to the caves from here?" Wolf asked.

"Maybe about a thirty-five-minute drive to Stackpole, then possibly a twenty-minute walk down to Stackpole Quay. There are caves all along that coastline. That's all I know." With that, Mrs Chivers slumped into an armchair and began to weep.

They had no time to comfort the woman. As they left the house, Wolf said to the dowager, "We are going to need all the help we can get. Lady Pembroke, I am going to drop you at the police station. I need you to tell Constable Tucker to gather whatever reinforcement he can and then have him go to the post office and telephone the hall. Ask Bear and Langley to bring men from the estate and meet us along the coast near Stackpole Quay. And make sure they are all armed."

For a moment, it seemed as if the dowager wanted to argue that she wouldn't be left behind to miss all the fun. But being the one to muster the local constabulary sounded more exciting than tramping along a beach. And, while she wouldn't admit it to anyone, a long walk just to get to those caves seemed more than she could handle.

Chapter 33

The carriage jolted along as it left the cobbles of Pembroke behind and started down the narrow country roads toward Stackpole. Tabitha leaned forward, trying to will the horses to gallop faster with her thoughts. This was one of the tensest situations she believed they'd ever faced during an investigation; they were rushing far from Pembroke to a site that might not even be where Hywel was holding Clarice. They could waste hours wandering along the coast only to realise they had been looking in the wrong place all along.

Adding to Tabitha's anxiety, Wolf said, "I wish we had started out earlier in the day. It will be almost four o'clock when we get to Stackpole Quay, and the tide will have already begun rising. We risk not being able to get to Clarice if that is where he's holding her."

They passed a quaint little village with an ancient church standing grey against the afternoon sky. Smoke curled from the squat cottages huddled at its base, and a pair of children paused in their game to stare at the Earl's carriage flying by. Tabitha's fingers clenched tight around her reticule. Clarice could be anywhere. They had to hope they were going in the right direction.

Speaking her fears aloud, Tabitha asked, "Do you think he means to hurt her?"

"We cannot know. Even if his mother is correct and Hywel's original intention was simply to isolate Clarice long enough to speak with her, once he realises she had no interest in a romance with him, who knows what direction his apparently deranged mind might take."

At Wolf's words, Tabitha was reminded of Maureen Prescott and how far her obsession with Wolf had gone. If they were right, Hywel Chivers had already killed one person in his pursuit of Clarice Hill.

Soon, they entered the orderly parkland at the edge of the Stackpole estate. Beyond the trees, Tabitha glimpsed the white façade of Stackpole Court overlooking its grounds. She barely paid it any mind. The air now carried a faint scent of cut hay and sea salt; the coast couldn't be far. In a field, two men paused their work, caps in hand, as the carriage rolled by. One shouted something, but the wind and the wheels drowned it out.

The road to Stackpole narrowed as the carriage rattled over the last stretch of lane. Tall hedgerows pressed in on either side, broken now and again by the whitewashed cottages of the estate village. The afternoon sun threw long shadows across the track, and Tabitha noted how the air grew sharper with each turn, carrying with it the tang of the sea. They travelled through the heart of Stackpole, where neat rows of cottages gave way to the larger stone building of the Stackpole Inn, its signboard creaking softly in the breeze. Wolf thumped on the carriage roof, and Madison slowed down to stop in front of the inn. The horses exhaled forcefully from the quick pace, and Tabitha was thankful for a moment's rest from the hurried carriage ride.

A pair of elderly men stood at the doorway with tankards in hand, casting curious looks as the Pembroke carriage drew up. Their curiosity was piqued even further when Wolf stepped down. They turned and called into the inn, and a moment later, a full-figured woman in an apron, probably the innkeeper's wife, appeared at the threshold and offered them a polite nod.

Wolf asked about the fastest way to the quay, and she directed them past the inn and down a narrow lane that sloped toward the woods. "Keep to the track, sir. It'll bring you out above the quay. Though your driver should be careful in a carriage this heavy and it's unlikely you'll be able to drive the whole way. Oh, and the tide's running strong today, so take care."

They were about to leave when Wolf suddenly had a thought and turned around. "Have you seen a young man and woman, possibly driving a cart, and heading toward the cliffs?"

The woman shook her head, but one of the elderly men piped up, "This morning. I saw a man driving a cart this morning. Didn't see a woman with him, though. Maybe about ten or eleven. Drove the cart down that path there, same direction you're going in. Didn't think much of it at the time."

Tabitha let out a sigh of relief; it seemed they were in the right place. If Hywel had left the cart nearby, then he was probably headed to one of the closer caves. They thanked the woman and headed in the direction she had indicated.

Soon, the inn and village were behind them. The path was quite wide at this point, and by driving slowly and carefully, Madison managed to guide the carriage along it. Still, the lane from the inn gradually became narrower, tightly bordered by hawthorn. The wheels jolted uncomfortably over stones and into ruts, and more than once the carriage lurched against the camber of the road. As they started down the hill, Tabitha gripped the side rail. Now, the path from the Stackpole Inn quickly narrowed, turning into little more than a dirt track.

"I suspect that woman was right; I doubt we can drive all the way down. But I trust Madison to take us as far as he can safely," Wolf observed.

No sooner had Wolf said this than the carriage slowed even more and, moments later, stopped. Madison called down, saying he didn't think he could take them any further, so Tabitha and Wolf got out. Madison mentioned that he kept a lantern in the carriage that they might want to take with them. Wolf gratefully accepted the offer. It occurred to him to bring Madison with them, but, on further reflection, he thought it better that the man stay with the carriage and direct Bear and Langley when they arrived. Then, he and Tabitha started on their way down the narrow path. They were now in quite thick woods, and the trees of the Stackpole estate closed in, offering welcome shade against the warm August day.

The path turned sandy under their feet as they approached the water. A gull screeched overhead, its cry sharp against the steady crash of waves in the distance. They walked for ten minutes until finally the trees parted, revealing the first glimpse of the coastline: jagged cliffs, the white line of surf curling against them, and out of sight, the dark entrances of sea caves. Would they find Clarice Hill in one of these?

"At least it's a beautiful, clear, sunny day," Tabitha said, noticing the mostly unbroken stretch of blue sky interrupted only by the occasional puffy white cloud. "We shall have enough light for our purpose."

"Light is one thing. The tide is quite another," Wolf replied anxiously. Suddenly, they came upon an abandoned cart. Was this what Hywel had used and left behind when the path became too narrow? They could only hope.

"It is a good sign that we are on the right track," Wolf said. Then added, "However, let us not get ahead of ourselves. We do not know for sure that this is the cart Hywel used, and, even if it is, they have many hours on us. He could have taken Clarice anywhere along this shoreline by now."

Tabitha knew he was right. Nonetheless, the cart gave her hope that they would find Clarice Hill.

Their vista suddenly opened as they moved closer to the edge of the fields where the land rolled down toward the sea. A small stile led onto a well-worn path that had been travelled by many generations of walkers. Wolf offered his hand to Tabitha to help her cross. The path, as much as the worn grass could be called that, curved upward through a meadow where calm cattle grazed. When they heard people approaching, some of the herd lazily lifted their heads, then went back to eating.

After they crossed another stile and left the meadow, the terrain became more rugged, with tufts of coarse grass sprinkled with bright summer wildflowers. Tabitha caught the scent of gorse as they passed a thick clump of it.

They walked side by side, the sound of the sea swelling as they neared the headland. Soon, the edge of the cliffs came into view, dropping straight down to the water. From this height, the ocean stretched out before them, sparkling in the sunlight. White-topped waves crashed onto the shore. As they moved closer to the cliff edge, they could more clearly see the numerous caves and inlets along the shoreline. Most of them appeared to be already filled with water.

Tabitha paused at the top, catching her breath. "It is beautiful.

Though I cannot imagine what sort of hiding place someone might contrive here."

Wolf narrowed his gaze toward the jagged indentations at the cliff's base. "He must have thought one of these caves would be safe. Or safe enough," he added ominously.

They began to follow a path that led down in a series of steep steps roughly cut into the earth and stone. They moved carefully, with Tabitha lifting her skirts to keep them from dragging, Wolf steadying her when the ground slipped beneath her boots. Finally, they reached a rock shelf just above the waterline. The tide was still low enough to allow navigation along the beach, although the waves slapped steadily, creeping further in with each minute.

The first cave they encountered was wide and shallow. They stepped inside and felt the cool, damp, and heavy air. Seaweed covered the floor in heaps, and the smell of it was rather overwhelming. Wolf lit the lantern and held it high, its light casting long streaks across the stone, but all it illuminated were bare walls worn down by centuries of tide.

They continued forward. The next cave was narrower, forcing them to walk single-file. Tabitha touched the wall with her gloved hand; it was slick and cold. The passage widened and ended in a natural chamber. The roof dripped steadily, and the sound echoed in the close air. Wolf moved the lantern's light across the floor, half expecting to find some sign of recent habitation, but there was nothing but rock and damp sand.

Chapter 34

Tabitha and Wolf emerged into the daylight, blinking against the brightness. The tide had edged higher already, pressing them further against the cliff. They made their way along to the next opening. This one required scrambling over a jumble of rocks, and Wolf offered his hand as Tabitha climbed, the hem of her skirt damp and heavy, the wind tugging at her hat. Inside, the cave arched higher, its roof black with soot from a long-past fire. Maybe fishermen had taken shelter here over the years. The floor was uneven, covered with pebbles and driftwood. A gull flapped away as they entered, its wings noisy in the tight space. They searched again, but only found signs of tide and storm. Tabitha wondered if they should yell out, but hesitated, questioning whether alerting Hywel to their presence was a good idea.

Tabitha exhaled with a hint of impatience. "Three caves, and not a hint of them."

Yet they did not turn back. Instead, they pressed on along the shoreline, even though the tide was rising quickly enough to soak their boots. The next cave was smaller, already half-flooded, and they couldn't enter. They looked into its dark opening, the waves crashing inside, then moved away swiftly before the water cut them off.

The final cave was farther around the headland. It was the biggest yet, with a jagged, tall opening. They stepped inside to find a space that could almost be mistaken for a ballroom; its floor was so wide, and the ceiling was high. Pools of seawater shimmered in its hollows, and limpets clung to the walls. The sound of the surf outside echoed loudly and insistently.

As they entered this cave, Wolf noticed something and crouched down to inspect it. "Here," he murmured. He touched a mark etched in the stone at the cave's entrance: a long scrape, as if something heavy had been dragged across it. "This looks freshly done. I think something has been hauled in."

They moved inside. The air cooled immediately, and the sound of the crashing waves was muffled somewhat, replaced by the steady drip of water. It took a moment for Tabitha's eyes to adjust, but then she saw it: a length of rope pulled taut across the rock. Wolf followed it with his hand until the shadows revealed a small rowboat. Its hull was damp, and its bow was wedged against a jut of stone. The boat was tied securely, and stones had been piled inside as ballast.

Tabitha drew closer. Something caught her eye. It was a length of pink chiffon, snagged on the thwart. She reached out and pulled it free. It was a woman's scarf.

"Clarice!" she whispered.

"It would seem we have found the right cave," Wolf agreed. "Let us go as quietly as possible. We want to retain the element of surprise as much as possible."

Wolf's jaw clenched. "The tide is coming in quickly." He nodded to the cave mouth, where the water rose higher with each roll of the waves. "There is no time to waste."

The cave reeked of salt and seaweed, perhaps even more than the other caves. The sound of incoming waves crashing against the rocks echoed through the cavern, and water was already washing around their boots in sudden surges. Although this cave let in more daylight than the previous ones, as they went further in, the light quickly dimmed to gloom, and Tabitha was thankful for Wolf's lantern, which cast long shadows on the wet rock.

Up until that point, the only sounds they'd heard besides their footsteps were waves crashing behind them, seagulls squawking, and water dripping from the cave roof and down the walls. Now, Tabitha stopped and whispered, "Did you hear that?"

Wolf hadn't before, but now he stood still and listened. "Yes, I think so. I hear voices."

To follow the sound, they would need to go deeper into the cave. They risked the lantern giving away their presence. However, without it, they would have no light by which to navigate the slippery, rocky area. Wolf made a decision and took off his cravat, throwing it over the lantern in the hope of dulling its brightness somewhat. Then, he took Tabitha's hand, and they followed the sound.

With the now dimmed lantern, it was more difficult to see where they were headed. More than once, one of them slipped. Finally, they reached a cluster of rocks that looked almost like stairs leading up to another level. The sounds they'd heard were louder now. Was that someone crying? A woman? Clarice?

Wolf paused at the rocks. He let go of Tabitha's hand and drew his revolver from his waistband. He would need both hands if he were to hold the lantern as well. "Take out your gun," he whispered. "Then stay behind me. And be careful on these rocks."

As they began to climb, Tabitha was thankful she had kept her gloves on. The soft kid leather provided padding and improved her grip as she pulled herself up. It was very clear where the water line was, as the rocks suddenly became less wet and slippery.

There was a kind of light ahead that provided cover for the illumination from their lantern. In fact, at some point, Wolf stopped and snuffed out his lamp; there was no need to give Hywel any more warning than necessary.

Now they were approaching the upper chamber, and the voice was much clearer. Wolf paused his climb and put out his hand to halt Tabitha's.

A male voice, presumably Hywel, was saying in an almost pleading tone, "I love you. How can you not see that? All I have ever wanted is for us to be together. I know you are scared, but there is no need to be. The last thing in the world I would ever do is to hurt you."

Then, a frightened female voice responded, "Hywel, if you love me, let me go. We can talk then."

"You keep saying that, but I know the truth." Suddenly, his tone grew colder and filled with venom. "I know what everyone thinks of me. Even James. He pretended to be my friend, but I know that the two of you laughed about me behind my back."

"I feel terrible, Hywel. I think I am sick. Please, can you not return me home so I might see a doctor?" the young woman asked in a plaintive voice.

"I promise there is nothing wrong with you," he replied suddenly. "It's just the chloroform and then the chloral hydrate I had to give you to keep you sedated enough to bring you here safely."

Clarice began to cry again. "Hywel, how can you not see that drugging and abducting me, and now holding me here bound with ropes, is not showing me that you love me?"

"I just needed to get you away from your father and everyone else who would turn you against me. I only want you to stay here long enough to see how special our love is. Look, I have food, drink, and a blanket. I used to play here as a boy, and I know the tide won't reach us. We are completely safe. You are safe. I won't let anything happen to you, my darling. I promise."

"Then at least untie me."

"My love. My angel. I wish I could. And eventually, once you realise that we should be wed, I will. I've already saved you once from James' propositions."

"James?" Clarice asked in a voice filled with shock and horror. "What did you do to James?"

Now, Hywel's voice grew proud. "All I did was save you, my petal. When he told me that he wished to marry you, I knew I had to do what I could to pry you away from him."

"I was never going to marry James Truegood," Clarice insisted through her tears.

With a sinister edge to his voice, Hywel replied, "And I made sure that remained the case."

As the true horror of what Hywel Chivers had done dawned on Clarice, her cries turned into sobs. Hearing the young woman weep in terror, Tabitha's heart broke for her. Clarice Hill might be a rather heartless flirt, but she didn't deserve to be kidnapped and confined in a damp cave for her actions.

Wolf considered what they'd heard and what it likely implied. Even if Hywel had some kind of weapon with him, he probably didn't have it out and trained on Clarice if he'd had her bound with ropes. However, could they be sure of that? The last thing Wolf wanted was to get into an exchange of gunfire in a small, dark cave.

What he was sure of was that he wanted to keep Tabitha out of sight until he was certain. Turning to her, he whispered, "I want to surprise him, but he might have a gun. Stay here until I am sure. But keep close and keep your gun ready, in case I need you."

Tabitha's first instinct was to argue, but she realised that with her skirts now even heavier from the water, she couldn't move as quickly and nimbly as Wolf could.

Chapter 35

Wolf was able to climb up to the ledge and peer over without alerting Hywel to his presence. He saw Clarice, her hands and feet bound with rope, sitting with her back against the cave wall. Hywel was sitting on a nearby rock. From what Wolf could see, he wasn't holding any kind of weapon; this was good. Even so, Wolf decided to proceed carefully. There was no doubt Hywel could reach Clarice faster than Wolf could, and if he had some sort of weapon ready, she might still be in danger.

It occurred to Wolf that he could just shoot Hywel from where he crouched, but that seemed like a drastic step unless it was absolutely necessary. He would rather arrest the man and see him stand trial for James Truegood's murder.

Wolf thought that if Hywel was sufficiently distracted by something, he might be able to get over the ledge and slide toward Clarice so that, by the time he confronted Hywel, he would be between him and the young woman. Of course, with the rising tide, there wasn't much time to spare. While they could use the boat to escape, they needed to reach where it was tethered.

About five minutes passed. Hywel kept ranting at Clarice, who continued crying. Finally, Hywel turned away and moved deeper into the cave, appearing to search for something.

"Are you hungry, my love?" he called back.

Wolf seized the opportunity and pushed himself over the ledge. Clarice saw him as he jumped up, and she gasped. Wolf worried Hywel would hear and rush back before he was in place. He quickly put his finger to his lips to signal she should be quiet. While her eyes were wide, Clarice seemed to understand what was needed.

Just as Wolf reached her, he heard Hywel returning and asking, "Would you like some bread and cheese, my sweets?" Then, when he saw Wolf standing in front of him, he yelled, "Who are you, dastard? What are you doing here? Leave this place."

Then, he noticed Wolf's gun pointed at him and shrank back. "What do you want? Money? I will give you what I have." As he said, Hywel seemed to realise who he was talking to. "Your lordship? What are you doing here?"

After a momentary pause, it dawned on him what Wolf was doing there. "No! You will not take her from me. She is mine!"

"Hywel, Miss Hill is no one's possession," Wolf said calmly. "You drugged and abducted her, and now you have her tied up and terrified in a damp cave. Is that love?" Even as he tried to calm the young man, Wolf kept his gun pointed at him.

Suddenly, before Wolf knew what was happening, Hywel had bent down and scooped up a handful of sand and loose grit from the cave floor. With a desperate snap of his wrist, he flung it at Wolf's face.

Wolf instinctively blinked and turned his head, raising his free hand to shield his eyes. In that split second, Hywel lunged, crashing into him. The pistol jerked sideways, metal scraping the stone as Hywel clawed at Wolf's wrist, both men grappling in the dim light.

From her spot on the rocks below the ledge, Tabitha heard the sound and pulled herself up. The light was so dim and the men's movements so hard to discern that she had paused before shooting. But now, with Wolf off balance and Hywel's hand nearly closing over the pistol, there was no time to weigh her options.

"Wolf, get down!" she shouted.

Wolf twisted his body sharply to the side, instinctively ducking low as

Tabitha took aim. Her revolver cracked, the shot echoing off the cave walls.

Hywel cried out, staggering backwards as the bullet hit his thigh. His grip on Wolf loosened, and the pistol clattered to the floor between them. Blood spread dark against his trousers as he collapsed to one knee, clutching at the wound, his face ashen.

Wolf grabbed his gun and aimed it again, his breathing ragged. Tabitha moved forward, steady as she closed the gap, her eyes fixed on Hywel.

"You have caused enough damage," she said, her voice steady but sharp as steel. "It stops now." Then, turning to Wolf, she said, "Give me your knife so I can free Clarice."

Without taking his eyes off the squirming, injured man, Wolf reached for the knife he had thought to loop to his belt and handed it to Tabitha. She bent down next to Clarice and began cutting the ropes. The girl's crying had quieted; now she was sniffing and occasionally hiccupping.

"Try to cut the ropes carefully so we can reuse them to bind Hywel," Wolf called to her. Tabitha followed his suggestion, and as she worked to free Clarice's legs.

Tabitha tried to calm Clarice as she cut the ropes. "You are safe now. This is almost over, Clarice. He cannot hurt you anymore." Her words helped, but even so, the girl seemed drained and unable to do anything to help Tabitha free her more quickly. Tabitha wondered how they were going to get her to the boat. She could imagine that if the girl had been drugged and her feet bound since that morning, it might take her a while to regain full control of her limbs. When she was finished, Tabitha threw the rope toward Wolf, then moved on to free the girl's arms.

As Tabitha had feared, even after she was free, Clarice still seemed unable to stand. Tabitha decided to leave her there for now while they restrained Hywel.

She said to Wolf, "I will keep my gun trained on him while you tie him up." In truth, the young man appeared sufficiently incapacitated by the gunshot and lay on the ground, groaning and whimpering in pain. Nonetheless, Tabitha didn't want to take any chances.

Wolf took the rope and quickly bound Hywel's hands, but not his feet. He realised they needed the man to be able to walk if they wanted to take him with them. From what he could see, they were already going to have enough trouble getting Clarice out of there.

When Hywel's hands were restrained, Wolf examined the wound on his leg. "Help me!" Hywel screamed. "I need a doctor."

"Well, there is no doctor here," Wolf replied flatly. "I think we are better off leaving the leg as it is instead of me trying to cut out the bullet." At Wolf's words, Hywel began crying.

Wolf was strongly tempted to leave Hywel Chivers behind. It would already be difficult enough to escape the cave with Clarice; the young man would only slow them down. They could send men to retrieve him later. As if Hywel could read Wolf's thoughts, his cries grew even more plaintive. Even though Wolf felt no pity for the man, he realised that Hywel's injuries needed urgent treatment.

Bending down, Wolf said, "I need your belt, Hywel." The injured man blinked at him, confused.

"Your belt," he repeated. "We need to tie your thigh, or you will bleed out."

Wolf unfastened the man's belt, tore a strip from his shirt, and wrapped Hywel's leg tightly above the wound. When he finished, he tried to help Hywel sit up. The man was trembling now, from pain, shock, or both.

"You need to stand. Put your arm around my shoulder and I will take the brunt of your weight," Wolf ordered. Hywel did what he had been told and, with Wolf's help, managed to stand. "In order to help you, I will have to put my gun away so I can carry the lantern. If you try anything, I will have no qualms about leaving you here, do you understand?"

Hywel grunted out his understanding and willingness to comply.

Tabitha made her own efforts to get Clarice to her feet. Finally, the young woman was standing, however shakily. Between her and Hywel, it was not going to be easy to get out of there.

Getting down from the ledge proved challenging. Tabitha went first, testing each step before shifting her weight. Below, the cave opened into a dark bowl of water. The tide was already filling it. The waves surged in a steady rhythm, each one sending a cold draft up the rock.

"Slowly," Wolf said behind her. His voice was even, but she could hear the strain in it. "Hywel, keep your weight on my shoulder. Miss Hill, lean into Lady Pembroke and try to hold onto the rocks if you can."

Clarice nodded without speaking. Her eyes were unfocused from the drug, and her breath came light and fast. Tabitha wrapped one arm tightly around the girl's waist and guided her down one step at a time. Every few steps, she paused to let Clarice catch her breath and assess the next grip. Hywel, white-lipped, hissed once when his wounded leg grazed the rock. Wolf steadied him with his free hand and said nothing.

It took much longer than Wolf hoped, but they finally managed to climb down the rocks to the rising water, which had now totally filled the space. Now what? Wolf realised there was no other option. Even if Tabitha, in her gown, could swim to the boat, Hywel and Clarice definitely could not.

"I am going to swim out and fetch the boat," Wolf said firmly. Tabitha would have argued with him, but it was clear there was no other option. The only alternative was to stay on the rocks until the tide went back out, and they didn't know how serious Hywel's injuries were. Additionally, Clarice looked so dizzy and confused from the drugs she'd been given, Tabitha thought it was best to get her to a doctor as soon as possible.

Wolf lowered Hywel onto the rocks, and Tabitha did the same with Clarice. There seemed to be no reason to keep the young woman on her feet longer than necessary. While Tabitha didn't think the injured man was in any shape to try anything, she decided not to take any chances, so she withdrew her revolver again and warned him she wouldn't have any problem shooting him in the other leg if needed. Her only reply was a whimper.

Chapter 36

A wave surged in, hitting the rocks just below their feet and splashing cold water onto their knees. At that moment, Wolf swung down, hanging from his hands, and dropped into the water. The cold shock ran through him. He went under, surfaced, and began swimming steadily toward the mouth of the river. For a moment, the surge pushed him sideways. He had left the lantern on the rock beside the others, and it cast enough light for Tabitha to see her husband almost being swept away. Her breath caught, but Wolf angled his body, made his way to the boat, and found the painter line. He wrapped the painter around one forearm and pulled himself hand over hand until he reached the boat. Then, he dragged himself into it.

Unsure if Tabitha would be able to hear him over the sound of the waves, Wolf nevertheless yelled out that he was safely in the boat and coming to get them.

Now that he had managed to get in the boat, Wolf still had to navigate it through the cave without wrecking it on a rock. As he'd swum, he'd tested the depth of the water, and it seemed as if the tide had come in sufficiently that it should be possible to row the boat back all the way to the shelf where Tabitha waited. However, that didn't account for any rocks that might be sticking up from the cave floor. If nothing else, he would have to row slowly and carefully, hoping for good luck.

Wolf untied the painter, settled into the boat, and took the oars. Being as careful as possible, he pushed off with the oar. The boat slid into the cave mouth on the back of a spent wave and then paused for a moment in a pool of turbulence. The next surge tried to push it sideways, scraping its gunwale along the stone. Wolf used the oar to push against the cave wall and the wave. The bow stayed on course and nosed toward the back of the cave. He rowed slowly, trying to feel for rocks beneath the boat with the oar. A couple of times, the boat seemed to hit something, but Wolf managed to push off with one of the oars, and there didn't appear to be any damage. Fortunately, this looked like it was a fisherman's boat, and it was sturdy and built for rough conditions. Wolf assumed Hywel had stolen it from Stackpole Quay.

Finally, Wolf could see the lantern clearly and Tabitha standing by it, illuminated by its light. The boat's bow bumped against the edge of the rocks. Wolf tossed the painter to Tabitha. She caught it, and the line went taut, humming with the strain. The next surge hit, lifting the boat and slamming it against the stone, but the turn held.

"Pull me as close as you are able," he yelled to Tabitha. She followed his instructions, but even then, it wouldn't be easy for them to climb into the boat. She looked around; was there anything she could tie the painter to? Surprisingly, as she looked at the rocks just above the waterline, she saw what appeared to be an iron ring. It seemed they were not the first people to bring a boat into this cave. At some point, some resourceful fisherman must have attached this ring. Whatever the reason, Tabitha gave thanks and moved to tie the rope securely to it. She looked at Wolf in the boat; did it make more sense for him to get out and help her guide Clarice and Hywel to it, or stay in to drag them in? In the end, she decided it was easier for her to push the others in with Wolf in the boat, pulling.

Tabitha decided to get Clarice into the boat first. All things being equal, she should be the easier of the two. Furthermore, Tabitha resolved that if someone had to be sacrificed, it would be the murderer, not the innocent young woman.

What Tabitha hadn't expected was for Clarice to be paralysed by fear. "I can't swim," the young woman said through her chattering teeth.

"Clarice, you will not have to swim, but you might get wet. My husband has brought the boat up as far as he can. I remember from making our way up here that there are more rocks below the water that we climbed on. Now, you are going to climb down them, even though they are submerged, to the boat. Then, Lord Pembroke will pull you in. Can you do this?"

The girl said nothing. It was clear this was going to be difficult. The women's skirts were getting wetter, and the water was weighing them down more. As she thought about this, Tabitha made a decision.

"Take your skirt off, Clarice. I will do the same."

Even in the young woman's drug-induced stupor, and despite her terror, she looked at Tabitha incredulously. "You wish me to strip to my petticoat?"

"Your skirt will be too heavy. It will drag you down. Doing this is our best chance of survival." It looked as if Clarice was going to refuse. Tabitha would not let this woman's extreme prudishness be the reason they drowned. She started to unbutton her own skirt, then let its material fall around her feet. Then, she began to unbutton Clarice's skirt.

As much as the other woman was appalled, she lacked the physical and emotional strength to fight and stood there as her skirt also fell, leaving her only in a petticoat. Tabitha stepped out of her skirt and immediately felt the relief of not being pulled down by the heavy, wet fabric.

Even as she helped Clarice step out of her skirt, all Tabitha could think about was how appalled the dowager would be by this story. Strangely, this thought gave her hope and pushed her to guide Clarice into the water and toward the boat.

The young woman was a burden, too muddled and frightened to help herself. Tabitha tried to guide her without losing her own balance. It wasn't easy, and it took strong will and determination to step one foot after another into the dark water, expecting there would be rocks beneath. She held onto the painter with one hand and Clarice with the other.

Just as they were nearly at the boat, the other woman started shrieking and flailing about, and Tabitha almost lost her grip on her. Wolf dangled over the edge of the prow and reached as far as he could, just managing to grab Clarice's arm. Somehow, he pulled the terrified, soaked woman into the boat. Tabitha breathed a sigh of relief; the hardest part was over, or so she hoped.

Getting herself out of the water and back to Hywel was more difficult than Tabitha had imagined. Even in only her petticoat, the wet fabric was hard to manoeuvre and pulled her down. She was tempted to rip the petticoat off as well, but she wasn't sure she could face disembarking the boat in Stackpole and making her way back to the carriage in her bloomers; she was progressive, but not that progressive.

Once again, Tabitha appreciated her gloves as she grabbed hold of wet, jagged rocks to pull herself up. Hywel hadn't spoken in a while, and Tabitha started to worry that the man had lost consciousness.

Now, she approached him and said sharply, "Hywel, you need to stay awake. Can you hear me?" There was no response. Bending down to the man lying motionless on the rocks, Tabitha pulled her hand back and slapped his face. Hywel's eyes sprang open at the unexpected pain.

"Hywel, you need to stay awake, and you need to stand up," she commanded as she grabbed hold of one of his arms. Somehow, she managed to haul him to his feet, but getting him to the boat was a bigger challenge.

By the time she and Wolf, working together, managed to get Hywel into the boat, Tabitha was exhausted and soaked. She wondered if she had the strength to go back to the rocks for the lantern, but decided she didn't. They would have to navigate their way out of the cave the best they could.

"Help me in," Tabitha called up to Wolf, who lowered himself down again as much as he could to pull her in. When she was finally in the boat, Wolf used his knife to cut the painter. He tried to leave as much rope as he could, but was unwilling to risk leaving the boat to untie the mooring.

Finally, they were all in the boat, wet, shivering, and exhausted, but still alive, at least for now. Now, all Wolf had to do was steer the boat out of the cave without hitting a rock or getting washed overboard by a wave. Somehow, they managed. Wolf let out a sigh of relief as they reached the open water. Luckily, the weather had held, and the water wasn't too rough.

Clarice and Hywel were both lying at the bottom of the boat, motionless. Wolf looked at them and wondered whether it was better to reach land quickly or row to Stackpole. He had just decided to go with the latter when he saw figures on the coastline.

As they drew closer, he said to Tabitha, "I think that is Bear and some of the men." His friend was so tall that he easily stood out. "I am going to row to meet them. I think it is better if have the men carry Miss Hill and Hywel to the carriage from here rather than trying to get all the way to Stackpole Quay and then having to manage alone." She agreed.

Rowing the bow to shore was hard work, and Wolf's muscles ached with every stroke, but he managed it. As they approached the shore, he and Tabitha called out, and once Bear realised who was in the boat, he and three footmen started to wade into the sea to help pull it out.

"It is good to see you, my friend," Wolf said wearily. "I will explain more later, but we need to get Miss Hill and Mr Chivers to a doctor, and then he needs to be arrested." Looking down the beach, he saw another group of men much farther up. "Is that Langley and the constable?" Bear indicated it was, and Wolf sent one footman to inform them of what was happening.

Chapter 37

Wolf had entrusted Bear and Langley to deal with Clarice and Hywel; neither he nor Tabitha were up for returning to Pembroke. They were soaked, and Tabitha was half-dressed. Langley promised to ensure that Clarice was taken home, and a doctor called to check her for any last effects from the chloral hydrate, to say nothing of the freezing water and shock.

Constable Tucker had enlisted police officers from nearby towns for the search, and now they took Hywel Chivers into custody. When he had seen the constable, Hywel had started to weep and essentially confessed to James Truegood's murder in his hysteria. Tabitha could only imagine that Mrs Chivers wouldn't be the branch president of the Parish Mothers' Union after this news got out. Tabitha would have felt sorrier for the woman if she weren't sure that, under different circumstances, she wouldn't have been the first person to pass judgement and then spread malicious gossip.

The carriage ride from Stackpole Quay to Glanwyddan Hall didn't take long, but even so, Tabitha and Wolf were grateful for the blankets it seemed Madison always had on hand.

Tabitha had hoped to enter the hall and make her way immediately to her bedchamber for a hot bath and a change of clothes. What she wanted least of all was to be met in the entrance hall by the dowager, a look of horror on her face.

The dowager looked Tabitha up and down and said, "What happened to your skirt?"

Sighing, Tabitha replied, "Mama, I am soaking wet, freezing cold, and exhausted. All I want is a bath and dry clothes. This conversation will have to wait."

Apparently, this was insufficient, and the old woman continued, "Please tell me you have not been seen in public in such a state of dishabille, Tabitha. Whatever will people think of their countess?"

Wolf had entered the hall just behind Tabitha, and now he answered for her, "Lady Pembroke, people will think that she is brave, resourceful, and the perfect partner when one is stuck in a perilous situation. If anyone is small-minded enough to think anything else, they will not be foolish enough to air those thoughts around me!"

It was rare that Wolf spoke so forcefully and plainly to the dowager. She was so taken aback that she said nothing more, and Tabitha and Wolf were able to escape to their room.

An hour later, after a long bath and two cups of steaming tea, Tabitha no longer felt chilled to the bone. Even so, she dressed far more warmly than she would normally have done on a mild summer's night. She and Wolf had decided they were too weary to dress for a formal dinner and would instead take trays in their room. Neither had the energy to face the dowager's interrogation just yet.

"I know we are taking the coward's way out and that the burden of satisfying her curiosity will fall on Langley, but I cannot find it in me to be sorry," Wolf admitted. Tabitha had to agree.

As they sat facing each other in the comfortable armchairs in their bedchamber, trays of food on their laps, they reflected on the conclusion of their investigation.

"Is there any way we can cancel tomorrow's hunt?" Tabitha wondered aloud. "After all, Sir Christopher is no longer a suspect, and we can use the excuse of exhaustion after today's travails."

Wolf sympathised with her sentiment, and it had even crossed his mind. However, he'd made a decision, which he now vocalised. "I would like to go ahead with it, if you can bear it. Certainly, if you want to swear off, I imagine everyone will understand. Still, I genuinely want to mend fences with Sir Christopher, but more than that, I have a proposal I want to put to him."

Tabitha quirked an eyebrow at this. "A proposal?"

"Yes. What if an important piece of British history is never found because Hywel Chivers murdered James Truegood in a jealous rage?"

"You are talking about his hopes to find a copy of the Magna Carta?" Tabitha asked.

"Indeed. I would like to honour Mr Truegood and help his death not be entirely in vain by continuing his hunt for the document."

"On Sir Christopher's land?" Tabitha theorised.

"And in Pembroke Castle. I want to fund Mr Goodge to pick up his friend's research in both locations."

Tabitha understood Wolf's motivation, but a possible problem occurred to her. "If the Magna Carta is found on Sir Christopher's land, will it not be his property? I assume such a rare and historic document would be very valuable and that certain collectors would pay a lot to have it in their collection."

Wolf nodded. He had considered this. "I want to make a telephone call to my solicitor to confirm, but my understanding of the law of treasure trove is that while coins, bullion, or precious metals found hidden with no known owner, usually revert to the crown, that is not true for documents, however valuable they might be."

This raised an interesting question. "If this is the case, then why did Sir Christopher assume he would own whatever treasure he thought James Truegood might find?"

Wolf shrugged. "Perhaps he did not understand the law, or perhaps he intended to flout it."

His words raised another concern. "So, what you are saying is that if a copy of the Magna Carta is found on his land, Sir Christopher would in fact own that, as opposed to what he imagined treasure to be."

"Under normal circumstances. And so, I would offer to buy it off him so I could then donate it to the crown."

"How much are you prepared to spend?" Tabitha asked, worried about what this might entail.

Wolf laughed. "The truth is that if such an incredibly historic document were found and authenticated, I can only imagine that there would be immense pressure, political, academic, and from the press, for it to be owned by the British Museum. I will point out that he will be a public hero and will forever be associated with this act of civic sacrifice, or infamy if he tries to sell it privately."

Tabitha sipped her wine and took a forkful of the hearty stew Mrs Budgers had sent up. "Did Sir Christopher strike you as the kind of man likely to be swayed by such considerations?"

"Not really," Wolf acknowledged. "Hence, I will sweeten the pot. While I will not offer him anything close to what he might eventually sell the Magna Carta for, I suspect that the prospect of ready money may sway him more than anything. Anyway, I thought that if I show him sufficient hospitality tomorrow, I might be able to persuade him."

"And if your fine claret and excellent table does not suffice, you can leave him alone with Mama for ten minutes, and that should be persuasion enough."

Wolf laughed. "The dowager countess will make an excellent fallback plan."

The following day, Tabitha decided she would take Wolf up on his suggestion and bow out of her hostess duties. In truth, every muscle in her body ached from her labours the day before, and the thought of spending her day making small talk with the local bores, lechers, and drunkards was more than she could face.

Instead, Tabitha allowed herself to indulge in the rare luxury of spending the day in bed with Ginny fussing over her. Wolf had assured her that he would keep the dowager busy enough that she would leave Tabitha in peace, and, true to his word, Tabitha enjoyed a day of rest and solitude.

When Wolf had finally bid adieu to his guests, he visited his wife. Tabitha felt guilty; she was sure he ached just as much, if not more so, than she did. After all, Wolf had done all the rowing. Still, he seemed in good spirits, even if weary.

"Well?" Tabitha inquired.

"He agreed. Finally. It took a lot of wine, and I did have to bring in the cavalry."

"Mama?"

"Indeed. She barely had to open her mouth, and the man was terrorised and agreed."

Smiling, Tabitha observed, "You might have been able to spare yourself the exhaustion of the day and just sent her to Ashling Hall to begin with." Wolf smiled in return.

Epilogue

A month later, Mr Goodge still had not found anything in the ruins. He had been keeping Wolf updated on his work. Mr Allen had been persuaded to review James Truegood's notes and, although he was not entirely convinced, had agreed to postpone his return to London for a few weeks to participate in the work. Occasionally, Wolf would stop by the ruins on Sir Christopher's land to check on any progress made. So far, it was all quite discouraging.

Over dinner, they discussed the ongoing work to clear the ruins while searching for anything buried there.

"Mr Goodge is determined that no harm come to the site," Wolf explained. "As it happens, it seems the men are discovering far more buildings as they carefully clear away the overgrowth and fallen rocks."

"So, even if the treasure is not found, a valuable historical site has been uncovered," Tabitha said with a smile. "It is good to know that something will come out of Mr Truegood's research."

"Indeed," Wolf agreed.

"However, I am sure that rogue Sir Christopher does not consider that any consolation," the dowager observed. "I assume you will not pay him unless a copy of the Magna Carta is discovered."

"That was our agreement," Wolf concurred. "Although so far, he is taking it in stride. He seems to think that the ruins will be significant enough for visitors to come to Lamphey just to see them, and that he could charge an entrance fee."

Wolf was sceptical of this idea, particularly as the ruins of Lamphey Bishop's Summer Palace were in the same village and could be viewed for free. Nevertheless, if the hope kept Sir Christopher happy and willing to allow the excavation to continue, then it was all well and good."

Langley had returned to London for a few weeks, and Tabitha was enjoying the slightly more intimate family group. She adored Maxwell Sandworth, Earl of Langley, but she was feeling so fatigued lately that even having one less person to interact with was a relief. While Tabitha had tried to hide her lethargy from Wolf, it was hard to pretend she wasn't taking naps most afternoons.

Finally, that evening, after dinner, when Tabitha had excused herself to go to bed at an almost embarrassingly early hour, Wolf followed her up to their bedchamber to check on her. The dowager was left alone in the drawing room, upset that she had no one to observe her knowing look.

Bored with the book she'd been pretending to be absorbed in for the last few evenings, she said to no one in particular, "Let us hope she finally makes the announcement. In my day, we did not make such a fuss. One would think she was the first woman ever to expect a child. Such a to-do over what Providence has arranged since Eve."

While her words were sharp, they were belied by the gentle smile on the dowager's face. And of course, she knew better than anyone why Tabitha might have been inclined to wait until further along in her confinement before saying anything, even to Wolf.

Continuing her conversation with herself, the dowager said, "If it is a girl, I think she should be called Julia!"

Want a sneak peek at book 12, An Anointed Woman? Keep reading...

Tabitha and Wolf have been invited to historic Salisbury for a scholarly lecture celebrating their recent discovery at Pembroke Castle. However, the occasion takes a dark turn when the lecturer is found dead beneath the towering ruins of Old Sarum.

As the couple begins to investigate, they are drawn into a labyrinth of ancient Druidic rites, shadowy Church intrigues, and secrets buried beneath the chalky plains. An excavation near Stonehenge uncovers more than bones, awakening old rivalries and new dangers.

In a landscape where myth and history intertwine, Tabitha and Wolf must navigate shifting allegiances and long-buried truths. As tensions rise and the past casts long shadows over the present, they race to uncover the killer before another body is claimed by secrets that are best left buried.

Afterword

Thank you for reading A Valiant Woman. I hope you enjoyed it. If you'd like to see what's coming next for Tabitha & Wolf, here are some ways to stay in touch:

SarahFNoel.com
Facebook
@sarahfNoelAuthor on BlueSky
sfnoel on Instagram
@sfnoel on Threads

If you enjoyed this book, I'd very much appreciate a review (but, please no spoilers).

About Sarah F. Noel

Originally from London, Sarah F. Noel now spends most of her time in Grenada in the Caribbean. Sarah loves reading historical mysteries with strong female characters. The Tabitha & Wolf Mystery Series and its spin-off, The Continental Capers of Melody Chesterton, are exactly the kind of books she loves to curl up with on a lazy Sunday.

Visit Sarah's website (sarahfnoel.com/) to join her mailing list, connect with her on social media, and see what's coming next!

Printed in Dunstable, United Kingdom

80075499R00127